ROGUE

GARGOYLES DEN BOOK TWO

Lisa Barry

Witching Hour Publishing Inc.

Witching Hour Publishing, Inc.

ISBN-13: 978-1-943121-53-3 (Ingram Spark)

Editor: Courtenay Dodds www.CourtenayDodds.com

To the lovers and writers of fiction

Without you I am not certain that I would have ever realized my passion for writing. It's the writers who allowed themselves to take a chance and create so many worlds beyond, that made me happy; and it is the lovers of those written words that encourage creative thought, making me believe that someone, somewhere, would enjoy the noisy imagination that clawed its way out of my mind and ended up on these pages.

Thank you.

My Music Muse

I often write to music. For me, music communicates things that cannot be captured in words. The emotion that is conjured with a note or a voice is part of what makes me tick. I listen to almost any type of music and I do seem to lean toward a certain type. My husband calls it 'vamp music' and that's good enough for me. I also happen to like it louder than even my children can tolerate. Go figure.

I wanted to acknowledge some of the artists whose songs went a little further for me on this particular book. Sometimes when I am cruising along in the car, a song will be playing and a scene will play out in my head. I will play that song over and over and over until I have completed the scene. This means that even my children know when I am mid something by how they never want to hear a particular song again whereas for me, it helped to create something I am proud of and it settles fondly in my heart.

Here are just a few honorable mentions…

Artists I listen to in the background that are just a good solid base depending on what I'm writing at the time:

Chillin' music is Pinback, Dramatic is definitely Audiomachine.

Adema: Giving In and Unstable. Both of these songs had their own playlist for a while there.

Mantis: Their song, The Aftermath, helped me write the fight scene that appeared near the end of book one (The Guardians).

Lindsey Stirling: Moontrance

Bassnectar: Timestretch (West Coast Lo Fi Remix)

Earshot: Headstrong

Motograter: Down

Phutureprimitive: Xotica

Chevelle: Forfeit, Grab Thy Hand, Family System

And for my victory dances:

Muse: Feeling Good

Nelly: Hot in Here

DNCE: Cake by the Ocean

Happy listening!

ACKNOWLEDGMENTS

There is so much activity that goes into the completion and release of a book and so many people that helped to bring this one to fruition, I hope that I do not forget anyone.

First, I would like to thank my writers group, the Ink Slingers Guild (check us out here: www. InkSlingersGuild.com!). You all are so inspiring, motivating and most of all supportive. I don't know how other authors do it without such tremendous backup.

As always, my editor, Courtenay. She allows me to have my voice and makes sure I don't do stupid things like have every single person in the story wearing a blue shirt. You know my voice and make it more beautiful. You are a wonderful editor and an even better friend. Thanks, babe.

My test readers. You've helped me to build a better story. Christina, you helped find the wrongs and make them right. You have all help me to get the story right and I can't thank you enough.

My family. You have always encouraged and supported me. <3

Thank you!

Chapter 1

L ying in a hotel room bed and listening to the man who made her heart beat about a million times faster than it should, may not be as good as it might sound. Not only was said man not entirely *man*…well, it would be better said that he was way *more* than just a man. But that was just Sloane Jacobs getting distracted. *As usual.*

"Come again?" Sloane said softly, her head reeling from the hangover headache.

"I've gone rogue," he said clearly.

Sloane continued to stare, trying to push the darkness away so she could see Liam McDougall's white, sculpted skin, fiery red hair, and penetrating blue eyes. Only his seated silhouette greeted her from a few feet away.

Now the hormones were just ticking her off. And the headache too. There were rumors about ways to get rid of those. Argh. His admission finally filtered through her hazy mind.

"Rogue?" Incredulous, Sloane's voice sliced through the silence. "You went rogue? That makes no sense. That's not like you." She paused as the memories came rushing in.

"I thought you were dead," she said. "Fuck. I *knew* you were dead. I don't know how but I felt it.

Literally."

Liam jumped out of the chair and knelt at the bedside, his face just lines and shadows in the dark. Startled, Sloane pulled away and covered her mouth. It was just a few hours ago that he'd held her hair out of her face while she had puked her guts out. Many thanks to a binge at the bar for that lovely experience. When she had thought he was gone forever, that she'd never see his quirky smile and messy red hair again, she'd headed straight to the bar.

"What do you mean you felt it?" he demanded.

"Well, let's see. I was innocently on my way to the kitchen when..." Sloane paused, remembering the shock and pain that had engulfed her before going comatose.

"When what?" Liam pushed.

Sloane waved a hand at him in annoyance. "When I felt like something ripped my fucking back open and shredded my guts, Liam. It sucked, okay?"

Liam pulled away from the side of the bed, crouching, his elbows resting on his knees. Right when Sloane really wished she could see his face, a blur of darkness moved before her. A click and then a dull light became a laser beam straight into her eyes.

"Jeez! A little warning would have been nice," she berated.

"Sorry," he said without feeling, "but you should see this."

"Give me a damn minute then."

Liam waited while she blinked at the ceiling. When she finally turned to him, she could only stare.

His beautiful creamy skin was sunken and bruised, and dark shadows creased his eyes.

"Liam," Sloane whispered softly, raising a hand tentatively toward him. He shook his head.

"That's not what I wanted to show you." He turned his back to her, sat on the edge of the bed, and started to pull his shirt up. Sloane's heart went into overdrive as she anticipated the alabaster masterpiece of muscles that she had been longing to see since the first time she'd ever laid eyes on him.

The last thing she expected was the long, jagged scar. She sucked in her shock along with an unfortunate gulp of spit that went straight down the wrong pipe. Sloane gasped and coughed uncontrollably.

Liam dropped his shirt and turned to her aid. She waved an embarrassed hand in front of her face. Leaving her side for a moment, he returned with a bottle of water. She drank it gratefully.

"Damn," she finally said. "How is that possible?"

"The coughing or the scar?" he asked, an eyebrow raised.

"That *you* have a scar that *I* felt."

"I'm not sure."

Sloane's eyes narrowed. "You're not sure? Well, someone had better know."

Liam watched her for so long she started to feel uncomfortable. To make matters worse, her body was letting her know it liked the look. It was a bit smoldering, wasn't it?

Sloane finally rolled her eyes. "I get it. You have an idea but you're not going to share. Well, okay then. That's awesome." She wished things hadn't gone this way. Maybe the day could start over?

"Will you tell me everything you can think of about your step-father?" he asked abruptly.

"He's not what did that to you." Sloane's skin crawled at the mention of *that* man.

"No. They will be taken care of by the Guardianship. But your step-father won't."

"Can we just call him Dr. J? I don't want to think of him as family if that's all right with you."

"Fine."

Releasing a long breath, Sloane's eyes rounded, and she turned her head as she remembered that her breath would likely kill an entire army. She nodded knowing he was still watching her. She suddenly felt really tired and snuggled back into the sheets.

"I'm going to get some supplies," he said. "Get some more sleep, it's early yet. We'll talk later."

He left the room without another word, a turn of the lock and then silence.

Sloane's head teamed with questions, but the haze of sleep was too strong. She mustered the energy to lean over and click off the light. She snuggled into the pillow and before she could attempt to breath in his scent, passed out cold.

Chapter 2

When Andy stepped out of the Bergerac airport in southeast France after catching four separate flights since Tampa, the last flight being a small plane which was just slightly less exciting than a four car pile-up, he was glad to smell fresh air again. He was just taking a second, deep breath when he noticed a black antique car by the curb. The darkly tinted windows obscured his view of the driver. On a hunch, he walked over and pulled open the back door.

"Good afternoon, Mr. Chamberlain," a breathy male soprano voice said from the shadows of the driver's side of the car.

"Good afternoon. Please call me Andy," Andy replied to the shadowed figure as he tossed his bag in and slid into the back seat. "What should I call you?"

The driver glanced back at Andy who, by using every skill he had, kept his face smooth. The driver was wearing your normal, everyday chauffeur's hat but his face was an odd greenish color. His nose was pushed in, like a pug. Something resembling gills moved beneath his ears and continued downward, disappearing beneath his stiff white shirt. His eyes were round and pale.

"You may call me Songue," he said. "Make yourself comfortable, Mr. Chamberlain. We have an hour drive to the Chateau."

"Sure," Andy said hoping he sounded at ease. He stared at the back of Songue's head until the countryside caught his attention. They drove in silence while Andy enjoyed the colorful flowers, crumbling castles, towers, and amazing greenery that swept past.

Had someone told him a year ago that he would be on his way to a secret school for gargoyle shape-shifters he would have laughed in their face. As an orphan, he had never dreamed of being part of something so big, never would have guessed his ancestry would be exceptional.

Andy Chamberlain had discovered that he was destined to become a Guardian, able to shift into gargoyle form in order to protect humans from the things that really and truly do go bump in the night. Guardians came in different gargoyle forms, some with faces more like a cat or a dog, and others with the more familiar dragon-like snout. Some had wings and other didn't. Most had at least one additional skill that set them apart, like super speed or extended hearing.

Andy found that he had the rare skill of a displacer, able to manipulate his body so he could pass through things like a ghost. He felt like he should be happy with that, but he couldn't help but wish for a set of wings so he could soar through the night sky as so many Guardians could.

The time seemed to fly by and the next thing Andy knew, Songue had pulled the car into a hard-packed dirt drive way. Standing before them was a tall electronic fence that was attached on each side to a cracked and vine covered stone wall which disappeared into the trees after several hundred feet. Songue clicked a button on the visor and the gate slowly opened outward. The car had been stopped only inches from the fully extended gate.

As soon as it was wide enough, Songue drove the car through. Andy looked out the back window as the gate automatically closed behind them. They drove another ten minutes through the trees, some areas so thick he couldn't see through them. He caught glimpses of open fields with the occasional grazing horse or sea of wild flowers in dazzling colors. One time Andy caught a glance of butterflies erupting from a hollow base in a large tree.

The car started to slow as they came around a hill and Andy watched awestruck as the Guardianships' abode came into view over the tree tops. Had there been less tree coverage and hills on the drive in, there would have been no way to miss the tops of the square towers and tall spires.

The spires disappeared as the car turned right onto a cobblestone drive, passing under more thick trees. Seconds later the trees opened displaying an old village and a great towering castle in the distance. They had to drive through the village to get to the castle. The road led them past two stables, one on either side, and then past two long buildings, also on each side of the road.

As they continued, the land widened into a vast grassy area on both sides with several large, rectangles of dirt, each boasting tall lamp posts.

Andy supposed them to be training areas, but they were empty now. The castle loomed ahead, the spires seeming much higher than when Andy had first observed them. He smiled as he caught sight of stone gargoyles spread in excess throughout the façade. He would have to get a closer look later.

"Welcome to Chateau le Gardien," Songue said as he pulled to a stop in front of the castle's tall wooden door, complete with medieval hinges. Andy let himself out, grabbed his bag and watched the car drive off and disappear around the side of the castle.

Chapter 3

The sun was up, that much Sloane could tell, though the room was still dim with the heavy drapes pulled shut. Her head had stopped throbbing, which was a lovely relief. Sloane wiped the sleep from her face and curled into the soft sheets, rubbing her face on the pillow. She caught a hint of his scent and memories flooded back.

Liam McDougall had gone rogue. He had gone off the radar of the Guardianship without permission to take on an opponent that he seemed to feel should be permanently relieved of duty. That opponent just happened to be her stepfather.

And the most bizarre thing, after months of wondering what had happened to Liam, he had shown up out of nowhere, kidnapped her and brought her to this motel room, while she was inebriated, no less.

Sloane noted that the shower was running. Before the hormones had anything further to say about that, she sat up and the unmistakable delight of a coffee aroma perked her senses. She closed her eyes and breathed in before reaching to the nightstand where a large Dunkin Donuts cup awaited her. It was still hot. Smiling at his thoughtfulness, she took a swig. Perfection.

After slugging down a quarter of the cup, enough to get her kick started, she was thrilled to find that the hotel sink was outside the bathroom, along with two new toothbrushes and paste. The shower shut off just as she was rinsing. She cringed at her tangled dark strands but there was not much that she could do for it. She quickly sat in the room's only chair and nursed her coffee.

The bathroom door opened a moment later and he stepped out. He wore only jeans, slung low on his hips, and his towel dried hair was doing its usual unpredictable thing of sticking every which way. Sloane felt a tightening in her stomach as her eyes traveled over his trim torso, his muscles sculpted and defined, a feast standing before her despite the deep blues and blacks of bruises still healing. Liam saw her in the mirror and nodded before taking the second toothbrush. As he leaned over the sink, Sloane beheld his back.

The scar ran from his right shoulder, down and across his spine, to his left hip. It was pink in some places and purple in others. Sloane puzzled over it. His kind healed crazy fast and if she understood correctly, this had happened months ago. There shouldn't be any evidence of it now.

As he finished at the sink, Sloane found herself standing directly behind him, her gaze roaming his torn skin. She gently touched the top of the scar at his right shoulder. He froze in place. She traced the injury gently, downward with just the tips of her fingers. When she reached the end, she realized something.

"You should have died from this," she said softly

as she lifted her hand away from his skin. Liam took a long breath and turned, looking down at her.

"I did," he said. Sloane frowned but was immediately distracted by his depthless blue eyes. She lifted her hand and traced the bruises on his forehead, then down his cheek. Liam closed his eyes, his breath shallow. He reached up and pressed her hand to his cheek.

"Woman," he growled, "must you?"

Sloane pulled her hand away and backed against the wall.

"Sorry," she whispered, "I wasn't thinking."

"Of course, you weren't thinking," he said his voice still low. He took a step toward her, his breath ragged. "It's the bond. You're aware of it?"

Sloane lifted her left shoulder in answer as she stared at the green carpet. "No one really explained it to me," she mumbled.

He stepped closer. "It connects two people. It *literally* bonds their souls." He took another step. He was so close. He put his hands on the wall to either side of her head and leaned into her face, his lips almost touching hers as he whispered. "It can consume you if you let it."

Sloane trembled. The oddest mix of stark fear and lust exuded from him, washing over her like a thunderstorm. She couldn't move without touching him and at that moment it was the only thing she wanted to do. She looked into his eyes and whispered back.

"So?"

Surprise flashed across his eyes and then his lips were on hers. Crushing her to the wall, his hands slipped beneath her shirt and grasped her hips. Sloane bent to him as his hands explored, searing her skin. She found her arms around his shoulders, her hand gripping his neck, desperate need consuming her as she tasted the sweetness of his mouth, his tongue making her swollen and woozy.

Her hand slid into his hair as she pulled her legs up and wrapped them around his waist. Liam groaned as he lifted her and swung her to the sink. Moving his hands further up her back, he paused, pulling away to gaze at her. He brushed a stray hair from her neck, allowing them to breathe for a heartbeat before trailing his lips down her neck, slowly, one hand melting her back, the other cupping her head as she leaned into it, her short gasps feeding his lust.

Leaning into him, Sloane shivered as he reached her shoulder. His musky scent called to her as her hands found his chest. She traced his hard curves, bringing her lips down to his smooth skin. She felt him freeze as he exhaled, long and deep before pulling her face up, his lips devouring hers once more.

Then they were floating, mingling on a plane of existence beyond the physical, entwined in a haze of spiritual warmth.

Slamming back to the physical world, Sloane's body felt heavy and she found that Liam had pulled away.

"I can't do this," he whispered. Still breathing heavily, she watched him pull on a shirt, grab his shoes and go out the door of the motel.

Sliding off the counter and onto the floor, Sloane stared at the door. An engine roared to life outside and she had no doubt who it was. The tears came quietly, sliding down her face and dripping to her knees. She just couldn't understand why he wouldn't just let go.

Standing, her legs like jello, she grabbed the counter with one hand to steady herself and wiped away tears with the other. She caught a glance of herself in the mirror. Her face was flushed, her lips slightly swollen. Even with her forlorn face, she was glowing. What could possibly be wrong with that? Before the tears came again, Sloane forced herself to get undressed and hit the shower, hoping to rinse away her heart. She wanted to trade it in for a solid core, so she wouldn't have to feel anymore.

Chapter 4

After turning on the truck, Liam sat staring at the door of the motel room, willing his lungs to calm, willing his heartbeat to normal. What an ass he was. He was only hurting her more. He simply could not do it. Could not do it to *her* though there was nothing he wanted more. Putting the truck into reverse, he slammed a hand on the steering wheel. Stupid bond was ruining him. Distracting him.

Chapter 5

"There, there. It will be all right," Dr. J said softly as he pet the soft green fur that had sprouted from Hal just hours after the injection.

Hal's wide fearful eyes blinked and then closed as another wave of pain racked his body. Dr. J gave his hand a squeeze before leaving to check on the next patient.

Chapter 6

Staring at the invite in her hand and then back at the biggest tree she had ever seen, Verity Applebee wondered what it meant by *walk through the door*. Noah had already inspected the note twice and stood next to her, arms akimbo, a frown etched across his otherwise perfect bronze skin.

The *Baranoff Oak* was estimated to be the oldest Oak tree in the county, between 300 and 500 years old. Despite its sprawling branches and thick leaves, the sun crept through, beating down on Verity's black hair, causing a thin sheen of sweat to make its way down her chest and arms. Looking at the invitation one last time she walked up to the foot of the tree.

Dragging a hand along the massive trunk, Verity made her way around it. Just as she was shaking her head in defeat, her hand vanished into the tree. Jumping back, Noah caught her before she fell on her ass.

"I see," he said. "It's a screen."

"A what?" Verity asked as she righted herself.

"You literally walk through it. But if you didn't know it was there, it wouldn't open for you. Let me go first to make sure it's safe."

Nodding her head, Verity watched carefully as Noah simply disappeared into the tree. A moment later, a tan, muscled arm appeared, floating alone in the air, the hand beckoning her forward.

Taking Noah's hand, she stepped forward and was instantly out of the sun, standing in a dimly lit cave entrance with a stairwell just a few feet ahead. Trickles of water could be faintly heard, and a light musky odor filled her nostrils. She gave Noah a half smile.

"It's kind of pleasant in sort of an odd way."

Noah sniffed in amusement and waved a hand forward.

They had not driven far to reach the tree, only twenty minutes to Safety Harbor. The quaint streets and small shops were gone from her mind as Verity stared down the dim, stone stairs.

The instructions in the invitation had seemed simple. Show up at the address listed. If desired, accompaniment of one Guardian was permitted. The address turned out to be a monster size tree. Then they were to walk through the door.

Noah headed down the stairs first. After two steps, he turned to her, his golden cat eyes showing no emotion as he waited for her to follow.

When Verity had shown him the invitation there had been emotion, quite a bit of it in fact. But she would not budge despite his concerns and he would not allow anyone else to accompany her.

It could have been a perfect romance. She had saved him from a horrible death. He had given her hope and guidance. After surviving the brutal circumstances of being enslaved by a man trying to understand and then destroy Noah's kind, Noah had called Verity his Dark Angel and hugged her like there was no tomorrow. Verity's rush of emotion toward him hadn't really been a surprise considering what they had been through together.

But he wasn't interested in her the way she was with him. Verity didn't think he even realized the affect his kind actions and soft words would have on her. In that way, he was very much from another world.

At first, she had felt like he had barely given her a chance, but then she got the idea that maybe someone else held his heart. She knew he cared deeply for her, but it just wasn't enough to redirect his attentions. He was simply a nice guy.

Then she had received the invitation. Both Aggie and Keanan were floored when she showed them. Like Verity's friend Sloane Jacobs, Aggie was an Aspie, which is short for the Latin word *aspicio* meaning 'to see'. Aggie had been around a long time and she could see people's Hues and read their feelings. Keanan was a gargoyle shapeshifter who was retired from the Guardianship, the group that protected Humans from the things that you don't want to meet in a dark alley.

They said it was a prestigious honor. The Goblin's were a noble species and did not invite people in on a whim. Noah did not agree. Verity wasn't sure who was right, but she wanted to see what it was all about for herself.

A soft glow somewhere near the bottom of the stairs was their only light. Noah could see in the dark, so the spook was all on Verity.

She stepped down, leaving the pseudo safety of reality behind. Expecting a dank, nose scrunching violation, Verity marveled at the musky, almost sweet air wafting around her.

Verity continued, her footsteps echoing around her. Noah's steps made no sound. They walked without conversation. When they reached the bottom they were greeted by a wall adorned with a scarred sconce that housed a strange round glow that flickered like a candle. The hall to the right disappeared into darkness. The hall to the left had a soft glow. Noah followed the light, Verity close behind. The path curved here and there with no other hallways or doors to catch their attention, just stone and dirt with the occasional sconced glow. After a time, the hall widened, and they were able to walk side-by-side. A wall dead ahead greeted them, corridors veering to the left and right.

Noah shoved Verity behind him as a shadow stepped out from the right corridor.

"Welcome," a deeply graveled voice penetrated the silence. Annoyed, Verity pushed her way forward and moved to better see the creature of myth. This was *her* adventure after all and no one was going to get in her way. Noah grunted.

The creature was a few inches shorter than she but twice as wide. The breadth of its shoulders seemed off kilter, top-heavy to the remaining stocky body, like it should fall over at any moment, yet it stood solid, arms stretched out in greeting. It was hard to tell in such bad lighting, but its skin looked to be black with a smattering of random brown hair patches. Its dark eyes were surrounded by a pale yellow light.

Willing her knees not to shake and attempting a smile Verity answered, "Thank you." She had come to help after all. If she could.

The creature nodded and waved for them to follow it into the goblin's lair.

Chapter 7

The huge castle door was surprisingly easy to open. Andy went inside, his eyes wide. It was right out of a faery tale. He walked into a large room, although not as large as he would have thought from the outside. The ceilings were high and covered with intricately carved stone. The room seemed sparsely furnished but only because it was so large. The main attraction, a small reception desk, was set up in the middle of the room about thirty feet in from the main entry. The desk was modern; it had a cherry wood finish and one of those high rails running around the top of it, like a fence to keep you from getting too close to the receptionist. As Andy approached the desk he didn't see anyone immediately. He took in the lush rugs on the stone floor and the heavy tapestries that hung on the walls depicting wars and heroes from long ago. There was a bell on the desk railing which he rang absently while he looked over a real suit of armor that was stationed near the desk, seemingly the solitary guard of the main room.

"I'm not deaf," a high-pitched voice came at him from somewhere behind the desk, "but possibly you are blind." Startled, Andy leaned over the railing and came eye to eye with the receptionist. He was sitting with two large books tucked underneath him, so he could reach the counter top. His jet black hair was perfectly combed and styled, and he had on a tailored gray, pinstriped suit.

"I'm sorry," Andy finally said, realizing he was staring, "I didn't realize you were there. I didn't know your kind could be a Guardian."

"I'm not a Guardian, you idiot," the man scoffed. "I am the Head Administrator."

"Oh...sorry about that," Andy smiled, trying to save face. "I'm..."

"Yes, Andy Chamberlain. Newly indoctrinated and ready to save the world. Have a seat and someone will be with you shortly." The man picked up a phone and pointed to several stiff backed velvet covered chairs to the right of the desk. Andy frowned and headed toward the chairs. Instead of sitting, he stood near them and continued his perusal of the room. A moment later another super short person click-clacked over to him in black, very high heels. She looked like a perfect blond model in a red blouse and black skirt, except that she was only about three feet tall. Andy stared.

"Hello!" she said, beaming as though he were an old friend she hadn't seen in years. "I'm Shana." She held out her hand. Andy pulled it together and quickly sat to be a bit more eye-level and took her hand.

"Andy Chamberlain. Nice to meet you." Her hand was the size of a three-year old's but with long, red fingernails.

"It's great to finally meet you!" she said, her blue eyes bright. Her voice was so high-pitched, Andy wondered if dogs would come running.

"Finally?" Andy asked cocking his head.

"You're a rarity, you know? The first male displacer to be born in your line in ages."

"Oh. My line?" Andy questioned. She knew more about his family than he did. His face must have been blank. Shana giggled at him and waved toward a hallway.

"In time. Come on, I'll show you around."

As they entered the hall Andy was again awed by the building: the ancient stones, the ornate rugs, the armor and weapon displays and the sconces where actual hand-held torches hung. Andy restrained himself from plucking one off the wall to see if it was real. Shana's heels click-clacked whenever they came off one of the thick rugs and would go silent when she got to the next one. Andy had to walk slowly so he wouldn't run her over, which was fine with him. He didn't know how often he would get to see The Castle.

"This is the main hall," Shana said.

"I think I upset the Head Administrator," Andy said as he glanced around the huge room.

"Oh, don't mind him. He's like that with everyone. You'll get to like him."

"I think I offended him though."

"You and everyone else. Once you understand that not being a Dwarf is offensive, you'll be much more comfortable with him."

"Ok. I guess that makes sense," Andy said although he wasn't totally sure that it did. "I thought Dwarves were bearded and mean." Shana giggled again.

"You spread a rumor or two to hide the truth and

it becomes fact," she said turning and waggling her blond eyebrows at him. When she had turned away, Andy raised his eyebrows.

"Are there a lot of Dwarves here?" he asked.

"No. There's just a few. Most of us prefer living in the mines," she added as an afterthought. "There are all sorts here. The Guardianship isn't prejudiced when it comes to species. They just want the best to help protect their family and forward their endeavors."

She continued walking and Andy found himself pondering family. He guessed that many of the kids here had grown up with their real parents, maybe had some inclination as to where they came from and how they might have ended up a Guardian, but Andy had none. Just memories of a life that could have been.

"Hello?" Shana asked as she stopped at a set of stairs.

"Oh sorry," Andy stammered, "this is a bit surreal." Shana gave him a sympathetic pat on the arm.

"You'll get used to it and the answers will come as they may," she said cryptically as they started up the stairs curving to the left of the great room. They were stone with lavish rugs perfectly fitted to the stairs.

"This leads to the third floor," Shana stated as she started up. Her legs were a blur while Andy followed slowly behind her. The stairs went up a floor then turned left and went up again.

Andy was surprised when he stepped off the stairs. It had the walls and floors of an old stone castle but that was where history ended. The open room was filled with the likes of a proper corporate office; modern black desks, leather swivel chairs, computers, and people. There was someone at every desk either standing or sitting, either engrossed at a computer or talking on a phone. A screen took up the majority of one wall and displayed a huge world map. There were hundreds, or perhaps even thousands of colored lights dotted throughout the map. Before Andy could take more in, he had to turn to follow Shana's click-clacking around a desk to the right and then he saw the office.

In the back right of the room, near a bank of windows, was a large glass office. Andy could clearly see the backs of two people who were standing close. One of them had a phone to her ear while the other, a man, was in front of a computer screen. There were more desks, more computers, and more people between Andy and the glass office. The lower floor was like a library at closing and this one was like a Saturday morning at Disney World.

Shana led Andy to the front of a desk just outside the glass office. A short stocky woman was on the other side with a cell phone to one ear, her head slightly bowed, and one hand held a finger in the other ear. She had short brown hair, slightly disheveled, and was wearing a bright green blouse. Something told Andy that her appearance didn't reflect how this particular lady was with her work. Her desk was perfectly organized, folders tabbed, papers tidy, messages laid out in lines; the dream secretary.

The woman hung up the phone, laid it down and started to move around the desk. Andy fought his instinct to run when she held out a hand. From the waist up, she was definitely a woman but from the waist down she seemed to be...Andy gulped...a snake. Her lower body was a roiling length of black scales complete with red and yellow rings. Andy fought off a shudder at the meaning of the warning colors in her rings and took her still outstretched hand. It was cold.

"Andy! How lovely to meet you!" the lady exclaimed, smiling widely. Her teeth were black and sharp. It was the kind of smile he imagined from meeting the principal for the first time. He knows your name and you're not sure if that's a good thing or not, so you smile back wondering whether or not he's going to eat you, rather, whether you're in trouble or not. Andy smiled back.

"My name is unpronounceable, so you can just call me Joy," she said with an extreme lisp. "I'm the Queen's Assistant." She shook heartily but professionally and let go. "The Queen is looking forward to meeting you." Once the words had settled in, Andy cocked his head.

"Queen?"

Chapter 8

When Liam came back, Sloane was sitting on the bed reviewing the notes she'd made on the motel notepad, hoping she had remembered everything about Dr. J. She stared at the paper, pretending to study it. He set a bag next to her and disappeared wordlessly into the bathroom. She wanted to ignore it, but the smell of eggs and toast assaulted her, and she was starving. She ripped into it and inhaled the freshly made food, chasing it with several gulps of coffee.

Once she had thrown the empty bag in the trash bin, he emerged from the bathroom. If she wasn't so pissed at him, she might have laughed. After upsetting a woman, it was very smart to feed her before talking to her.

He sat on the chair. Searching his face for any emotion, she found only a statue, void of life.

"Take me home," she said.

He looked at her so long her skin started to sizzle with need.

"I will. But we have one thing to do together first."

"What? What else could you possibly need me for?"

Sloane threw the small notepad at him. His arm moved gracefully and caught it easily.

"There's what I know. Now take me home," she said.

He read over it and nodded. "This is good. You say you think he went to Ireland? Why Ireland?"

Sloane bristled. "He's always wanted to take my mother and apparently he's got some office there. It's not like we sat down and had a fucking chat about it."

Liam studied the list a moment longer before bringing his gaze to her.

"We have something to take care of. Would you like to stop and get some fresh clothes before we head out?"

"Of course I would. Take. Me. Home. I have lots of clothes *there*."

"You didn't say fuck. Are you sure you don't want to fit that in somewhere?"

"You asshole. What did I ever see in you?"

"You didn't. It's the bond."

"Do you really think that?" Sloane snarled as she stood. Liam pulled his head back in surprise. "How do you think we ended up bonded in the first fucking place?" She shook her head. "You're the most brilliant idiot I know."

A scratching noise brought Sloane's attention to the window. She instantly shrunk down and looked at Liam. The muscles and tendons in his body rippled in defense as he went to the window. Scratch, scratch. After a second his head dropped and shook slightly. He went to the door and swung it open, bending his upper body out and down and then came back in with something grasped in his hand. He held it out to Sloane.

"Look familiar?"

She gasped at the big-eyed squirrel shaking in his grip. Her mouth opened to say something but then closed again quietly. Assuming it was the same one, this squirrel had been living behind her apartment and trying to communicate with her all this time. She had always thought she was just crazy.

Liam chuckled and tossed the squirrel to the bed.

"She's been indoctrinated," he said to the squirrel, "so you might as well explain it to her."

Sloane looked frantically between Liam and the squirrel. The squirrel removed an imaginary hat and bowed to her. His voice was deep with an edge of squeak.

"My Mistress, I bring you tidings." He stood straight and somehow dignified before placing a hand over his heart. "They are coming for you."

Chapter 9

The walkway in the goblin's lair curved sharply, left and right through more halls and doors to the point where Verity was lost and knew she could never find her way out without help. Their guide had said not another word. Noah walked next to her, silent and brooding, an unusual mood compared to his more common cheerful demeanor.

After roughly a quarter of an hour, they reached two large and weathered double doors. Verity whistled at the craftsmanship; the wooden doors were adorned with metal that was somehow entwined within the wood.

The Goblin held out a hand and they stopped. He opened one of the doors easily and slipped inside, the door closing behind him with a heavy thud. They stood in silence until his return a moment later when he beckoned them in.

The cavern was huge, shaped together by roots, packed rocks, shells, and dirt. The center was filled with the very backbone of the ancient tree above, the trunk of the root twisting its way into the ground. Vines crisscrossed the ceiling and floor, some blooming with odd flowers, others with deep green leaves.

As they made their way around the trunk, the real

attraction came into view. A throne, formed from roots and large leaves, covered in gems of varying colors, sparkled softly in the dim light. The occupant stood, mouth partially open with long yellowed fangs hanging low over its bottom lip. Verity hoped that was a smile.

She made her way toward him over the uneven ground, Noah at her heels. When she was just a few feet away, the King gave a low graceful bow before holding out his hands to her. He was an inch or two taller than Verity. She wondered briefly if size mattered around here as she reached out tentatively. He closed his hands around hers and it was like they were enclosed by the softest, furriest stuffed animal she'd had as a child. She smiled and met the King's yellowed eyes.

"Welcome to my home, Verity Applebee, human healer." Verity's eyes widened. Not only had he spoken in perfect English, he had a lovely British accent.

"Thank you, Lord King of the Goblin Lair. I am pleased to accept your invitation." Verity quoted the memorized words.

"Please, call me King," he replied. His eyes shone with a spirit and humor she had not expected. Even the fact that he still had her hands was not uncomfortable. She smiled.

Noah cleared his throat behind her. King's eyes narrowed, and he finally released her hands, leaving them to cool after his warmth.

"*Guardian*," King acknowledged Noah, an odd tone in his voice as if he was mocking Noah. "Your place is there." King pointed to the main root where four goblins stood quietly at attention. They each held some type of spear and had metal gadgets strapped here and there on their hairy bodies. Verity watched as Noah moved to speak and shook her head at him. Pursing his lips and frowning, he backed away to stand with King's security. Verity turned back to King as a small Goblin set a heavy wooden chair down next to her.

The King flourished his hand toward the chair as he made himself comfortable on his throne. Verity expected the wood to be hard but instead it felt soft and cushioned, setting her even more at ease. King placed his large hands together and leaned forward like a small child might except, of course, that with those enormously muscled arms he could probably break her in half if he felt like it.

"So, tell me Miss Applebee, how are you adjusting to the real world hidden around you?"

His English, accent and all, was so amazing Verity would have sworn she was speaking to a human if she hadn't been looking at his fur covered, odd-shaped body with her own eyes.

"Actually," Verity began, "it almost seems like it's always been this way. It makes sense to me, I'm enjoying it."

He smiled broadly and nodded his head. "And your healing? Have you had the opportunity to put it further to use?"

Verity dropped her head briefly and looked at the pale hands resting in her lap. "I seem to get more and more control each time I heal. I'm not surprised I ended up on this path, it's always been part of me. I just didn't know it. Though it does still surprise me when it works so consistently."

"Excellent! I wish to see it in action."

Before Verity could respond, King pulled a long, curved blade from within the armrest of his throne and held it up. Verity squealed in alarm, shrinking into her chair while a loud commotion broke out behind her and then abruptly went silent. Frozen, Verity watched the same small goblin who had brought her a chair approach King and hold out his arm. The blade came down slicing four inches long and an inch deep into the goblin's flesh, just below his elbow. The goblin made no sound as dark liquid oozed from the wound and dripped to the ground.

Chapter 10

"They were faster than I thought," Liam said as he started throwing the few things lying around into a black backpack.

"Who?" Sloane asked without taking her eyes off the squirrel.

"The Guardianship," Liam answered.

"Why would they care?"

"You're one of their own now. You're in training with a very old and very talented Aspie. You'll be on the work roster soon. They are going to want to take care of you and they don't know you're in safe hands."

"They don't know you're alive, do they?"

"I'm not sure."

"What are we going to do about him?" Sloane didn't have to point at the squirrel who sat patiently on his haunches, a smile across his furry face.

"I'll tell you while we drive."

"Wait, why don't you leave me here? I told you what I know."

"We still have something to handle first," Liam stood by the door, "Let's go."

Sloane didn't move. Her mind raced. She desperately wanted to go with him, and at the same time she couldn't bear to go with him. It was so painful. If Sloane went back to the Guardianship, she could perfect her skills, use them for work. For her entire life the ability to read people's thoughts and emotions had kept her from fitting in. As much as she wished she and Liam could work it out, the opportunity to stop hiding was not just enticing but she needed it to survive. Liam had been alone, loving ladies and leaving them for so long that maybe he really couldn't handle the idea of changing. She sighed. It made sense even if she hated it.

"Well?" Liam's voice cut through her thoughts and she looked at him with a bit less vinegar.

"I don't want to go with you," she said. His face didn't crack, not even a twitch.

"Sloane," he said. His voice was soft but gone was any of the emotion he had allowed earlier. "Just this one last thing and I will bring you home and you don't ever have to hear from me again."

"Fine," she mumbled. It seemed like the only way she could eventually be free. She picked up her purse, which he had kindly thought to grab for her during her inebriated state and headed out the door. The squirrel scampered along at her feet. When she climbed into the truck, the squirrel didn't follow. He sat on the sidewalk watching. Sloane looked at Liam in the driver's seat and then back at the squirrel.

"He'll find you again," Liam said so she shut the door.

"I'm still trying to figure out why he's following me around," she muttered as Liam pulled onto the road.

Florida was flat and pretty much looked the same everywhere you went but Sloane definitely didn't recognize any of the street signs.

"Where are we anyway?" She asked.

"We're near Crystal Springs," he said keeping his eyes on the road.

Sloane tried the silent treatment, but she sucked at it. She turned to Liam.

"Why is a talking squirrel stalking me?"

His lip curled up slightly and then vanished.

"He's a Brownie."

"A what?" Sloane frowned.

"Brownies are a kind of faery. They generally take on the form of animals. It makes it easy for them to get around. They're different because when they hit a certain age, they choose a master." He paused, eyes never leaving the road, and ran a hand through his hair. "Well, master's not really the right word. Close enough though. That little guy has chosen you."

Sloane took a minute to let it sink in. "Why on earth would he choose me?"

Liam shrugged. "They're a member of the Fae family. Who knows why they do anything. As far as I know, they usually choose people who are gifted in some way and they only do what *they* think is beneficial."

Sloane remembered when the squirrel was at her apartment. She had thought Liam was at her door. She had jumped up and seen the squirrel outside her window frantically shaking its head. It had tried to warn her. It hadn't been Liam at the door. Instead, her step-father had drugged her and brought her to his mental institute. Sloane shivered.

"AC too high?" Liam asked.

"No, it's fine," Sloane answered. She stared out

the window, watching the trees and occasional cow or horse filled field go by when a thought struck her.

"Back at the motel, what did you mean when you said you *did* die?"

Liam didn't stiffen particularly but his easy demeanor vanished, and all the walls flew up. Sloane waited for him to answer. Here she thought women were the ones all gummed up with stress.

"For someone who has trained his whole life to lock in emotion, you are one emotional guy," she said.

"Only around you, Sloane," he said with a sigh, "Only with you."

More understanding eased its way into her heart. She was a distraction. For probably the first time in his life, Liam had something that took him away from doing his job. Deep inside, Sloane laughed painfully. It wasn't *her*.

"I don't know exactly what happened, but I do know that I was very dead. And then I wasn't."

Sloane didn't like that thought and changed the subject. "Where are we going? What's this last thing that you need me for?"

"We're going to see someone," he said, his eyes never leaving the road. In fact, she didn't think he'd looked at her once since they'd been driving.

"About?" Sloane pushed.

"He's the only one I know who has successfully broken a bond."

Chapter 11

The Goblin King wiped the blade clean and then slid it back out of sight before waiting expectantly, his eyes roving between Verity and the young goblin. Verity glanced behind her chair only to breath in sharply at the sight. Noah was held solidly in place not by the guards but by the tree root itself. Thick vines of gnarled root were wrapped around his legs and arms, leaving him no room to move.

Slowly turning back, Verity saw the young goblin's wide eyes and quivering mouth. Instinct switched on. She turned to the bag she had brought along and took out gauze, ointment, tape, and a small flashlight.

She stood, placed the flashlight in her mouth and gently took the goblin's arm. It trembled beneath her touch and she winked at him hoping to calm him. After blotting as much excess blood away as possible, Verity placed a thumb on either side of the cut. Closing her eyes, she envisioned the blood flow calming, the cut pulling itself together. Opening her eyes, she leaned in to inspect the skin. It was similar to human skin, but more dense and rubbery. She forced the skin together with her thumbs and after a quick glance at Noah, she blew on the broken skin.

After confirming that the cells were indeed reaching out to one another, Verity looked up at her patient. He watched in awe as his skin slowly mended itself. She turned to King.

"Can you let Noah go now, please?" she asked. King nodded, and she turned around, verifying Noah's release. Verity watched him scowl and rub his arms for a moment before a thought struck her and she turned back to King.

"You have a healer, don't you? Why do you need me?" she asked, her brows creased, fear forgotten.

King leaned back in his throne lazily. "You are human. To say that your gift is unusual is an understatement."

Verity frowned briefly before turning back to the young goblin. The wound had knitted enough that it would heal fine on its own. She placed an ointment-covered gauze on the cut, having no idea if the ointment would help his kind or not, and wrapped it up, patting the goblin gently on the arm when she was done. King clapped.

"Miss Applebee! Meet my son Matthew."

Surprise that King would so casually slice up his own son streaked down Verity's back. She smiled at the goblin boy with the common human name. He bowed before disappearing down a corridor. Verity sat down, uncertain what to say. King sat forward and spoke quietly.

"He did offer."

Verity frowned. "He offered to be sliced open like a guinea pig by his own father?"

King laughed, hard and long.

"I should like to see these guinea pigs you

humans speak of."

Verity tried not to laugh but ended up producing a squelched snort which made King laugh even more.

"They're not very interesting," she commented turning around to check on Noah. He was leaning casually against the mammoth tree trunk, his arms crossed over his broad chest. Verity gave him a small smile before turning back to King, whose face had gone serious.

"You mentioned earlier that I had a healer. Then you have some knowledge of us?"

Verity shrugged. "Only a little."

"Tell me what you know so I may save time explaining why I chose to invite you to our home."

"Well, I've heard that you are a very well-mannered people with a strict ethics code but downright mean when someone crosses you. I heard that your healer was the best on this coast and that many species visit you for help."

King smiled, at least what she had determined was a smile with his huge teeth. "You know the gist then, good. What no one knows yet is that our healer has moved on to wherever elves end up when they lay to rest."

Verity brought her hand to her mouth, eyes wide. King lifted a finger and shook it at her briefly. "He died of old age, young one."

Verity nodded and realized her heart was about to pound out of her chest. She waited for it to slow before speaking.

"I am so sorry to hear that."

King nodded. "Yes, we were sad of his exit but

of all the things one can combat, age is not one of them. He was over four hundred years old, of which two hundred were spent with us. His service, his dedication was both admirable and stupid."

"What do you mean?"

"He had barely lived, young one. Before coming to us, he had lived in the same place, studied for more than half his lifetime and then settled here, never leaving. I would not wish that of you, child, but I would invite you to stay with us and be our healer until we find another to take your place. It would not be so urgent, you see, but we have an important patient who needs constant care."

"I would be happy to do whatever I can, King." Verity quaked inside but the challenge was perfect.

"I am pleased. Thank you," he said as he stood slowly. "Then let me show you our patient, shall I?"

Chapter 12

"The Queen?" Andy asked again.

Shana was flirting with one of the guys at a nearby desk and Joy had reached over her desk to grab a ringing phone.

Perplexed, Andy gazed at the glass office. He had always heard people refer to the Director when they spoke of the Guardianship. He'd never heard of a Queen.

Joy hung up and ushered him to the door of the glass office. He glanced over his shoulder and Shana waved before heading out of the busy room.

The woman was tall and had shoulder length white blond hair. She was still on the phone with her back to them, but the man had moved to the side. He was also tall and trim, wearing a dark suit. He smiled and gestured for them to enter. Andy thought him to be in his mid-thirties with brown hair, pale skin and dark eyes. When they came through the door the woman didn't turn. The man pulled a folder out from under her hand. She half nodded to him. The man made his way behind them and out the door. Joy motioned her head at him after he passed.

"That was the Director," she whispered. Andy dipped his head in acknowledgment and turned to watch the man leave the floor toward the stairs.

Finally, the lady said her good-byes and turned to them. She looked at him for a long moment; he could almost feel her scanning him. She was exceptionally tall for a woman. She looked like she was in her forties, but something made him doubt she was that young. Her hair was perfectly styled, and she wore a light blue dress and matching jacket. The dress brought out her periwinkle eyes. She had high cheek bones and thin lips that were just starting to turn into a smile.

"Well, now that we've appraised each other, hello Andy. It is good to meet you. I am Helen Barrows." She held out her hand. He took it and was relieved that it was warm.

"Good to meet you too," he said, holding tight to his training of manners and trying desperately not to let his knees shake. The Queen turned to Joy.

"Thank you, Joy. I think we'll be fine for now," she said. Joy bowed slightly and slithered out of the room, closing the door behind her with a hush.

"Now, Andy. I bet you have a few questions?"

"I don't even know where to start. So much of this is new to me." Mrs. Barrows nodded in understanding.

"I don't normally meet the students before they start classes, but I made an exception in your case. Not only is being a displacer rare, but Brick seems to be quite fond of you." She smiled for a moment at something Andy couldn't see before placing a finger under his chin and bringing his face up.

"You look like your father," she murmured as she inspected his face. She frowned and then shook her head. "I can't help but wonder how different your life might have been if he hadn't been taken so early."

Andy felt emotion swell in his chest. "I miss him... them," he whispered.

Helen pulled away and he watched some emotion wash over her.

"Me too," she said and then turned to sit at her desk. She waved him to a guest seat.

"We keep a lot of things secret, Andy. Not because they are bad but because most people wouldn't understand. Those who don't understand often will try to do harm before gaining the truth." Helen eyed him to ensure understanding before she continued. He nodded.

"I wish it were not something we had to deal with, but it is how it is for now. It protects everyone." Helen sighed sadly.

"I understand that completely," Andy said, "but I am still not sure why I am here. I mean I know why I'm at the school but you...you're the Queen. You have like, Queenly things to do."

Helen chuckled. "True. The reason you're here, Andy... Well, let me explain. We have been losing Guardians for hundreds of years now. One here, one there, a number that is small enough to be...well... normal. In the last twenty years, those numbers have risen by thirty percent. In the last ten they have risen one hundred percent and in the last five? Over two hundred percent. Andy, we are losing over a hundred Guardians a year." Helen paused and gave Andy a hard look. Andy spluttered.

"How is that possible? How many join each year? How do you know they're gone?"

"Excellent questions, Andy, just another reason

why I brought you here." She smiled brightly. Andy felt himself overwhelmed by the strangest desire to protect the woman sitting in front of him. He felt a strange pull and his eyes widened, his mouth formed an 'o'.

"You're a...but how?" Andy stopped himself before he could look like a complete idiot.

"Yes, Andy, I'm a Guardian. I too shift into a Gargoyle form. I am the only female Guardian alive currently, at least that we know about. We only show up every hundred years or so. When a new one is found, she is brought here and trained to take over the Guardianship. It's been that way since the beginning."

"Wow," he said quietly and then felt like he was eight again. Wow? That was all he could come up with? Helen made one of those adult noises like "hmp" that he thought was a short laugh. Then she straightened up and gave him a hard look. She was just about to start talking again when her phone rang.

"Barrows," she answered quickly, and he watched her lip quirk slightly before she ended off and put the phone on the desk. She stood and Andy moved to stand as well. She motioned for him to stay seated and went over to the corner of the room where there was a beige screen set up. It was over eight feet high and blocked his view from the desk as well as the view by anyone from the office side of the glass. She vanished behind the screen but continued to speak.

"I'm sorry I don't have more time to visit right now. We have a few things to take care of and then we'll get together and I will tell you some great stories about your father. I'm afraid I never met your mother."

When she stepped out from the screen Andy jumped from his chair. In full gargoyle form with a tuft of blond hair, she smiled and waved daintily at him. It was the oddest sight Andy had ever seen. She went to balcony doors that Andy hadn't noticed before and unlatched them.

She turned to Andy, her voice rough, "Once you get through some of your studies, you'll be able to join us on these little jaunts."

Before Andy could answer, she stepped out the door, jumped onto the balcony wall and pushed off into the sky.

"She loves her job." Joy's voice startled him. She snickered behind him. "The hobgoblins are messing with the mermen again. Technically it's not her job to handle that sort of thing but there is so much tactical planning and paper pushing around here that it's nice to see her get out once in a while."

Chapter 13

Sloane was so surprised she kept her mouth shut. Would breaking the bond mend her heart too? Or would she lose that odd yet comfortable feeling and still have the pain? She didn't even bother to ask where they were going. Bringing her legs up, she leaned against the door and dozed.

The next time she opened her eyes it was dark.

"Whatever happened to getting me some clothes?" she mumbled as she rubbed the sleep from her eyes.

"Oh. I forgot about that," Liam said without a glance, "but I think it's time to stop for something to eat. I saw a Cracker Barrel sign not long ago. Up for it?"

Sloane smiled. There was something about their hash brown casserole that made her downright happy.

"Yes, please," she said just as her stomach rumbled. They barely spoke during the meal. The casserole was as good as she remembered though. Afterward, they swung through a mall just before closing and Liam stood like a rock at the checkout counter while Sloane tried on jeans and tee shirts. She had insisted much to his irritation. You just have to try jeans on, the sizes vary too much.

The lady at the counter, a cute young blond, was doing the ogle-eye and trying to make conversation. He ignored her as his eyes followed Sloane around the store. Yep, Sloane noticed. She grabbed a couple pairs of underwear and a bra, hallelujah there was one in her larger size. When she hit the counter, Liam tossed an extra black shirt in the pile and paid for everything in cash without batting an eye. The ogle girl's eyes narrowed at Sloane as they left the store. Sloane changed into a complete new set of clothes in the bathroom. They were just leaving when Sloane slowed down to admire a pair of amazing high heeled black boots that caught her attention.

"What size are you?" he asked.

"Nine. Big ass feet on this girl."

Liam nodded and stepped into the shop. She stood watching him through the window. He went to the counter and flashed a smile as he spoke. A petite red-head smiled at him and quickly went to retrieve a box. She looked over some socks carefully and chose a pair placing both on the counter. Liam paid and walked out. His eyes met Sloane's with a challenge and then he continued to the mall exit. Sloane admired his backside as he went. Nice. Then she remembered she shouldn't be doing that and caught up with him. Silently they hit the road again. After a mile or two, Liam spoke.

"Do you always shop like that?"

"Yep," Sloane answered, "in and out. I hate shopping. Why?" She gave him a sharp look. He shrugged.

"Just curious."

"Okay, so I have a question about the squirrel/

brownie thing. Why did he call me Mistress? That was really weird."

"Truthfully, I didn't spend a lot of time studying up on them since they are relatively harmless. Like I said, they attach themselves to someone who is gifted and in their own way, help them. He obviously picked you."

"He tried to help me once."

"Did he?"

"Yes." Sloane didn't feel like relating that particular story. Maybe Liam would enjoy some cryptic silence for a change. She stole a glance at him. He watched the road like it was a beast to be slayed. Sloane didn't say another word for the rest of the drive.

~~*~~

Liam could feel her glance. The sheer force of her intention was clear. He could feel the turmoil boiling inside her. It was eating his insides too and it hurt in a way he had never experienced before. He had been convinced that it was the bond. But what was it she had said? *How do you think we were bonded in the first place*? No...*first fucking place.* When he had first seen her at the book store he was enraptured, wasn't he? He hadn't even thought twice about following her.

Fighting the urge to punch himself in the face, Liam stole a look. He rolled his eyes. He should have known she was asleep again. Her breathing had evened out and he was so caught up in his thoughts he didn't even notice. She was curled up on the door as far from him as she could get. He fought the ridiculous urge to reach out to her. This was *not* him.

He contemplated how others had handled the bond without losing their mind. There were great warriors and leaders in history that were bonded. Liam could not fathom how they accomplished anything. He suddenly wished he had paid attention during those lessons.

Chapter 14

"I thought I saw you on the roster this evening," Nikki purred after opening the door. She took in Simon's tall, trim physique openly. His current hair color, a medium brown, reflected in the harsh fluorescent light; his blond hair hidden. Even the blue eyes she stared at were not his own, his deep green hidden by a bit of plastic. His skin, having a pale, stone-like quality, was the only thing, besides his general size, that he couldn't change. She grasped his muscled right arm with her left hand and squeezed. Her right arm opened the door further and she "pulled" him inside.

"Yep," Simon said and headed toward his locker. Nikki was a flash back to the 80's. Her bleach blond hair was cut short and styled a little bit messy. Her small eyes always had a thin line of dark blue eyeliner around them making her eyes look even smaller. Hot pink lipstick, a blue mini-skirt, and tank top finished her ensemble.

Simon pulled a purple vest from the locker, indicating His Bouncerness, and put it on over his form fitting long-sleeve black tee before turning to Nikki. He knew she had watched his every move. She had placed herself on the greeting stool near the back door. She sat with her legs open, inviting.

Unfortunately for her, Simon was not even slightly interested. He appropriately flashed a melting smile. Nikki smiled back at him like the cat that got her cream. One thing Simon did not have a problem with was women, unless you counted too many choices a problem.

He started out the Employees Only door, hearing her loud sigh before it snicked shut behind him. Right now, Simon was bouncer extraordinaire at a posh club, named after it's illustrious owner, Kitten Lanagan. Kitten's Play was your standard, upper-class meat market for the young, playful, and often foolish. It was not Simon's first run as a bouncer, as he found the human interaction in such an establishment fairly entertaining and surprisingly well paying.

It was half an hour before the doors opened for the rich, frivolous, and well-connected New Orleans patrons. They would get an hour of mingling amongst themselves before the doors opened to the lucky public the bouncers decided to let in.

Simon made his rounds to all the party rooms ensuring they were in order before show time. He surveyed the main dance area and saw everything as it should be. The huge floor was open and waiting, the band; some group of pop wonders he had vaguely heard of, were doing their final sound checks on the stage. Three raised platforms, one on each side of the stage and one in front would soon be filled with writhing bodies. The other side of the dance floor was now filled with empty tables and loveseats, clean and waiting to accommodate. No one talked to him. They left him alone while he did his silent inspection. The servers milled about waiting for the masses. The owner herself, Madame Kitten, would be in a hidden dressing room preparing to make her grand entrance.

For fifteen years now, Simon had lived a normal life and loved every minute of it. Well, most of it. Never staying in one place for very long, he never had the opportunity to relax and fit in. Truth was, it would be dangerous for anyone around him if he stayed too long. His instincts would come out sooner or later no matter how much he buried them. He would always have to move on.

Essentially, he was an outcast. It was of his own choosing, but he made the best of it and enjoyed watching, and sometimes participating, in their petty games all the while keeping a sharp eye over his shoulder. He changed his last name each place he went, moving on when his gut told him to and keeping an acceptable distance from everyone.

A moment before eight, Simon stuck his head out the front door. Behind him, the main lights of Kitten's Play had been dimmed, the strobe lights were pulsing, and the band broke out with their first song of the evening. Ezra and Chuck glanced at him. Ezra was a medium height, small-boned wiry guy. Even his hair was wiry. His wide eyes stared at Simon for a moment, out of fear or admiration Simon wasn't sure, then he nodded. Chuck was his opposite. Short but big and beefy, biker-like with a shiny bald head and piercing blue eyes. He also nodded, and Simon stepped back inside to watch the peacocks parade through the door.

It was generally interesting. He got to scrutinize

them as they came in. Observe. His knowledge of them had grown tremendously by now. This job was a perfect fit for learning and yet he still didn't understand them. Humans were an emotionally volatile lot.

Laura, a regular, came through first with her boy toy of the week. She wasn't very pretty, but being the daughter of a very wealthy businessman had its advantages. She leered at him.

"Hey, Simon," she drew out slowly but loudly.

"Evening, Miss Laura," Simon answered, his baritone almost swallowed by the loud thumping of the music. She did her best to slink by while holding on to her toy's arm. He guessed their drinking evening had started early. Simon knew they would head straight to the bar where Nikki would pour their first drinks heavy enough to keep them spending for a while.

The masses came through a few at a time and Simon settled in to his standard menacing posture and watched. An hour later he felt his replacements behind him. He turned and nodded at the Bobsy Twins. Joe and Guido, two dark and burly Italian brothers stepped up to either side of the door allowing Simon to start his rounds.

It must have been a good three or four hours later when Simon came to the startling realization that something was wrong.

Madame Kitten had come out in her blond and sparkling splendor hours ago, but he hadn't seen her since. He was slipping. He had just finished a pass through of the party rooms, broken up a fight between two guys over a very proud girl, stopped someone from being sick in a corner plant and sent one overly pushy big girl wearing almost nothing out the back door to sober up.

He leaned against the left end of the long bar and motioned to Nikki. She was happy to oblige.

"Have you seen the Madame?" He spoke loud enough to get through the mind-numbing noise. Nikki smiled knowingly and wagged her eyebrows.

"She said she didn't feel well and was escorted to her room by a young little hottie."

Alarms went off in the back of Simon's head. In his four months at Kitten's Play the Madame had never done such a thing. He frowned as Nikki left him to serve the patrons.

Someone touched his elbow and he forced himself not to startle. No one snuck up on him, ever. His senses were turned up too high for it. Well, except for right now apparently. He turned and had to look down to meet the eyes of the petite lady standing before him. Her eyes were a deep ginger color; each slanted like one half of a yin and yang. Her nose was a gentle curve on her face and her lips were shiny and full. Dark hair fell down the sides of her face and continued, making him want to turn her about for closer inspection. A small, lithe body was covered with black leather pants and a tube top, showing her tanned, muscled shoulders. The sultry lips were moving. The music that had momentarily vanished flooded into Simon's ears and he almost flinched from the pain of it.

Coming back to his senses he leaned down to hear her better. He froze for just a second when he caught her scent; a musky, forest smell that could

only mean one thing.
   Werecat.

Chapter 15

"Clara, my love. You get more and more beautiful with each passing day, did you know that?" Dr. J told her.

She smiled at him and brushed her hand down his arm. Tugging her into his arms he kissed her forehead. She leaned into him as his phone announced a text message.

He released her and scanned the room, taking in the unopened paints and blank canvasses piled against one wall.

"I have to get back to work, but maybe you'll paint today?" he asked for the first time. He had hoped by putting them out for her she might decide to do something with them on her own.

"I'll try," she said and waved him goodbye. Closing the door behind him he wondered if, especially after the drug hypnosis mind-alterations he had done, she would still be able to paint at all.

Chapter 16

"She's human?" Verity asked when she entered the room. It wasn't so much of a room as it was a cave formed of thick roots and wide leaves. The bed was centered against one wall. Modern equipment was on one side of the bed, a table covered in odd flowers and herbs on the other. It was hard to tell but the woman lying on the bed seemed fairly tall. Her hair was light and pieces of it floated in the air as though being blown by a breeze. She was thinner than Verity thought was healthy save the very large lump under the covers at her midsection.

King walked to the side of the bed and took the unmoving hand, covering it with both of his. Her lids fluttered open revealing startling green eyes. Her pink lips turned slowly to a thin smile as though the very effort of it was tiring. Verity went to the side of the bed opposite King, concerned about the pale skin and lethargy.

"My dear," King spoke to the woman, "I have brought you an incredibly skilled healer. Do not judge her age. She will be able to help you." She turned her head ever so slowly and met Verity's eyes. Verity did her best not to squirm as the woman bore into her, giving the feeling that the woman could see her core.

"Verity," King said, "meet my Queen."

Chills ran down Verity's arms and legs. The woman spoke, so softly Verity had to lean in to hear.

"Hello," was all she said. In response, Verity took the Queen's free hand in her own and, closing her eyes, felt the Queen's physical condition. Whatever essence or power Verity had, she pushed it through the Queen's hand, up her arm and throughout her entire body. It didn't tell her exactly what was wrong as much as it gave her the symptoms, so she could deduce the problem and do what was needed to help. The Queen seemed to be in dire need of nutrients, but Verity needed more time to fully understand.

"King, before we get started, might I see my room?" Verity asked. "I'd like to freshen up." And think about the best course of action.

The Queen's body shook slightly. Verity thought she might be having a seizure until, with a quick look at the King's amused face, she realized the Queen was laughing. Verity stood uncertainly. Did she not get a room? Was it horrible? Did she have to share with someone strange?

King leaned down and rubbed his face on the Queen's cheek before turning away. He went to the door and poked his head out, nodding at some unseen hallway lurker before gesturing Verity out of the room. A goblin with mahogany fur and bright eyes waited for her. Further down the hall, Noah waited patiently. He fell in behind them as they passed. Verity frowned to herself. She almost wished another Guardian had come. The small heart tugs were not really wanted right now. They didn't go far before the goblin turned down another hall, through a wooden door and into an antechamber.

"This is for your Guardian," the goblin said while gesturing with one long hairy arm around the room. Verity took in the room, a large bed and dresser in beautiful wood workmanship and what appeared to be a closet. She cocked her head and frowned at the modern TV stand and medium sized flat screen TV. Didn't expect that.

Noah sat on the bed and smiled for the first time since their arrival at the goblin, who nodded in what looked like mutual understanding. The exact understanding was lost on Verity. The goblin made his way to a wooden door on the far left corner of the room. He pushed it open and Verity followed him into the massive room. A bed larger even than Noah's was centered in the room. Thick vines came up from each corner of the bed and wove together above it in an exquisite weave covered in leaves and flowers in shades of ivory, pinks and reds. She went to one corner and ran her hand over the vine.

"It's absolutely beautiful," she said in awe.

"One of many things that my family is capable of."

Verity tore her eyes from the art she would sleep in and glanced over the remaining ornate furniture. Everything you would find in a hotel room, including a small door that led to a moderately sized bathroom with a tub and shower. Everything looked to be hand built and felt alive save the TV stand and TV. Turning to Noah, who had not entered the room but leaned against the doorway watching, Verity smiled like a school girl. Noah grinned in return, but the smile didn't reach his face. Turning from him, Verity couldn't understand his strange attitude. He really didn't seem to like it here at all.

"I'll go get our things," he said and vanished from the room. Verity turned to the goblin.

"Once you're settled in, the King will be pleased to have you join him for afternoon tea." He said. Or she. Verity wasn't sure.

"Thank you. What's your name?"

"I am called Shyann by your people." Ah. Pretty sure that would be a female.

"Well, it's nice to know you, Shyann."

Shyann bowed her head and left Verity to the splendor of her quarters. She opened up drawers, tested lamps and checked the bathroom amenities. Everything she could possibly need save her clothing was available. Her thoughts went to the Queen as she started out the bathroom and ran smack into Noah. His muscled arms caught her and moved her to the side. Verity's heart sputtered for a moment.

"Sorry, didn't know you were there," she said. "That was fast."

"I didn't want to leave you for long, so I hurried."

Verity raised her eyebrows. "What's the deal? You don't seem to like these guys at all."

"I don't trust them. There's a difference."

Rolling her eyes, Verity walked to the bed where Noah had left her suitcase. "Why?" she asked.

"Experience."

Opening the case, Verity was going to ask but he spoke again. "I'll unpack. Just knock when you're ready." He went into the antechamber, his room, and closed the door behind him. Verity turned and stared at the door. With a heavy sigh she made a mental note to get these arrangements changed. There was no way she wanted to walk through his room every time she wanted to go somewhere. No way indeed.

Chapter 17

Simon's defenses kicked in hard, aware of her every move. The werecat's scent, her exotic look, and the gleam in her eye was almost a drug. It took almost everything he had to focus. And it bothered him. Only once before had a woman screwed with him like this. He was the one that did the screwing.

As he brought his head down to hear her, he scanned the crowd on the dance floor. There were several males cruising the floor methodically, looking over each person and moving on. He counted five. The low seductive voice in his ear almost made his heart stop.

"Would you like to join me in one of the back rooms?" she asked. Oh boy did he. Simon almost stomped his foot through the floor; he was so annoyed at his lack of control.

"I don't know what you're up to," he whispered to her, "but I'm going to find out." Her pouty face flashed with surprise and then became hard. He knew that look. She put one arm on his shoulder seductively and started to bring the other down fast and hard. A smart move. One hit in the right place and he would be down, nerves scrambled, and she could carry on with whatever she was here for knowing he wouldn't be able to move for a while.

Except for one problem. He was faster. He grabbed the incoming straightedge hand and twisted it behind her back. She snarled at him. He smiled his best shiny smile and looked into her eyes.

"What do you think you're doing?" he asked softly, knowing her catlike ears would hear just fine.

"What the hell are you?" she spat, her pupils large and dark.

"Possibly a friend. Tell me what you're looking for, Kitty Cat, and maybe I can help you."

Her eyes narrowed to slits. He waited to see if she would pounce or try something sensible, there was always a chance with cats. After a long moment she stopped struggling. He took a moment to scan the floor. They hadn't found what they were looking for yet. He wondered if it was even there. He looked back at the bomb he held firmly in his grip. A puzzled look vanished from her face and determination set in. He almost laughed. If you can't beat 'em, join 'em. He was starting to enjoy this. It reminded him of the old days before he had gone rogue.

"A man, a dangerous man, is here and we need to find him," she finally said, "and we need to find him fast."

"What is he and what has he done?" Simon asked. He could almost see the fur bristling under her skin. She was about to answer when he spotted one of her sentries from the dance floor heading straight toward them with malice in his eyes. He was trying to be inconspicuous and failing miserably; his impressive size and anger pushed him through the crowds. She saw him too.

"Let me go and Kasuchi there won't turn you into a snack," she hissed. Simon smiled at her.

"Now what fun would that be?" He pulled her around in front of him, keeping her arm almost to a breaking point behind her back. Kasuchi walked right up to them and stopped a hair away from touching her.

"Let her go or we will have issues," he said arrogantly. Simon flashed a smile that made his new friend pull his head back.

"Come with me," Simon ordered. He stepped backward and to the right, keeping the girl held in front of him. He found the door he was looking for and backed through it, Kasuchi following close. When the door shut, Simon released the girl. She rubbed her arm and he noticed her claws sinking back into her hands. Huh. He hadn't noticed them before. What was his problem?

"Cough it up. If you're doing something pack related, I can probably help." The two cats stared him down for long moments. He was getting annoyed.

"Oh, come on," he let his annoyance show, "you'll rarely run into the likes of me and I'm one of the good guys."

Kasuchi glanced at the girl. She was frowning.

"Sheba?" Kasuchi queried. Simon held his lips together tight so he wouldn't laugh. She caught it and glared at him. Despite the emotion boiling from her she acquiesced.

"We have a stray on the loose. He's eaten three people in the last two days and we finally tracked him here. We have to find him before..." she trailed off. No imagination needed there. Simon nodded.

"Good looking, young?" Simon asked. Sheba nodded and concern flickered across her face.

"I know where he is and I hope we're not too late." Simon went to another door in one fluid move. He heard Kasuchi hiss behind him and Sheba take a sharp breath. They had no idea what they were dealing with yet. It came back to him as easily as sucking through a straw.

Sheba stuck her head out the door they had just come through and waved to the four remaining in the crowd who quickly made their way over. Simon went through the other door before they could regroup, and they hurried to keep up.

Simon led them through a narrow hallway to a closet door. He opened it. Brooms hung along one wall with a shelf above loaded with cleaning supplies. Mops and buckets leaned against the other wall. The back wall had shelves of maintenance items; light bulbs, tools, etcetera. Simon pressed the screw beneath the light switch and waited as the shelved wall lurched back leaving a three-foot gap.

He went through first and quickly covered the short distance to Madame Kitten's hideaway room. He stopped and looked at Sheba who was standing so near her scent made his skin flame up. He smiled and touched her cheek. She startled and pulled back for a moment. Their eyes met, and she allowed a small smile to tell him what he wanted to know. He glanced at the others. They couldn't possibly know what he was, but they knew enough. He waved them in close, leaving only enough room for him to kick the door. He brought his fist up.

One finger went up, then two. At three his leg

shot out with blinding speed and the door flew off its hinges. A loud snarl from inside greeted them as they spun into the room like practiced dancers. A man rose from kneeling on the other side of the bed. He smiled at Simon as he licked blood from one of his sharp and deadly claws. Simon shook his head.

"Now, now," Simon said condescendingly, "it's not nice to play rough with kittens."

Chapter 18

Sitting on his new bed and staring blankly at his school schedule, Andy thought about his parents. So, his dad had been a Guardian. Andy blinked back the threatening tears and his mouth curled into a sad smile. He had no doubt that his parents would be proud of him. He had found his way home; a place he could belong.

He hadn't even hit class yet and knew that when he did he would find the same things as any other school; the jocks, the nerds, the goth, the rockers. He was pretty certain that no matter who you were or where you came from, that never changed. For some reason, it brought him great comfort.

He put the schedule on his desk and took a good look at his dorm room. His roommate, James something-or-other was in class. Andy would start tomorrow and had hours before James came back. Each side of the room was set up identically. A single, extra-long bed, desk and chair, and large free-standing closet.

His roommate had pictures of half-naked girls taped to the wall along his bed, the sheets striped in alternating black and dark blue with a thin gold line between. James' desk was covered in books and papers, a shiny computer in the center of it all.

The comforter on Andy's bed was a faded blue but the fabric was soft. He thought about crashing but instead, tossed his backpack on the bed and unzipped it.

A knock at the door gave him pause. He opened the door and a box floated before him. He leaned down and plucked it from the air.

"Awesome, thanks. That was heavy," a high-pitched voice said. Andy found a young Goblin, smaller than Shana even, shaking out his arms.

"Ah sure," Andy said.

"That's been sitting in package claim for a few days but I heard that you'd arrived and thought I would bring it up for you."

"For me?" Andy asked as he peered at the box looking for a name.

The Goblin laughed. "Your name's on the bottom."

Andy flipped the box. "Sure enough, there it is." He smiled and holding the box in one hand, held the other out to the Goblin.

"I'm Andy," he said.

"I know," the Goblin said. "My name is Eroch Greyfeld Bohan Stiggers, but if you're not a dick, you can call me E."

E put his hands on his hips and looked at Andy expectantly.

"Well, ah. I'm going to bet that I could probably get away with calling you E."

The Goblin nodded. "I'll let you know if anything changes. Ok then, I'm off to the package room. Have a nice day, Andy!"

"Thanks, E. You too."

Andy closed the door and blinked a few times.

He had a lot to get used to. He put the box on his desk and grew out one of his claws to rip through the packing tape. There was no return address or indication of where it had come from.

He lifted the brown packing paper and was greeted with a gift-wrapped box. He took it out, set it on his bed and found two more smaller wrapped gifts and a card. He smiled as he ripped the card from the envelope.

The moment he laid eyes on the card he laughed heartily. The top of the card read "Good luck to the College Bound" and he could tell the card originally had a picture of an overloaded car, but someone had pasted over it with a picture of a scantily dressed woman with fake black wings.

He opened the card. "Congratulations!" the printed words read.

In a graceful script was written:

May the sun shine broadly for you and the waters be calm. Your future is untold, make it as you see fit. We'll be proud. ~ Aggie

Then in a hard-to-read block:

See you there, Andy. Lots of trouble, I mean fun, to be had! K

The third set of handwritten notes were in red.

Brick did that and you know what I am talking about. Good luck at school! You're crammed full of greatness and I am so pleased that you're my friend. Next time I see you, the Poker Queen shall reign! Have fun, Andy! Love, Sloane

Then there were the words written in tiny black print:

Andy, I know you will have some tough luck and

sometimes school can be a real bear. Even I remember some of those times too well but there was always hope, always the knowledge that we save the world from itself every day. I am proud to have you by my side. Learn well. See you soon. Brick

Andy blinked back the tears. If he didn't feel at home earlier, he sure did now. He sat on the bed and wiped the wetness from his face. After a moment he breathed out a long sigh and picked up the nearest gift. It was about the size of a tie box. He ripped away the paper and found a simple rough brown box. He slid the top off and stared at the beautiful knife. It was about twelve inches long with a five-inch black handle. The blade itself was flat black with a smooth edge.

Holding the knife up, Andy found that it fit his hand perfectly. He made a faux jab and smiled. Glancing back in the box he saw that it had a nylon storage pouch. He pushed the knife into the pouch and tucked it into the inside pocket of his back pack. There were some things that he thought should probably stay hidden for now.

He picked up the next gift, the size of a new phone case. He opened it up and found a sleek over-sized watch. It was silver with clear glass over the inner workings. The gears, pins, and other intricate parts exhibited a fascinating array of motion. It displayed both digital and analog time. Andy loved it. He put it on before reaching for the biggest and last gift.

He knew what he wanted it to be. But that would be too much. He needed to not get his hopes up.

He tore the paper off a little slower, hesitant to look until he knew the paper was off. When he looked down, he gave a shout. Tossing the laptop onto his bed he shook his hips and moved his arms, thanking the gods for granting him family once more. He laughed and sat down, again reaching for the box, when a motion at the window caught his attention.

A five-inch tall winged humanesque form was looking in while shaking its bootie and laughing. Andy's eyes went round and the creature took flight and vanished. Andy ran to the window and peered out, searching but seeing nothing but lush green vines and flowers.

Chapter 19

They hit New Orleans just before midnight. Liam stopped in front of a 24-hour Walgreens and handed Sloane a fifty. She raised an eyebrow at him.

"Go get whatever you need to..." he paused looking for the right word but apparently couldn't find it, "whatever you need to make yourself super-hot."

Sloane blinked and left her gaze on him a bit too long before leaving the truck and heading inside. It took her ten minutes to replace the make-up bag that was sitting on her bathroom sink at home. She grabbed a couple of jeweled combs for her hair and a brush.

When she climbed back into the truck Liam was smiling.

"What?" she demanded.

"That was a lot faster than I expected."

"Not all chicks are vain."

Liam nodded, his lopsided smile causing a temporary short circuit and she laughed. The mood was lighter as they stopped at a quaint three-story hotel. It was covered in beautiful iron work and had small balconies at each upper level room. Their room was on the third floor overlooking a street that boasted coffee shops and mom and pop stores. A tourist area obviously and Sloane loved it. When she turned from the view Liam was pouring the bag of clothes from the mall onto the bed. She frowned. Why did they keep ending up with one-bed rooms? Before she had a chance to speak her mind, Liam took out the boots and socks. He pointed at the other pair of jeans she had bought. They were skinny jeans with some snags and holes in them. He tossed a black shirt onto them.

"Wear that," he said, "with the boots."

Sloane picked up the shirt. She had thought he had thrown one in the pile for himself, but she was wrong. It was made from a thin, stretchy material and had a deep vee-neck. It would be skin tight. Her shoulders slumped and she pouted.

"Why?" she whined.

Liam's mouth twitched. "He likes girls a lot."

"Must run in the fucking family," Sloane mumbled as she scooped up the pile and went into the bathroom.

~~*~~

Liam changed into all black. Black jeans, his favored black Doc Martens, and a black long-sleeve netted shirt with two small silver buckles and suspender-like straps. The shirt was a bit much, but he would fit in perfectly where they were going. He went to the bathroom door.

"I'll meet you in the lobby, just pop down when you're ready. I have a key, the other is on the desk."

"Okay," she said softly. He could hear her breathing. Liam realized his hand was on the door and pulled it away like it burned. Shaking his head, he took the stairs and made his way to the lobby.

As he exited the stairwell something slammed into the back of his head. It wasn't enough to do a large amount of damage to him in particular but it was meant to. That pissed him off. His skin started to swirl into shadows as he turned to meet the assailant. Three large human men stood with two-by-fours glaring at him.

"Give us the girl and we might let you live," one of them commanded him. An unamused laugh coughed from Liam's throat.

"Who sent you?" he growled.

"Now that be none of your concern, huh, skinny white boy?"

They laughed. Liam shook his head slowly and looked around the stairwell. Seeing no one, he moved.

The man standing nearest to him went down with a swift cut to the neck. The other two rushed forward swinging their wooden sticks. Child's play. Blocking one easily with an arm, he swung his foot up and planted it into the others groin, then slammed his elbow into the man's face. As soon as that one was down, the one he had blocked backed up and ran, disappearing through the side exit. Liam dragged the two sleeping beauties out the exit and dumped them on the sidewalk before running to meet Sloane.

Thankfully, he saw her first which gave him a few seconds to clamp down his control and crush any reaction into a pocket at the back of his mind. As she walked from the elevator he felt the urge to throw her over his shoulder and carry her right back upstairs. She always looked good enough to eat but seeing her in the tight jeans, her shirt straining over her chest and the boots...it was almost too much. She had her hair up with sexy loose strands brushing her shoulders. He mentally patted himself on the back for the foresight to meet her in the lobby. That shit should not be left alone.

She saw him then, standing near the large picture window by the front door. She stopped and covered her mouth, her eyes wide. Invisible mental restraints covering him from head to toe, Liam walked over to her and held out an arm. She took it but didn't stop staring. He smiled inside, just before a frown washed over his face as he wondered if he was doing the right thing.

~~*~~

Liam stopped and pointed across the street. Sloane followed his hand and laughed.

"You have got to be kidding me. *Kitten's Play?* You're not taking me to a strip club, are you? That would just piss me off."

Liam laughed. "No. It's your standard dance club."

Sloane breathed out in relief. Liam abruptly realized that Sloane's hand had never left his arm during the four-block walk. She still held on while her infectious laugh made his heart warm up like a new toaster.

As he started to smile he realized he hadn't done much of that lately. Overcome by the bond and the challenge he was embarking on, he'd forgotten one thing. To live a little. He squeezed Sloane's hand and led her across the street to the entry. He gave her a wry smile.

"Let's have some fun," he said. Sloane raised an eyebrow, which only served to broaden his grin. "Since we're going to see Simon at some point this evening, I think we should let loose a little. Enjoy the moment."

Sloane frowned, and her boots suddenly seemed to hold great interest. Liam reached out and lifted her chin with a finger. She met his eyes and he saw pain. Pain he wanted to erase even for a short time.

"If you really don't want to, I understand. But I think after all this time, we owe it to ourselves to have some fun."

Glancing at the club door, Sloane answered, "A club wasn't quite what I had in mind."

Liam understood that all too well. He shrugged. "A close second?"

Her laugh melted the tightness that had been collecting in his shoulders since they'd left Florida.

"You think you can keep up with me?" she asked. It was Liam's turn to raise an eyebrow.

"I think you're about to be shamed."

"You're on, you cocky bastard," she snarled but her eyes shined.

The bouncers let them in, the music loud and pumping; one of the latest catchy dance songs. Liam hadn't been paying attention to the names of the artists for quite a while, which made it a pain in the arse when he wanted to fill his iPod. He partially blocked his over-sensitive hearing so the music wouldn't be as painfully loud and followed Sloane in. He paid for their cover and led her to a corner. Sloane leaned back into the wall and looked at him expectantly.

Liam moved in next to her and scanned the club. He liked the look of the dance floor right in front of the stage. He leaned down to get close to Sloane's ear.

"Center floor?" he asked. Sloane looked thoughtfully around the club before flipping her body directly in front of him and pressing him back into the wall. His heart rate skyrocketed into the outer-sphere as he met her eyes. She was smiling in that way girls smile when they are up to absolutely no good. His defenses started to slam up when she shook her head at him.

"Fun doesn't work when you block me out. Here's the deal. You and I have *fun* for one hour. That means fuck the should-nots, fuck the barriers, and especially fuck all the rules save one: we don't complete the bond. We play like it's real. Those are my requirements for *fun* this evening. Take it or leave it."

Stupefied, Liam searched her face for the joke. When he met only the intensity of her gaze, he considered the terms. She knew he would still try to break the bond, didn't she? He didn't know how to be what she wanted. Did he?

She was still there. She wasn't giving up on him yet. Everything in his being told him to run away. To find Simon and get out. But her body, so warm and inviting, pressed close. Her eyes were too beautiful and expectant. Her fierceness made his nerves zap and tingle. He didn't want to run. He wanted this hour like he needed his next breath.

Nodding, he put his arms around her and crushed her to him. Her arms snaked around his neck and she gave him a smile that melted any remnants of the barriers he'd worked so hard to hold.

He leaned over and kissed her shoulder, heat filling him like an active volcano. He moved up her neck with his lips, feeling her heartbeat quicken, feeling her meld into his embrace. When he reached her ear, he whispered, "One hour."

She turned into him, brushing her cheek against his, sending lightning into his groin.

"One hour," she said, husky and seductive. Liam almost pulled back, but the game was on and he *really* wanted to play. He moved to kiss her, and she pulled back with a wicked smile. Grabbing his hand, she pulled him to the dance floor.

Knowing that what he really wanted would break their one rule, Liam entered the floor and the largest challenge in his life. Dancing came naturally to him. Years of experience in the club scene and many more with the waltz, the rumba, and countless others. He watched her like a stake out and didn't miss a thing. Whether those moves came naturally to her or whether they were earned with hard work, tonight, they were just for him.

A light sheen of sweat appeared on her forehead as she glided and grinded with the pumping sounds of the music. Liam allowed his body to breath a bit and soon he too was covered in a moist sheen. No one came near as they blended and moved together like a symphony.

Liam was disappointed when the song ended, until an older slow song he knew came on. An impish smile touched his lips and he pulled her close. She didn't resist, instead she fused to him like melted caramel. He felt her emotions filling him and realized that she had learned to block them from him. How had he not noticed? The warmth and trust. The love.

Brushing off his fear, fully tucking his barriers away, he allowed his emotion to flow freely, allowed truth to reach out to her, hoping it would be received as he intended. Though he was completely and devastatingly in love with her, it could not be.

He knew the second it hit her. Her body tensed in his arms for a heartbeat before she pulled her head up and studied him. He gave her a sad smile, which she returned, before pressing her lips to his.

His legs almost bucked at the pure ecstasy her lips drove through him. He returned her kiss gently, as tenderly as he could manage while keeping wild lust and the bond at bay. She was slowly killing him. Arms trembling with effort not to scoop her up and run to the nearest private room to seal the bond, Liam continued to sway to the powerful song, basking in her warmth.

Pulling away from his lips, Sloane laid her head on his shoulder and even through the music he heard her whisper. "Heaven."

Liam found that he could not agree more which made it even sadder. Sloane's sharp intake of breath brought him back to earth.

Barriers flew up around him like automatic doors in a prison, as he opened his senses to the building.

Sloane withdrew from him, eyes alert, a deep frown etched across her face. She pointed toward the other side of the building.

"There is some weird shit going on in there, Liam."

Chapter 20

During tea with the King, Verity was inundated with questions about news on the outside while Noah stood aloof near the door. Afterward, Verity and King visited the Queen. Verity was concerned. She would need to learn quite a bit more about the goblins before she would feel confident in helping the Queen. King pulled up a chair next to the Queen and gently took her hand in his own. She was sleeping soundly. Verity took up a seat on the other side of the bed. The King's concerned gaze fell on her.

"How many children has she born?" Verity asked.

"This will be number three. You've met Matthew. Johnathan is away. I encourage all children to leave the lair when they are of age, and live outside these walls before deciding their path." He smiled. "Most come home."

Verity nodded. "And how long is gestation? Same as humans?"

"No. My species is twelve months, yours nine. Together it seems to be eleven."

Whistling, Verity looked the Queen over again. "This is one strong lady."

King smiled broadly and appreciatively at his wife. "That is why I chose her."

Verity couldn't control the stab of a jealous pang before she pushed it away, intentionally not looking at the door where she knew Noah loomed.

"So, what am I dealing with here?" Verity looked at King.

King's smile vanished. He took his time answering. Verity waited patiently, listening to the soft rasping of his wife.

"The child is healthy. Her body feeds him well. But he steals from her. Energy, food. The light. She must be nurtured but only the healers know what to do. Someone must determine what she needs to survive. I do not know."

Frowning, Verity nodded and watched Queen's pale hair float oddly about. King continued.

"Then there is the delivery. The child is too large for a normal birth. She will die without magic. You have about a week to prepare."

Keeping her wits took every effort and Verity felt like she pulled it off. She took Queen's hand while letting out a deep breath, ready to feel the Queen's needs with a new view. The King's presence was like a strobe light. Taking just a moment to clear her mind, Verity closed her eyes and let her energy loose, following the rush through the Queen. Touching the nerves, the cells, and listening to their screams Verity started to get a better idea of what was needed.

Finally pulling back, she opened her eyes and gently put Queen's hand down. The King had not moved.

"I need to know everything she's consumed in the last two days. Food, liquids, vitamins, IVs, everything. Who's been caring for her since…?"

"I have. I trust no one else with my wife. It has been nine days since the loss of our healer. There have been no IVs, for no one would know how to use them. There are no vitamins as she can't keep them down. Her foods have been liquids only. Water and juice."

"All right, well that makes sense. She needs protein, King. And calcium. Her body is giving it to the child and she's extremely deficient. It takes her energy away and could affect them both adversely. Luckily the child is almost to term, so the drain is slowing but this is one hefty child."

The King had what looked to be a pained smile on his face.

"And what do you propose?"

"I'll make a list of what we need. We should get it today if we can, it will make the birth easier."

Chapter 21

The werecat stopped licking his claw to hiss at them. Simon felt a pang of pity. This one was just a kitten himself. One of the weres closed the door and the rest fanned out to the left and right. Simon knew there was no hope for this one. Sheba moved to stand in front of them all.

"Simba," she said, her voice more a plea. If it had been a different time, Simon might have laughed. Another appropriately named cat but obviously one that meant something to this beautiful were which bothered Simon more than he cared to admit. She moved forward slowly and held out a hand. "Come home."

The half-man dropped his hand and cocked his head. Sadness ran over his face. "It's too late," he said softly, his large teeth giving him a lisp. Before Simon's very eyes Simba's pupils dilated and hate overtook his gentle features. He wondered if this was the were version of rabies. Simon stepped up behind Sheba and put a hand on her shoulder. She didn't flinch.

"It's too late for him," he whispered for her ears only. He watched a tear roll down one exotic cheek. She wiped it off angrily and crouched. Simba pounced at her, soaring over the bed. She growled and prepared to take the tackle, take the fight. Simon's deeply buried protection instincts emerged with a fine edge.

Before Simba could land on the crouching Sheba, Simon's left arm shifted in one fluid motion. His pale arm exploded into a thick gray leather, claws ripped through his fingers, the sleeve of his shirt turning to shreds as it went. He grabbed Simba out of the air and with a one-handed twist broke his neck.

The thrill of being himself, even if just an arms worth, rushed through him. He knew they were staring at him. He would have to leave again, sooner then he wanted. He quickly formed his arm back to human and arranged the broken werecat in a dignified manner on the floor. He pointed at the back door. "Take him and vanish. I will take care of the rest."

Three of the men picked up the body and a fourth let them out. Kasuchi held the door for Sheba. She motioned for a minute and he stepped out.

Sheba met Simon's eyes, igniting things in him that were surprising and scary. She walked to him and touched the strips of shredded cloth hanging from his left shoulder. She took his arm and looked it over, turning it this way and that. Simon kept breathing in, breathing out. Still holding his hand, she looked up at him again, searching his guarded face.

"You're a..." he put his finger to her amazing lips, feeling a jolt through his fingers as he cut her off. She backed away, pulling his hand with her for a moment before letting it go. He slowly brought it down to rest at his side, never dropping his pointed gaze. She backed to the door, stepped out and then she was gone.

Simon rubbed his temple while he walked to the other side of the bed to see what had become of Madame Kitten. She lay on the floor; eyes closed, pulse slow and unsteady. Her stomach was torn up and oozing with thick red blood. He was glad she was still breathing; tough broad. He went to the bedside table, picked up her phone, dialed 911 and left it off the hook.

He didn't glance back when he let himself out the back door into the alley. Head down, he headed away from the club.

Not ten feet down the alley he smelled her; the thick, rich musk and something that was just her, greeted him. She was crouched, hidden behind an air conditioner, waiting. He approached slowly, reaching down before she could react and pulled Sheba to him. She started to struggle but then stopped, burying her face in his chest with a sob. He held her close and smelled her hair, explored her back gently.

Simba had been her kin. He knew it like he knew the sun would rise. The scents didn't lie. He turned, cradling her with his left arm and started moving down the alley, away from the club. Away from one life toward another. She pulled away and stood in front of him, blocking further progress.

"We must go," he said softly.

"Show me," she demanded. The tears were drying, and her invincible cat face was back on. He touched her face, traced her lips. She caught his hand, gently licked his palm and then bit down without breaking skin and shoved it back at him. He smiled. There was something very intoxicating about the mating ritual of cats. He never would have thought his true mate would end up being one. He started to pull off his vest. He would have to go back to his other life now. He couldn't stay with her and keep running from his destiny. She knew about his world, his worth. But stay with her he would. He pulled off his shirt and wished he was wearing sweats instead of jeans. They ripped a heck of a lot easier.

As they stood in the shadows of the alley, the sirens still in the distance, he started the change. Slowly so she could see exactly what she was getting into. His body became a roiling mass of gray shadow, his muscles bulged and expanded, his skin smoothed into a tough leather. His hair pulled into his scalp as thick skin and horns sprouted. He reveled in the feeling; it had been so long since he had been himself. He pushed ridges from his back and whipped his spiked tail around behind him. Jeans hung in shreds, he pulled them off. Sheba watched in silence; her eyes wide.

Simon had held the best for last. He stretched out his arms, for looks of course, and sprouted wings; almost double his height, leathered and veined. He gave them a quick flap and then folded them tight to his back. Sheba stepped up and ran her hand down his chest, touched his protruding jaw, ran a finger down a three-inch fang. She stepped away and took him all in, her eyes devouring him. He stood still as a statue; the sirens getting closer and closer. Sheba pressed her body against his, snaked her arms around his torso.

He put his arms around her protectively, and jumped straight up, pushing his wings out and catching the air in one smooth motion. He swelled with a feeling that he had almost forgotten. Joy.

Chapter 22

L iam rushed through the hallway, Sloane trailing behind him as she tried to run in her heels. Her heart pounded, half fear and half excitement. Never a dull moment around Liam. He found the closet and pushed through before her. The sirens were coming, and she had a good idea where they were going. She could feel a faint breath of life from somewhere ahead, it was mixed with distress and fear. When she finally entered the room, she barely caught a glimpse of a body on the floor before a squeal escaped her lips as Liam scooped her up and ran out a back door.

As soon as they hit the alley she saw the faint swoop of a shadow head into the sky.

Liam swore but kept running until he had reached the back of the dark alley. Sloane watched quizzically while he untied his shoes with superhuman speed and kicked them off. He tore off his shirt and a sock at the same time, which for some reason amused Sloane to no end.

"Turn around," he growled as his skin started to swirl. Sloane turned. You don't question that.

A moment later a thick leather arm grasped her, and they were in the air. Sloane threw her arms around his neck and buried her face in his chest. A second arm showed up and pulled her close. The wind whipped around her for a moment and then smoothed out as he cradled her. Sloane kept her eyes squeezed tight as she spoke, "We're chasing him, aren't we?"

"Yes." His voice was gruff and had lowered several octaves. A chill went down her back. Sloane dearly wanted to throw something, annoyed that her hormones were awake at a time like this.

~~*~~

Liam could see him clearly and knew it wouldn't be long before Simon noticed. Unless he was out of practice, but Liam didn't think that was likely. Sure enough, after about a mile, Simon landed on top of a several story's tall building. Liam was surprised to make out a small female released from his arms. She immediately crouched into fighting stance next to Simon. Liam landed twenty feet from them. He lowered Sloane gently to the ground, who immediately ducked behind him. He kept his wings partially spread to help keep her separated.

"Simon," he said. The other gargoyle lowered his head and sniffed the wind. A smile broke out on his elongated mouth, his sharp teeth gleaming. He chuckled.

"Liam. Of all the people I expected to see today, your name was definitely not at the top of the list. They finally found me, eh? Come to drag me back then?"

"Not really," Liam said and shrugged, a massive shoulder. "I actually came to ask a favor."

Simon cocked his head, black eyes shining. "A favor? Well, this day was already going quite well," he glanced at the girl who had straightened up to watch, arms folded, "and now this. I think I shall remember this one for a very long time."

It was Liam's turn to look puzzled. Simon ignored it and strode over to Liam. Simon put his hands on his hips.

"I would say you look good, but you look the same, you old scoundrel. I think I missed you." Simon held out a clawed hand. Liam took it with one of his own and they shook. Sloane peeked around at them.

Simon turned his head and looked her over. He started to laugh as he addressed Liam. "You hunted me down in what, a day? When the Guardianship's been looking for fifteen years, you found me in no time to talk to me about bonding?" Simon was really laughing now. "Tell me I'm wrong, Liam." Simon put his hands on his knees and shook with laughter.

Liam folded his wings back and glared. "So what if I did?" Simon almost fell in his amusement. The girl with Simon was smiling. Liam caught her scent and knew what she was. He waited for Simon to chill. It took a few minutes, but he finally pulled himself together, wiping the tears from his face. Liam stared.

"Fine, fine. But you won't believe me. No one does."

"Just tell me how to break it."

"Why man? She looks like a damn good fit for you."

"I. Don't. Fit. Now, tell me. *Please.*"

Simon pulled the werecat to him and rested an arm around her. "It's too simple. No one has believed me yet. There's only one way to break a bond. You both have to wish it."

Liam looked at Simon for a long moment while it registered. It was too simple and yet it made sense. He nodded.

"Thank you, Simon."

"That's not quite all," Simon said, "you have to both wish it so, but at the same time and I don't know exactly for how long, but it's not just a minute. It's more like for a couple of days. I can't be sure because I didn't talk to her after it broke. It was just gone."

Liam sighed and went into a crouch. He glanced at Sloane. She had turned away from them all and was staring off into the darkness.

"Sorry, man," Simon said as he put a hand on Liam's shoulder. "I guess you got it bad. You realize that it simmers way the heck down once it's consummated, right?"

Liam's head snapped up. "What?"

"You didn't pay any attention in class, did you?"

"Only if they talked about hunting and maiming big scary things."

Simon chuckled and crouched down as well. The girl stood next to him comfortably.

"Meet my soon to be bonded, Liam. This is Sheba."

Liam didn't hide his surprise. Simon grinned. "I broke a bond accidentally, Liam. I can't explain it, but the relationship wouldn't have worked. I just met this one an hour ago and I can tell you without reservation that this one will. We were just off to get that going, so if you could speed this up it would be just lovely." Sheba leaned into Simon.

Liam glanced up to where Sloane had recovered

and was watching their banter with a blank face. She was getting good at that.

"Meet Sloane, my bonded," he said. Simon and Sheba smiled and nodded. Sloane showed a few teeth in return before her eyes went back to Liam.

"How long? A week, a day?" Simon asked.

Sloane interjected, "About six months, give or take."

"Damn, Liam. And you haven't shagged her yet? You must..."

Liam growled. Simon laughed. "You must have guts of iron, seriously. That's unheard of."

"Not helping, Simon."

"Fair enough. Read a book on it. If you don't need me, I have some business to attend to." He scooped up Sheba in his arms and backed away. He flung his wings out for lift off when Liam called his name. Simon paused.

"You don't have anyone looking for you. You never will unless you get into trouble."

Simon gazed at Liam for a long moment before he nodded and took to the sky. Liam turned to Sloane and opened his mouth. She held a hand up.

"Nothing," she said and shook her head, "Say absolutely *nothing.*"

<h1 style="text-align:center">Chapter 23</h1>

"James Tally," the boy said, easy to understand despite the strong British accent. He stretched out a tentative hand. Andy looked at it for a moment before taking it. *It was just so proper.* The boy before him was about the same age but white, very, very white. He had brown hair that fell limply over his forehead and large brown eyes. He was about four inches shorter than Andy's six feet, and where Andy was rippled lean with muscle, this boy was soft, almost doughy. It was like he was still growing but the body hadn't decided which way to go yet.

His shake was firm however. Andy smiled.

"Andy Chamberlain. Nice to meet you James. I hope I haven't inconvenienced you too much."

James waved a hand as though brushing away Andy's concern. "It's part of our duty in the Den. We watch over each other." He paused and lifted a shoulder, looking at the ground. "If we don't, we'd never be able protect our brethren."

Brows raised, Andy waited for James to meet his eyes. When he did, Andy spoke. "Thank you, James. That means a lot to me."

"It does to me too. Watch out for some of the bullies here though, they think they *own*." James shuffled to his bed and tossed his book bag to it before sitting with a sigh.

Andy sat on his own bed and cocked his head. "Bullies, huh? I would've thought they left that shit at home."

James looked up sharply. "They frown on cursing."

It was Andy's turn to shrug. He smiled broadly, mischievously. "James, I'm not a bully but I've been hiding my whole life. This is the first time where I can just be me. And I am damn well going to do just that."

"Well, just make sure…"

"Don't worry, man. If there's one thing I've learned, I respect my superiors until they give me a reason not to."

This time James smiled. "Well, things just may work out then."

"You have no idea how glad I am to be here," Andy said picking up his laptop and settling it on his knees. "Do you know the wifi password?"

Chapter 24

It was late, at least it felt late. Verity didn't really know for sure, having no sun or moon to tell her. In a fit of crankiness, she had yelled at Noah to get lost. She felt bad about it but at the same time, she needed to be left the hell alone for a while. Since they'd arrived, grumpy Noah had lurked around the corner or in doorways and she could not take one more moment. He had raised his brows at her but actually gave in and left her alone with the Queen.

After three days of a nourishing IV, chocolate protein drinks which had pleased the Queen immensely, and fresh fruit the Queen's coloring was much better. The baby was so big Verity could watch him move, and could make out feet and hands as he tried to get comfortable. She knew that he would want to come out soon and it took everything she'd learned in the last few months to give her even the smallest confidence that she would be able to handle it. Telling bodies to heal, seal a wound, or encourage blood cells to perform was one thing. But telling a body to literally *think big* was a whole different animal.

Verity needed a distraction. She left Queen's room and started to wander. The waiting was driving her crazy. There was a time when she thought living in caves, dark and mysterious, was up her alley but she was wrong. She wouldn't be one of the healers that stayed in the lair for life. Especially if things didn't go well with the Queen.

Verity stopped and looked around. The lights were dim, the pleasant smell of old wood and moss was gone, and the scent of wet dog pervaded her senses. Fear shot through her legs as she eyed the three hallways presented her. Turning around abruptly, Verity stopped, eyes wide, heart pounding.

The creature was not a dog, but it did have four feet. Covered in fluorescent green fur, it's red eyes glowed at her. The teeth were bared, and thick strands of saliva dripped low.

"Good doggy," Verity purred hoping she sounded friendly. She hadn't listened much when the boys were explaining to Noah the things to look out for in the caves. She hadn't considered being in them alone. Backing up a step, her eyes never left the blood lust reflecting in the red gaze. A strange low moaning emitted from it, joined by another from behind her. Tears welled in her eyes as she thought about the life she had hoped for. Her lip quivered, not sure whether to scream or not. Would the scream bring them on? If she yelled at them would they go away? Struck with indecision Verity found herself shriveling inside.

She heard a scrape come from behind her.

Something tore into the back of her calf. Throwing out her hands and yelping in pain, Verity caught herself before bashing her head into the rocky ground. She screamed as teeth sank further into her leg. Verity tried to turn only to have her wrist grabbed by the second beast. Pain seared as it pulled her forward leaving her stretched between the two.

I want to live. "Get off me!" she screamed. The urge to escape, to survive, kicked in. With her free leg she began to kick the beast on her calf. An odd moaning erupted as she hit a tender spot. Encouraged she threw out her free fist only to have it hit the cold floor delivering even more pain.

Tears leaked as she screamed. The beasts started to moan together, sending peels of terror and fear through her.

And then they let go. Face down, Verity froze. She waited for several moments, breath heavy. The pressure was gone from her leg, but the pain throbbed, the nerves on fire, alerting her mind to a big problem. Lifting a tentative head, Verity looked up to find one of the beasts sitting three feet away, like a dog might, with its tail giving the random shake. Meeting its eyes, the creature whined and went to its haunches, tucking its head between its front paws. Wincing, Verity sat up and turned to see the other doing the same.

"You should know better than to wander the caves without the password," a deep voice said from behind her. Verity whipped her head around to find herself face to face with a pair of lace-up black boots. Raising her eyes slowly, she followed muscled legs hugged by black jeans to a white tee shirt with a black leather vest fitted perfectly over a trim muscular chest. Jet black, shoulder length hair framed a perfectly sculpted pale face. Arrogant purple eyes looked her over, finally settling on her leg. He shook his head.

"I didn't know there was a password," she whispered.

"Obviously," he replied snidely. He kneeled and reached out to her leg. Verity pulled it away, shrinking from him. Rolling his eyes, he leaned over and scooped her up effortlessly. Verity struggled.

"Oh stop," he said, "I will bring you to safety."

Relaxing, Verity settled into his arms, resting her head on his shoulder. Vanilla and wild flowers invaded her senses as pain and unconsciousness overtook her sensibilities.

Chapter 25

Liam dropped to the darkness of an alley just a block from their hotel. He had not spoken a word which Sloane was grateful for. She needed to think, and she was angry at him, so it was easier to stave off the seemingly unquenchable hormonal outbursts. She turned away, so he could change shape and get dressed.

"Done," he said, the gruffness of his other form gone. Sloane turned to him.

"So, besides Simon's solution to breaking the bond, there's only one way, is that correct?"

Liam nodded. They started the walk back to the hotel.

"Well, I for one am not all that excited about jumping off a cliff. And you can fly so that wouldn't work for you either."

Liam's lip curled up as he nodded.

"Well, shit."

Arriving at the hotel, they went to the room in silence. Sitting on the bed, Sloane pulled off the boots with a groan. She shook her head.

"Beautiful boots but damn. Hell of a way to break them in." She stared at the floor for a moment, wriggling her feet before bringing her gaze to Liam. He was leaning against the wall near the door.

"I think you should get me my own hotel room," Sloane said.

Liam was slow to answer but when it came, it was crystal clear. "No."

Sloane threw her hands up. "Why? I mean, I get it. You don't want me. I'm down with that, but why this torture?" She waved a hand at the single bed.

Leaning his head against the wall, eyes closed, Liam breathed in deep and let it out slowly.

"You don't understand the complexities. You don't know *me*." He brought his eyes down to meet hers. "And there is someone or something looking for you and I will not leave you in a room alone without protection."

"Gawd. Don't remind me. I had forgotten about that."

Standing, Sloane walked around the room, her toes luxuriating in the fibers of the carpet. She ended up near Liam and watched him back up toward the door.

"I'll leave for now and won't return until you're asleep. But I'll be watching."

Bringing her arms up, Sloane hugged herself and leaned her head to the side as she looked at him.

"Am I really that horrible to you? Am I so sub-standard?"

Liam's eyes flashed, and he growled, "*Don't* say that. There is nothing about you that I don't want, but I *can't* have you." His eyes widened, and Sloane thought she might have seen a hint of pink blossom on his colorless cheeks before he turned away. He grabbed his backpack and left the room, closing the door gently behind him.

Staring at the door, a smile spread across Sloane's face. Stifling a schoolgirl giggle she turned away only to hear the softest knock. She paused, listening. When it came again, she followed it to the balcony door. The heavy curtain was the one thing separating her from someone who wanted to remove her head from her neck.

Laying on the ground, Sloane was about to attempt to peer up behind the curtain when the balcony door slid open. Before Sloane could get out of the way, the curtain was pulled aside. Liam looked down at her.

"What are you doing?" he asked.

"I...ah...was trying to see..."

"In the future, do not try and see anything, just lock yourself in the bathroom until I arrive," he said sternly. Sloane pulled herself up nodding.

"Your slave is here, *Mistress*," he said as he pointed a thumb behind him. "Make sure you lock the door when you go back inside." He reached up and grabbed part of the iron decor, then swung himself up and over the building. Sloane leaned out and glanced upward to where he had disappeared. That was a seriously hot move. A twittering sound pulled her attention back.

The squirrel sat near the far left corner of the balcony. Sloane settled herself in a chair near the door, not too eager to be seen by any prying eyes below.

"Mistress," the squirrel said as he bowed.

"Hello again," Sloane answered. "First thing, you need to tell me your name. It just doesn't seem right to know you as 'the squirrel.'"

The squirrel just stared at her, looking slightly horrified.

"Wait," Sloane held up a finger and glanced at the sky, "let me guess. There's truth to that whole thing about how names are power or whatever."

The squirrel smiled and nodded vigorously.

"Then I'm going to call you Bob," Sloane said. Bob smiled and puffed his chest out. "Good, now that that's out of the way. How the heck did you get here?"

"Quick travel," he said with his deep squeak.

"That's helpful, thanks," Sloane said, eyes rolling. Then it hit her, and she stood. "They're coming, aren't they?"

"No, no!" Bob said, waving his short arms. Sloane sighed and sat back down. She was suddenly very tired.

Bob inched his way over to her before sitting on his haunches and looking up, his eyes big and round.

"They are sent by the Sinister," he said.

"The what?" Sloane frowned.

"The Sinister. He wants your body laid to rest. He must be removed for the sake of all. You and the red one can do it. In the ancient land. The Shades tell us so."

Sloane stared at him. "Come again?" she whispered.

Chapter 26

Verity came to awareness with a start, eyes flying open. Intricate vines crossed above her and the soft bed cradled her gently. She waited a moment for the pain to seep in. When nothing felt out of the ordinary she inspected her hands only to find them unscathed. Sitting up, she pulled her leg up. The jeans were shredded but her skin was closed and slightly pink where the bite had been.

Loud voices pulled her attention to the door. She stood tentatively, relieved to find that there was no pain. She rushed to the door as the voices got louder and yanked it open. Noah was standing at the outside doorway to the hall yelling at someone. He turned to look at her when her savior, the black-haired man, attempted to step inside. Noah flung his hand out to stop him.

"What are you doing?" Verity shrieked at him. "He saved me from being torn apart by those…those things!"

Not moving his arm, Noah turned his head back to her. "Do you know what he is? Do you know why he came here?"

"No. What difference does it make?"

The alluring man stood smirking at Noah, his arms clasped behind his back.

"See? I told you," the man commented, clearly amused.

Verity walked over and pulled Noah's hand away. She gave him a fake smile, took the stranger's arm and guided him to her room.

"He can explain it to me directly," she said to Noah as she closed the door, ignoring the concerned plea on his face.

She motioned to the only chair in the room while she sat on the edge of her bed.

"You healed me?"

The man sat down, one eyebrow raised, and his lips curved into a crooked smile. He nodded as he tucked a loose hair behind his ear. It was then that Verity noticed them. His ears were delicately curved into a point.

"Ah. You're one of the Fae."

"Indeed. You win a prize. Oh, never mind, you already cashed it in."

Confusion clouded Verity's face. The man laughed. It was light and airy but flowed out like a low-pitched door chime.

"Of course, it wouldn't make sense to you. I have paid a debt today," he said.

"A debt? For what?"

"My mother owed you a blood debt. I have paid it for her. Now she owes me."

Verity muddled through pictures flashing through her mind when an image of a young Fae became clear. Half a year ago she had helped to save the youngster from the clutches of a deranged psychiatrist. She had delivered him to his mother and he had bitten her, some type of blood bond. His mother had promised to help her when in need. It was pretty creepy but intriguing at the same time. She looked at her arm where the bite had been. There was no scar, but the memory was as clear as the Fae man sitting before her.

"Good, you recall it," he commented. Verity nodded.

"Is he your little brother then? I would have liked to see him again."

"He would have come but there was a ceremony. Considering it was *his* ceremony, he couldn't really leave. But I could. He was quite upset. For some reason he quite likes you. Said something silly about a horse."

Verity smiled. She had told the little guy a story about a horse who had found home again. She met the Fae man's violet eyes.

"What's his name?"

The man smirked at her, both eyebrows flew up. Verity waved a dismissive hand in the air. "Right, right. Bad karma or whatever. I called him Little One."

"Not so little anymore," the man commented as he stood. "My job is done. I shall take my leave now."

Verity stood to see him out when a thought occurred to her.

"Before you go, I am curious about something."

"I might answer," he said derisively. His manner irked Verity, a tingle in the jaw, but she persisted.

"What...what was it like when you healed me? When you heal? Do you feel it in your bones?"

The man paused and looked her over. "You are a healer."

It wasn't a question but a statement. Verity nodded anyway. He didn't say anything for some time, but he kept looking at her as though trying to get answers from her silent form. She started to feel self-conscious. Just before she felt the need to bolt from his prying eyes he answered.

"It comes from the heart," he said and lifted his arm, pressing two fingers firmly over her heart. He didn't move his hand as he looked down at her, his eyes darkening to a deep eggplant. "And I feel it everywhere."

Verity's heart started to pump a bit faster, his fingers warm. He pulled his head up with a jolt and moved away, pulling the door open. Noah was waiting like a cat ready to pounce. Verity sighed and shook her head at him as the strange Fae disappeared into the hallway.

Chapter 27

"Again!" he yelled. The monsters in front of Dr. J went at each other, swords held high. They danced around the mat, each trying to bring down the other. The newly changed creatures stood to the side to watch. To learn.

Blood squirted from Myra's eyebrow. His previous secretary was now an oddly scaled and bulky creature. Gore gushed from her head wound thanks to the hilt of Hal's sword. Hal used to be his human assistant but now he was a worthy opponent to any demon creature. He was huge, with large patches of thick blue fur and round black eyes.

"Watch and learn, my pets," Dr. J said. "It won't be long until you too will be fighting for your life. We *will* bring down the abominations."

The hoots and hollers did little to bring up his spirits. He would train these genetically modified humans to kill, and kill they would. Every single non-human creature would die, and he would rid the world of their foulness. It pained him just slightly to know that these humans were now also just that. A foulness to be extracted. But only after they did their duty for mankind.

Chapter 28

Andy had been right. The classes were pretty much the same save one awesome thing. Powers.

The boys who had already learned to use their gift, their ability, would often use them between classes or to get to classes. One boy, Jona, was able to leap mind bogglingly high. He would jump from any level of the castle down to the practice grounds and beat everyone else to get the first weapon of choice for combat training.

Another boy, Roshan, could control sand or dirt. He would create waves when outside and use them for transport. And yet another had speed like a vampire, which Andy discovered didn't exist, at least not like what you read in the fantasy books. Seldin was so fast he could run on water. Andy loved it. He was proud to be the only one who could walk through walls.

Three days in, Keppin finally arrived. Like Andy, Keppin was from Florida and they had met when Andy had discovered the Clearwater den and been introduced to their world by Liam McDougall. Keppin was born into the Guardianship world that was so new to Andy. They had become great friends.

Keppin was supposed to have been on the same

flight as Andy but his parents had made him stay to handle something first. From Andy's perspective, Keppin got in trouble with his parents *a lot*. Keppin ended up rooming with Roshan and the three of them became fast friends. They ate together, fought together, and studied together. James occasionally joined them, but he had been at the school for two years and had already established his group of friends. They played a lot of interactive games like D&D that Andy couldn't wrap his head around. He did much better with the outdoor sports and physical action.

Leaning against the wall, Andy paid little attention to the chatter that surrounded him. Keppin and Roshan were fighting over whether or not Zeus was cooler than Poseidon. They were in the lunch line, but Andy didn't allow himself to leave his friends behind and walk through the mess hall wall when he was with them. He frowned as he thought of his last class. It was history, but it wasn't the class he was confounded by but the teacher.

Mr. Shirtell was a displacer. He was also the grumpiest, most annoying teacher that Andy had. He was always correcting every little thing that was said incorrectly, and if you had most of the answer right and were just a tad off, he would still decimate you verbally. The one thing that Andy liked was that he never doubted where he stood with that teacher. You never stood tall. Andy stayed to himself and did as little as possible. He was always relieved to get out unscathed.

Miss Harper on the other hand taught his favorite class, *Creatures of Earth*. She was the only female teacher in the school and per the rumors, she was some kind of shapeshifter, but no one seemed to know what kind. As far as Andy could tell, she knew *everything*. No matter what she was asked; "do sprites really grow things just by touch" (they do) to "do female dragons have breasts?" (they don't).

"Andy, what do you think?" Roshan asked. Andy looked down. Keppin was almost his height now but Roshan was barely as tall as an average girl. He was lucky he had such an interesting power otherwise he would definitely get picked on.

"I'm gonna have to go with Zeus," Andy said.

"What? How can you say that?" Keppin crinkled his nose and threw his arms outward.

"We're not even talking about that anymore," Roshan said as he shook his head at Keppin. "Do you think the dance is going to be worthwhile?"

Andy raised a brow. The dance was an annual affair held by an all-girls school in the next town. The school also happened to be a coven so apparently it was a witchy affair. A way for the two schools to break loose a bit. Andy appraised Roshan, not sure how to answer.

"Don't even say it!" Roshan held up a hand. "My size does not mean I don't know how to handle the ladies."

Keppin snorted. Andy was grateful the line moved so he was finally in front of the buffet and he started piling food onto his plate.

"You just wait," Roshan said, "when..."

"Move, you runt."

Andy turned to see one of the third-year students shove in front of Roshan. Andy didn't know him, just *of* him.

"Dude, we waited like everyone else, so can you," Andy said meeting the creep's eyes.

"Well, what do we have here? Are you his body guard?"

"Seriously, man. We're all here for the same reason and will likely fight side by side someday. So how about a little class?"

"Are you saying I don't have class?" The boy stood straighter, tucked his chin slightly and crossed his arms. He was a big guy Andy noticed.

"I'm saying we need to dial it down a notch."

"I don't think so," the boy said. A shadow appeared next to him, one of the kids using his gift to fluctuate in space. Before Andy could move, a fist materialized from the shadow and caught him in the jaw. Andy's head whipped back but not so fast that he didn't see Keppin jump into the shadow with a holler.

Andy growled and reached a hand out, setting it on the big guy's shoulder. Then he displaced and pulled them down through the concrete. The big guy screamed. They fell through the open floor below them and then continued through more concrete, all the way down to the main entry before Andy stopped. As soon as his feet were solid on the ground he shot out his right fist and met the big guys head. He felt the bones in his hand crack and pulled back cradling it to his chest.

The guy leaned his hands on bent knees and let his head hang for a moment while he took in long cleansing breathes and let them out again. Finally, he straightened up and met Andy's narrowed eyes.

His mouth quirked up slightly.

"Nice one," he said and held out a hand. "Name's Ben."

"Andy," Andy said and took the hand with his left hand since his right was still healing. They shook awkwardly.

Ben pointed at his head. "Basically like hitting steel. Now that you've thoroughly scared the shit out of me, can you get us back up? I'm starving."

"Sorry, man. We've got to go the old fashion way."

Ben sighed. "Fine. See you later then."

Frowning, Andy watched Ben turn to the staircase and take the steps three at a time, vanishing around the bend in seconds, before he followed at a lesser pace.

Chapter 29

Eyes blinking, Sloane groggily recalled dozing off in the comfortable hotel bed. Without looking, she knew he was at her side. Breathing in his scent, feeling his warmth so close, the pull was painfully intoxicating. Emotion flooded her. Sloane realized how much Aggie's training had paid off, when she knew it wasn't her emotion but his. It was a warm and fuzzy feeling, comfort. It felt nice. No, it felt wonderful.

It was confusing.

Turning her head slightly, she could see him. Could it be that for the first time, she had woken first? She watched him, admired him. For all his faults, he was a good man. And hot as hell. She noticed how long his eyelashes were, the curve of his lips and his dark eyebrows. He was truly, mind-bendingly nice to look at. In her haze, she pulled up an elbow to gaze down upon him. One blink and Sloane found his half-lidded blues registering her gaze.

Quickly turning away, Sloane pulled herself out of the bed and slipped into the bathroom, closing the door with a soft click. She leaned against it only for a moment before climbing into the shower.

When she came out, he wasn't in the room. Grateful to be alone for a time, she brushed her teeth, got dressed in simple jeans and a black tank and applied some light make up. She ignored her coffee craving and thought about what Bob had said. It hadn't taken her long to figure out what he meant. Now she had to figure out how to handle it. Liam would freak. He was so damn touchy. It was nice on the one hand but a real pain in the ass on the other.

She had just emptied one of the two drawers onto the bed when the door to the room opened and he walked in with two coffee cups and a plastic bag.

"Ah, my savior," Sloane said as she jumped up to relieve him of one cup of delight. She sat on the edge of the bed and sipped at it, allowing a small moan. When nothing else looks up, there was always coffee.

Liam dropped the bag next to her and leaned against the chest of drawers in front of her. She glanced at him. His navy shirt clung to his muscled torso and his jeans hugged all the right places, ending with his heavy black boots. Damn. She needed something besides coffee to clear her head of him. She glanced in the bag and found a black backpack.

"We need to get out of here. It's time to get you home," Liam said.

"I'm not going home just yet," Sloane commented as she stood up, put down her coffee and started to fold her clothes.

"What do you mean?"

"You and I both know that you overheard Bob. It took me a few minutes, but I figured out what he was talking about."

She looked at him. His body had gone to stone, not literally. She rolled her eyes and held up her hand, counting off on her fingers as she continued.

"Sinister is Dr. J." One finger went up. "You are obviously red." A second finger went up. "And the ancient land has got to be Ireland."

Liam didn't move.

"You're going to Ireland, Liam. And I'm coming with you."

Liam started shaking his head. Sloane pointed a finger at him.

"Don't you dare," she commanded. "I have wished for death most of my miserable life. Instead of death, I find a Gray One in my trunk. He leads me to the Guardianship who has helped me want to live. I want to *live*, Liam. I can't do this until Dr. J is out of my life. And I will do whatever I have to so that happens."

"Sloane, you don't know what you're saying..."

"The hell I don't! I am going, with or without you. Now, get out of my way."

"I am not moving."

"Well...actually I need to get to that drawer."

Liam moved slowly and carefully away from the drawers. "I am your protector until I get you home."

"No, Liam. You're not."

Sloane pulled the rest of her clothes from the drawer and tossed them on the bed. She started to fold them. "You are not my anything. You can bring me home and I will go anyway. Now we can go about this as partners or not. It's up to you."

Sloane couldn't look at him. Her face felt like fire from the angry heat in her blood. She was done being babied. She had said she would take charge and she was going to. No more bullshit.

~~*~~

Liam walked down the alley with Sloane at his side. Her announcement to follow Dr. J had frozen his analytical mind. He hadn't spoken a word since. His need to get her somewhere safe was overwhelming but he couldn't exactly lock her in a closet. He almost wished he had given in and consummated their bond, so he could think. The desire, fear, and uncertainty was eating away at him. He was barely able to find his emotional lock down when she was near. How would he save her?

Detached emotion. Analytics full on. That's what he needed. He had to concentrate so she didn't ruin them both. They had almost reached the end of the alley and would soon be at the restaurant. He needed to figure it out now. He could allow her to accompany him so he could protect her, but then he would have a weakness that someone could easily take advantage. Could he send her home despite her wrath? Or maybe it wouldn't be wrath. Maybe it would be a hurt that he couldn't fix? The idea tore him up. It wasn't a difficult decision and it angered him that she wouldn't just cooperate. But then that had been one of her endearing qualities, hadn't it?

In front of them, a figure swung around the ally entrance and leaned against the wall, watching them. Tucking his internal debate away, Liam stopped, throwing out an arm to halt Sloane. She started to protest but quieted as soon as she saw the man. He was just over six feet, built like a truck but without an ounce of fat. His black hair was styled in one of the current semi-short popular cuts and his skin was tanned. Flicking a hand up in greeting, he started slowly toward them. Liam's hackles went up as he waited for the man to get close enough to speak.

"Hello, Lady and Gent," he said with a smile, "Name's Dustin." He pointed at himself and then stopped a few feet away, hands hanging at his sides, a sign of peace.

"What can I do for you today, Dustin?" Liam asked.

"Kind of a coincidence that there's a stray in my town and two suckers are found bashed up on the sidewalk, huh?"

Liam raised an eyebrow. "A stray?"

"A rogue or a *lost* Guardian," Dustin said with a shrug.

"I would venture that you too are a *stray*."

"Was. Was a stray. Now I'm home. Been here for years keeping tabs on everyone. Just want to ensure we don't get any trouble, you see?"

Liam laughed, startling Sloane and amusing Dustin. "A rogue Guardian who is being a Guardian. Nice, man." He held out a hand to Dustin. "Liam McDougall."

"Well, the pleasure is mine," Dustin said eying Liam's bright hair. "Been a long time since I heard your name. Still at it then? Or was I right?"

Liam dipped his head. "You were right."

Dustin chuckled. "Well, then. I hope I won't have to worry about any more sidewalk bodies?"

Liam turned serious, "Can't guarantee that. But we're just heading over for some breakfast before leaving town, so hopefully the bodies will leave us be until we're gone." He glanced at Sloane, who was watching with interest.

Dustin straightened up. "Where you headed?"

"LaPeniche," Sloane voiced.

"Good place," Dustin said as he thrust his hand at her.

"I'm Sloane, by the way," she said, giving Dustin her hand. He brought it up slowly and kissed the back of it before letting it go.

"It's my pleasure," he said with an admiring smile. Liam watched Sloane smile in return. He felt a pang flair up and shoot through his chest. He quickly tucked it away or tried to.

"Would you like to join us?" Sloane asked. Liam narrowed his eyes at her. She smiled and blinked a few times at him before turning back to Dustin, who was smiling like a puppy except bigger, way bigger.

"I would love to," he said holding out an arm for Sloane. She giggled and took it, ignoring Liam's raised eyebrow, and continued walking down the alley.

Chapter 30

Dustin was hands down one of the most gorgeous guys Sloane had ever had the pleasure to lay eyes on. His skin was tanned but not overly so and his light blue eyes smiled even when he wasn't. His dark hair was the stunning topping to almost perfection. Perfection being the pale skinned, red-head that had stolen her heart. But Dustin's look wasn't really what she was interested in. He was an excellent distraction. Liam had made it painfully clear that they were not going to happen and maybe taking her attention away from that pain and focusing it on something else would help. Maybe she could break their bond. Or maybe she was being overly optimistic. Truthfully, she wanted to see if Liam would break or at least squirm a little bit.

When she had taken Dustin's arm, the relief to have something else to focus on acted as balm on her overwrought heart. She strode casually through the remaining alley making small talk with Dustin, knowing Liam was trailing behind.

The restaurant was pretty packed, but they scored the last open table tucked in the back near the restrooms. Never the best spot in the house but hopefully it wouldn't be too annoying. Sloane sat near the wall, Liam sat scowling to her left, and

Dustin took the spot in front of her.

"So, Sloane," Dustin said, "you're not a Guardian or a rogue, what brought you to be hanging out with the likes of him?" He pointed a thumb at Liam. Sloane didn't dare look at Liam. She smiled innocently.

"Well, I think Liam would need to answer that," she said. Dustin raised a dark brow and glanced at Liam.

"She's an Aspie," Liam commented. Understanding dawned on Dustin's face.

"Ahh. I haven't talked to an Aspie in ages. How's the training going?"

"How do you know I haven't finished it?" Sloane asked.

Dustin glanced at Liam and they answered at the same time. "Too young."

It was Sloane's turn to raise an eyebrow. "They didn't tell me training was never ending," she mumbled. Dustin laughed.

"It's not never ending, sweetheart, it just might seem like it." He turned to Liam. "I thought our training was forever until I met an Aspie."

"Ditto," Liam answered. Sloane stole a glance. His face was unreadable and not a lick of emotion came through to her. She bit off a sigh and brought her gaze back to Dustin just as the waitress arrived. Dustin insisted they all try the Eggs Benedict and they ordered as recommended.

"It's my understanding that you start training at fifteen or sixteen, right?" Sloane asked Dustin.

He nodded. "Our parents are contacted as soon as the Guardianship clues in that a Guardian is coming of age. Most of the time the parents are happy to send their child to a prestigious school for free even if it's not well known. Then the kids get the training they need to understand what's happening and the parents don't have a clue."

"That's the best and simplest explanation I've been given yet. Thank you." Sloane smiled. Dustin beamed.

"And how long has it been since you first trained?"

Dustin laughed and looked at Liam. "Clever, isn't she? That's a much nicer way to ask how old I am." He brought his green eyes back to Sloane. "I'm pushing sixty, Sweetheart."

Sloane's jaw dropped. "But how can that be? You don't look a day over 30."

"Honey, they seriously need to bring up your education. Once we hit around twenty years, our aging slows down to about 3 years to every ten. So, assuming we don't get ourselves killed, we can live up to a hundred and eighty years or so."

Sloane sat back and let that sink in. The Guardians that protect the houses of their kin must be newer graduates of the school. Then they either retire, maybe start a family or they go into the secret service version of the Guardianship and start handling the bigger issues, like Liam. It was nice to finally get a better understanding of the hierarchy. But then, if Dustin was almost sixty years' old that would likely mean…

Sloane turned to Liam. "How old are you and don't avoid the question." Liam sat back and glared at Dustin who shrugged an apology.

"Forty-nine," Liam answered softly. Sloane sat stunned for a full minute before speaking again.

"So many things make sense now," she said thoughtfully and turned to Dustin. "You have no idea how helpful you have been."

Dustin smiled and gave her a wink as the food arrived. She ate half the meal ranting about the amazingness of the Eggs Benedict and the other half thinking. What the hell? Liam was forty-nine? Was it considered robbing the cradle if they were bonded? How the hell did that work? She really didn't know him, did she?

She had met quite a few Guardians. She silently guessed their ages with this new information. And then Brick came to mind. Brick wasn't tall like Liam, but he was built like a tree trunk with hulking muscles and ebony skin. That said, he was one of the most caring Guardians she knew. Always ready with a smile, he had even offered to become Andy's Guardian. Andy was an orphan who hadn't been discovered by the Guardianship but who had found them instead. Brick was also a bad ass fighter. And once, he had been bonded. No one talked about it, only insinuated that his bonded was no longer amongst the living. She turned to Liam. "What about Brick? How old is he?"

Liam was in the middle of chewing so she waited, glancing at Dustin with a small smile. He surprised her by answering.

"He's probably over a hundred by now. He wasn't a spring chicken when I knew him."

"Small circles, huh?" Sloane asked.

Dustin shrugged. "We all go to the same school, everyone runs through it before assignment."

"So how come you went rogue?"

"Now *that* is a story for another time." Dustin smiled without mirth. Sloane watched him for a moment before nodding. Dustin excused himself to the restroom and Liam didn't move or speak. Sloane bumped Liam's shoulder with her own.

"Ah, come on. It wasn't that bad was it?" she asked and nudged him again. He relaxed marginally.

"I told you that you didn't know me, and you don't."

It must have been the full belly and scored point of gleaning information from Dustin, but Liam's comment only made her laugh. She surprised him with a kiss on the cheek.

"Whatever, Liam. I know enough."

At that moment Dustin came back to the table. Liam stood and threw two twenties on the table.

"Dustin, do you have plans for the next few hours?" he asked.

"That depends." Dustin smiled at Sloane who raised her brows.

"Can you hang with her for a bit while I take care of a couple of things? I promise I won't leave a wake of bodies behind me." Liam managed a tight smile.

Dustin chuckled. "I think I can take care of that."

"Where are you going?" Sloane asked, hurt that he would so readily leave her alone with someone they'd just met.

"Nothing to worry about. I'll find you soon."

He nodded at Dustin and headed to the exit. Sloane watched until he was gone and then turned to Dustin. "Well, this is a bit awkward."

"Not at all," he said with a wave of his hand. "Do you like poker?"

"I love poker," Sloane said. She couldn't help but smile when she thought of Andy teaching her the game just months ago.

"Well, I think we should find two more players and put a few games under our belt. It will pass the time quite nicely."

~~*~~

For some reason, Sloane felt uncomfortable. Maybe it was the fact that the guy to her left, at least Sloane thought it was a man, was covered in forest green fur and used sign language to communicate, or maybe it was the fact that the man sitting comfortably to her right was decked out completely in upscale garb from the 1800's, had a cigar hanging out of his mouth, and was maybe three feet tall.

Across the table sat Dustin. His dark hair covered part of his face while he studied the cards in his hand. Three cards on the table and it was his turn to bet. His blue eyes met hers, but his face was like stone. It occurred to Sloane that trained Guardians could potentially be really good at poker. Dustin didn't seem to be in the high percentile though. Out of six games, he hadn't won any yet.

Dustin pushed a blue token into the pot and looked at Simian, the short, regal dude. Simian didn't even glance at his cards but pushed in a blue chip from his perfectly stacked colors. Sloane followed with a blue chip from her small pile and looked at the furry guy. He made a strange huffing noise before laying his cards down on the table.

"Yee is out," Dustin said as he watched the furry guy, who was dealing, flip the fourth card.

Sloane frowned when she saw the eight of hearts, forgetting her poker face. Looking again at the cards she held in her hands she got the strangest feeling of sorrow. Of lost love and...Sloane put her cards face down on the table and giggled. She wondered why she was giggling when life was so miserable.

"Are you out?" Dustin asked. Sloane giggled again and Dustin raised a brow. Yee made a noise that could have been amusement while Simian sighed in annoyance.

Something must have dawned on Dustin because he stood abruptly. Sloane heaved in a heavy sigh and a tear ran down her cheek. She wiped her face and frowned at her moist fingertips.

"What the...?" she whispered.

"Where is he, Sloane?" Dustin asked.

"He...what? How should I know?"

"You're bonded aren't you?"

"Sort of. So?"

"So? We should probably go find him before he gets into trouble. Now."

Chapter 31

The witches dance was held in the ballroom of a huge manor that also housed the girls. The dance itself was attended by the high school teens, the younger kids were corralled off somewhere for a movie night. The boys, there were thirty-nine of them, waited in the corridors for access to the ballroom. The noises of final touches, the clinks of glasses, and the smell of food drifted into the halls.

Andy felt awkward and stiff in his suit. It was dark blue and had a slight sheen to it. He was pretty sure that Brick had picked it out because he would have never thought to bring such a thing to school.

Ben stood nearby flicking the back of Rashan's ear. As hostile as their initial encounter had been, they had developed a surprising affinity. Rashan would build solid miniature sandcastles and Ben would practice tearing them apart with his seemingly steel appendages. Andy couldn't fathom the powers that they yielded and watched them in awe. Now he just shook his head at Rashan swatting Ben away from his ears.

Keppin was leaning against the wall with a slight smile on his face. He had on a black pinstriped suit that fit him to a T. He was looking out the window, but Andy was pretty sure he was seeing something else.

Andy was about to ditch them and take a walk outside when the doors opened. A tall, gray haired woman walked out, the doors closing softly behind her. She squinted out over the boys, looking at each of them in turn, meeting their eyes before turning to the next. Quietly. When she met Andy's eyes he felt like a deeply seated x-ray with a very long memory had been performed. He shivered.

"Jeez," Keppin pulled away from the wall and shook his head. "Why do I feel like I've just been raped?"

Ben chuckled nervously and tucked his hands into his pocket while Rashan stood a bit taller, as impossible as it might seem. Andy smiled to himself. He watched the gray haired lady finish her sweep of the boys, leaving them startled and feeling a bit naked. She clasped her hands in front her and smiled broadly.

"Now that I have imprinted each of you on my mind, let the dance begin." The maniacal smile never left her face and the doors behind her opened on their own accord. She turned and strode through the doorway, vanishing to the left out of sight.

No one moved for a moment. Andy was certain that some of these guys had attended before, so he wasn't sure what they were waiting for. Ben must have felt the same way. He grumbled something derogatory before pushing ahead and into the room.

The music started the moment he stepped over the threshold. The crowd surged into the room only to stop and stare.

The ballroom was ginormous. The ceiling was at least thirty feet high, draped with sparkly white fabric and silver chandeliers. The floors and pillars set throughout the room were marble. In the center of the room was a dance floor set in a pattern Andy couldn't quite make out through the crowd. Tables were set up on the outer perimeter of the dance floor and on the right a buffet ran over half the length of the room.

The real attention grabber, however, was the rainbow of colors rustling gently together on the other side of the room. The girls. They were all lined up in row, facing the boys, and each wore a flowing gown of a different color. Their hair was worn long and loose and their faces were void of make-up. They were colorful, young, bright and…

Ben left the group and beelined toward the girls. He stopped about ten feet from them and bowed, low to the ground. He strode purposely to a stunning Asian girl and holding one clasped hand behind him, he held out a hand to the girl and spoke. He was too far to hear, but everyone could guess what he was asking. The girl smiled timidly and took his hand. She left the safety of her coven and Ben brought her to the beverage table and started to pour her a punch.

Andy looked at Keppin who stared with wide eyes, bringing them to meet Andy's.

"Did you see that?" he asked. Andy nodded. "Then let's go! Remember, walk slow enough so's you can pick the one you want to dance with, ok?"

Before Andy could answer, Keppin took off. Several of the other boys started over too. Andy wasn't really sure what he wanted to do. He liked girls, but he didn't *need* to have one like other guys seemed to. A song came on that he liked, and the thought of dancing actually seemed fun. He needed someone who liked to dance. Starting across the floor, he didn't look at faces but looked for the one that was moving. Someone who liked the song and seemed like, just maybe, they would like to hit the floor.

A few couples had already started dancing when Andy found her. She was near the far left and was dancing with the girl next to her. Andy found her face and almost stopped. She was looking straight at him, a shy smile on her beautiful bronze skin. Straight, chestnut hair flowed down to her waist and the emerald green dress, though it wasn't form fitting by any means, complimented her natural beauty. Andy was struck.

He held his hand out to her, couldn't even speak. She looked at his hand with large eyes, the color matching her hair and then glanced at her friend. The friend, a short blond girl, tipped her head to the side and pursed her lips. Andy guessed this meant something as his golden beauty slipped her hand into his and he led her to the dance floor.

Chapter 32

Walking into the bar with Dustin, Sloane looked around with mixed feelings. A familiar song tore through the speakers and touched her heart, making her smile. It quickly turned to a frown when she thought of the many times she had drunk her ability to read Hues into oblivion. She sighed and searched the room for Liam. The few patrons of the bar appeared to be drinking away their sorrows, a blue-green cloud floating about their bodies. One man was surrounded by a billowing red and she wondered what had happened to make him so hateful.

She had never thought to try to track Liam before and was surprised at how simple it was. At least this time. She could feel him close, all of his carefully placed emotional guards down and flowing like a river at spring. She always wondered how he so easily tracked her and now she knew. You followed the feeling, the pull of the bond.

Dustin headed toward the back of the dimly lit bar and Sloane followed, checking the booths slowly as she went. She bumped into a solid mass and heard Dustin mutter under his breath. The mass being Dustin, she peered around him, pondering briefly why her heart rate didn't spike at their closeness, when she saw what had stopped him.

Lounging on a couch in a dark corner was Liam. One leg was thrown over the arm of the black leather couch, the other stretched lazily in front of him. His hand was wrapped around a tall orange drink, a dazed expression hung on his face. He looked sad. Sloane frowned deeper.

"I thought you guys couldn't get drunk."

"We can't," Dustin sighed, "on alcohol." Sloane narrowed her eyes, glancing between them and then at the bar.

"What the hell else can he get here?"

"Orange juice."

"Orange juice? Are you fucking kidding me? Nobody gets drunk off orange juice."

Dustin's shoulders twitched. "We tend to steer clear of it for that exact reason."

"This is ridiculous. I'm rescuing my bonded, who doesn't want a damn thing to do with me, from a severe *orange juice* hangover."

"I think it's too late for that, sweetheart."

Sloane wondered which part he was referring to and strode toward Liam. The moment he saw her he stood, fluidly, like a cat. Sloane doubted how drunk he could possibly be until, reaching him, he pulled her close, wrapping his arms around her and into a tight bear hug. Sloane hugged back, reveling in the intensity of the affinity he poured into her. He pulled away, leaving her heady and bubbly before gently pressing his lips onto hers. He was light and careful until he felt her respond. His tongue traced her lips, zaps of lightning exploded throughout her body.

Someone cleared his throat behind her. Sloane

suddenly wished Dustin hadn't come. Liam pulled away, a lazy smile lighting up his face. He caught her gaze and held it for a long moment before holding a hand out to Dustin. They shook before Liam sat on the couch, pulling Sloane with him.

His glazed, baby blues took her in, starting with her eyes and moving down her body like a scanner. Her heart sped up and skin prickled. His left arm came around her shoulder and pulled her to him, so her head rested on his shoulder, his cheek in her hair. His other hand left the drink on the table and took her hand, engulfing it with a gentle squeeze.

This was how it was meant to be, Sloane thought as he breathed in deeply, letting it out with a whoosh and whispering her name at the same time. Heaven!

Liam registered Dustin still standing before them. He waived a hand at the chair in front of him.

"Dustin, my friend..." he slurred with a strong Irish lilt. Sloane pulled her head back at the sudden accent change and inspected Liam's face as he continued. "'Ave a seat. I'd like to tell you how I met the most amazing, headstrong, frustrating, and sexiest woman I've ever known."

Dustin stood indecisive for a moment but finally gave in, sinking down into the velvet plush chair. He must have been as intrigued as Sloane by this turn of events. A tale from the man who kept words, and apparently his heritage, to himself.

Expecting Liam to explain how she had turned up unexpected at one of their den meetings, Sloane smiled to herself. She had been brought to the meeting by a Guardian's younger brother and it hadn't gone all that well but at the same time, the meeting had saved her life. Maybe he would even mention when they had first laid eyes on each other at the coffee shop. She certainly didn't expect what he did end up saying.

"So, I arrived in Florida for an assignment. Got meself a bike hire, a sweet Ducati."

Dustin made the appropriate man admiration noise and Liam continued. "I zipped over to the book store to pick up a map. I'm sitting there minding me own business, memorizing the map when the most intoxicating scent drifts through the air. I glance up and see...this vision."

He slurred the last word so much, Sloane had to replay it in her mind a time or two and then wondered what the hell he was going on about. There should be a coffee shop in this story.

"I saw her legs first. They just went up and up. These beautiful, smooth..." Liam shook his head and made a noise, a cross between a kitten mewl and a growl. Dustin chuckled. Sloane frowned.

"Then I see her stacks. Gawd. Need I say more? But if that wasn't enough, I saw these lips, pouty and full. A smorgasbord. And then her eyes, Dustin. Intelligent and full of life. Devastating, I tell you."

Dustin's smile was perplexed as he looked back and forth between her and Liam, completely amused. If her frown got any deeper, Sloane's face was liable to implode on itself. Who was Liam even talking about?

"You sure you want to keep going there, Liam?" Dustin asked, the amusement never leaving his face.

"Of course!" Liam said as he took his hand from Sloane's and downed half the OJ in his cup before continuing. "She's looking at books. She picks one up, reads the back and puts it down. Does this over and over till she finds one that grabs her fancy. Then she turns and bolts, straight to check-out. Well now, at this point, I can't stand the idea of not knowing her. I even forgot what the hell I was supposed to be doing in Florida. I NEVER do that. So, I follow her. She leaves in her car and I follow on the bike. It was awesome. Dustin, this girl drives like a bat out of hell. So refreshing."

Liam squeezed Sloane's shoulder at the same moment she flashed back to that day and realized that he *was* talking about her.

"I follow her to this great little coffee shop, Cafe Bliss, that I've since frequented. If you ever end up in Clearwater, I recommend it highly. Anyway, she was curled up in a chair in the back. I ordered my coffee and waited but I *know* she saw me. And when our eyes finally met..."

Sloane stiffened. She knew what he would say. She ran. Like the fucking wind. Sitting here and hearing this was killing her. She couldn't exactly keep Liam drunk forever so she could always have *this* man.

"She left, Dustin. But I followed her, she lived right behind the coffee shop in an apartment," he said. Dustin kept smiling and nodding. And then Liam's face dropped.

"And then I remembered what I was doing in Clearwater. And I tucked everything away."

Sloane's mouth hung open. Liam was oblivious to her reaction and the fact that he had just let her in on a very big, fucking huge secret. And he had tried to tell her it was just the bond. They were peanut butter and fucking jelly before the bond was ever in place.

Liam then told Dustin about actually meeting her; when Keppin had arrived at a Den meeting completely unannounced and introduced her. Liam found out that she was an Aspie and was told he had to maintain a professional relationship with her. Hands off.

A sinking feeling started to seep into her stomach until Liam pulled her in for a hug and sloppily kissed her cheek.

"But none of that matters now," he stated. "We're going to war soon so who knows what will happen."

Dustin perked up at the mention of war.

"What war?" he asked. Liam told him about Dr. J's experiments, the deaths of his brethren and the impending trip to Ireland to bring him down once and for all. Sloane was relieved that he didn't call Dr. J her father.

Dustin sat back and considered them before seeming to come to some decision.

"I'm coming with you," he said.

Chapter 33

Checking in on the Queen was an hourly endeavor as Verity waited patiently and with some trepidation for the Queen to go into labor. The comely Fae's admittance of her healing power had given her as much faith as it did peace of mind, though the fear of messing it up was not far from her mind. The King had given her a hard time about her walk in the cave and subsequent Vigilo bites. He said she was lucky they weren't poisonous and had wandered off laughing. No one had given her the password yet and she was miffed about that, but she was pretty sure they were waiting for the Queen to have the baby before letting her go far. So, Verity stayed close, making friends with some of the younger Goblins. They had so many questions about the goings on above ground. She grinned at their enthusiasm as she turned down the corridor toward the Queen's room.

The wildflower and vanilla scent floated in the air outside the room. Verity stopped and breathed in the smell before shaking her head, attempting to clear it of sultry thoughts before entering the room.

He was perched in a chair across from the Queen, who slept soundly.

"Ah, the healer with a death wish returns," the

Fae man said snidely. Whatever allure he may have had earlier vanished. Verity ignored him and went to the Queen's side. Her coloring was much better, and she was doing well with the protein drinks, but anything solid was useless. Verity was still concerned about how much she was sleeping. King said the same thing happened before and Verity was driving herself crazy trying to figure out why. Her glands seemed fine, her thyroid was functioning properly and there didn't seem to be any viral or bad bacterial activity. So why was the Queen so tired?

"A body is being built from limited resources that is unlike her own. It steals her energy," he said as though reading her mind. Verity turned to him.

"Why are you still here? Didn't you do your job? Didn't you gain your favor? Feel free to exit whenever you like."

Surprised at her own lack of accord, Verity blushed, turning back to the Queen to avoid his gaze. The Queen's bright green eyes were crinkled in a grin.

"I see you've met Duran," she said. Verity frowned causing the Queen to laugh. "Since they don't share names, we had to call him something." She looked fondly at Duran. "He's been around for a long time. Duran seemed fitting."

"Why fitting?" Verity asked. It certainly wasn't a name she would have come up with. The Queen brought her eyes to Verity and shrugged.

"It means *enduring*. That's what the Fae do."

Verity smiled. Fair enough and apparently true.

"And how are you feeling today?" Verity asked.

"Not bad, considering. I keep wanting to get

up and take a walk but then think better of it." She laughed without mirth. Verity took her hand and gave it a squeeze.

"It won't be long now. Soon you'll be chasing King around like a school girl."

The Queen gurgled with laughter, alarming Verity who only got waved away. The Queen calmed down and waved once more.

"Go on, girl. Go find something else to do for a while. I am glad to see Duran and I will speak with him for a time."

Verity thought the speech odd but nodded and turned to leave.

"Verity?" the Queen asked. Verity turned back.

"He will be helpful when the time comes. Try not to run him off too quickly." Her mouth didn't show it, but laughter danced in her eyes.

"Yes, ma'am," Verity replied and left the room possibly more confused than when she arrived. Though she was pleased that the Queen's body was just in overdrive. There wasn't much else she could do to help until the time came.

She turned into Noah's antechamber and ran smack into him.

"Geez. Sorry, Noah," she said patting him on the chest. He smiled at her.

"I'm just running out to get a bite. Do you want anything from the kitchen?"

Verity thought for a moment. When had she eaten last?

"I'd love something. Maybe a sandwich?"

"Sure thing. Be back soon."

As Verity stepped over the threshold to her room

her hand flew to her chest. That was first time her heart didn't give at least a weak flutter at Noah's presence. It was both a painful and happy thought.

~~*~~

When Verity returned an hour later, Duran was gone, and the Queen was asleep again. Verity checked the Queen's vitals before curling up in the chair next to her with the latest vampire novel she had found in the King's library. Verity thought it was funny that she had met so many unearthly creatures and yet no vampires. She should probably be glad that there weren't any, or none that she knew of, but still it did have some kind of weird romantic curve to it. She opened up the book and started to read. She was just getting to an interesting scene with a vampire named Lance and his love interest Rebecca when she was rudely interrupted.

"*Morning's Death*? Isn't that a bit cliché?" It was Duran. Verity blushed, annoyed that she hadn't heard him come in the room. She prepared an unkind retort only to hold her tongue in light of what the Queen had said earlier.

"Can I help you, *Duran*?" she said instead of something that she was pretty sure was not even mildly clever.

"No, actually. I take care of myself quite well." He smiled at her and sat in the same chair she had found him in earlier.

"Fine then." Verity answered and pulled the book up again. She tried to read but found herself wanting to look up. She sighed and read another line that she didn't register. He had ruined the reading moment.

"It is useless. You had better give me the attention," he said quietly. Verity looked up and met his gaze.

"What, are you a mind reader?" she asked, acid biting her tongue. He brought out the worst in her and she regretted the question as soon as it left her lips. He smiled.

"No. But I have been around long enough to know things."

"Been around a lot of humans?"

"Oh, yes. Very interesting study. No two are exactly alike."

Verity couldn't help but laugh. "That is very true," she commented.

"So, Verity Applebee. Tell me about yourself. How did you come to know about our world?" He settled back into the chair like he was planning on staying for a while. Verity really wanted to make a comment but chose to answer him instead.

"I got a job as a nurse in a mental health institute thinking I could help the people there. The problem I found was that no one really knows *how* to help them. You learn about these various drugs that are supposed to help balance out the chemicals in the brain. But after watching people get worse, some of them dying, some of them just listless and sad and, well…after a ridiculous amount of research and experience, I found that there is absolutely no truth to it. There are no brain chemicals that are altered. There are only the after effects of the drugs that are far worse than I could have imagined." She paused, and the tall Fae simply nodded her on.

"I worked in the institute for several weeks, coming to these realizations, when one day the head doctor, the owner, brought me down several floors and tried to hypnotize me."

"Tried to?" the Fae asked, leaning forward, placing an elbow on his knee and propping his chin on his open palm.

"Yes, tried to. It didn't take. I just pretended that it had worked. He then told me that I would be caring for monsters from then on out. He listed out my duties and told me that I would go through the motions every day and only remember that I had helped the patients feel better."

"Intriguing," he commented.

"I ended up caring for all kinds of different creatures. One of them was a little Fae boy..." He nodded and waited for her to continue.

"Then I received a Guardian to look after. He was in bad shape too. But for some reason the others were excited about him being there."

"The Guardians have some worth," he commented, sadness tinging his voice.

"That they do. I found another Guardian on the outside with Noah's help, of course."

"Noah?"

"The Guardian who was trapped there. He's the one who's here with me."

"Yes, of course. A debt. Go on."

Verity frowned. *A debt? Well, I suppose it could come across that way.*

"A plan was put together and we were able to rescue most of them. I met quite a few non-humans, including your Fae Queen. The strange thing was, even though it was scary, it seemed right to me. That they…that *you* exist."

Duran smiled at her. "You are clearly one of the opened minded humans."

"I don't know about open minded but I'm willing to see and believe the truth."

"Ah. Now there is a whole different thing altogether. Truth can be twisted."

Verity met his eyes. "I guess you have been betrayed."

"Ah, *and* she is clever to boot. Tell me how you realized you were a healer."

Verity chuckled, causing Duran to lift a brow.

"You said *to boot* and for some reason I find that funny."

He raised the other brow. "I have been around many humans, for a very, long time."

"So I gather." She chuckled again. "I didn't realize I was a healer until after we left the hospital. It turned out that Noah only survived because of the powers I didn't know I was using. Somehow, I was healing him enough to get him through the torture. When he was rescued and cared for, only then did the doctors wonder how he had survived. That's when eyes turned to me."

"Interesting," Duran commented. "And then what? How did you figure it out?"

"I practiced. I got a position at a local hospital, the hours were horrendous, but the joy I felt every time I was able to feel what was wrong with someone… well, that was something I will never forget. Once I felt it, their energy, the physical flows of their body, I could find where the damage was and help heal it.

After that, the Guardianship sent me to work with some healers where I was able to learn so much more. I'm sure there's more to it but I am very confident with what I *do* know."

"That is a good story," he commented as he looked over at the Queen. Verity felt a little bit like she had been talking to hear herself speak when he rose.

"Come join me for tea time."

"What?" Verity asked, startled. "Tea time?" she repeated. He held a long slender hand out to her.

"The child is restless. He'll be arriving soon, and I have just the tea to prepare us."

Chapter 34

After dancing for several songs, taking a break and then dancing some more, Andy and Charlese took what ended up being their last break for the evening. Charlese, he had learned her name in between the second and third songs, was gulping down her second punch while he downed a bottle of water.

"We never get sugar here, so I take it when I can get it." She smiled. Andy wondered if he was supposed to point out the red mustache she now wore. He panicked a bit before deciding to speak.

"Uh, you have a, some punch above your, eh, lip."

"Oh, silly me," she said and grabbed a napkin to wipe it away. Andy had the strangest thought of licking the punch away and was horrified. The boys talked about girls all the time, but Andy hadn't ever really joined in. He'd always been too worried about everything else going on.

The horror faded and turned to something like melted butter and warm biscuits.

And now, Charlese looked better than a triple cheeseburger.

Somewhere a bell tolled in the distance. The look on Charlese's face turned from joy to sadness in a blink.

"What is it?" Andy asked, his brows pulled down. He had barely looked at anyone else since he'd led her to the dance floor.

The loud ding of the last bell echoed and faded as a sad smile appeared on her face. Before Andy could ask again, she reached up and grabbed his shoulders, pulling herself up on her tippy toes and pressed her lips into his.

Before Andy could reciprocate she pulled away, clasping her hands in front of her, a mischievous smile playing on her lips. Andy closed his surprised mouth.

The dim lights went out, covering them in darkness and then every candle in the place lit at once. The walls were lined with countless sconces that turned the ballroom back into a study hall.

"Thank you for coming, Guardians," the gray-haired woman's voice boomed over them. "I hope you had a pleasant evening. The doors are this way."

Andy pulled his eyes from Charlese and searched the room. He found the woman across the way, hustling his brethren out. He looked back to Charlese and saw that several feet already separated them as she backed away, heading to the other side of the room. She smiled, head bent slightly and waved to him, her hand near her hip.

Andy wanted to say something, wanted to whoop and holler. He wanted to try that again. But instead, he waved back, winked and turned to leave. He looked back once and watched her grab her friend's hand, laughing at something. She turned back then, catching his eye and gave him one last glowing smile. Something jolted in his gut. He stopped walking and watched her hug her friend's arm and walk out the opposite door.

"Relax, dude," Keppin said from behind. Andy turned and belted his friend gently in the stomach.

"Easy," Keppin said and punched Andy's shoulder. "You'd think you'd never seen a girl before."

Andy rolled his eyes and walked toward the door, purposely banging his shoulder into Keppin. They laughed and walked out. Andy only looked back once more.

Chapter 35

After throwing Liam over his shoulder as though he weighed no more than a small child, Dustin led Sloane back to his apartment. The poker table was just as they had left it but without the extra players. Dustin disappeared into a room with Liam and returned empty handed a moment later. When Sloane went after Liam, Dustin threw an arm out to block her and shook his head.

"I don't think so, honey," he said. He gently turned her around and pulled her toward his beige couch. "Don't know how appreciative he would be when his sound mind returns."

Sloane rolled her eyes, kicked off her boots and plopped down on the couch. A yawn burst forth. She felt drained. Liam's emotions still poured into her, pulling her to him but she knew Dustin was right. Thinking of the devil, Dustin handed her a thick, soft blanket and a down pillow. He pointed to the couch she was perched on. Pouting, Sloane placed the pillow at one end and laid down on the plush couch pulling the blanket around her. A heavy cloud hung over her, infused by Liam's strong emotion. She sighed. Dustin turned off the light and sunk into one of the nearby chairs. Fucking babysitter.

Sleep took her quickly, but it didn't last. The

room was pitch as she blinked trying to see if Dustin's figure still perched nearby. The chair was empty. Sloane pulled the blanket off and padded over to Liam's room. The room was dark, but she could see well enough. Liam was on his side, fully clothed, facing away. Sloane gingerly sat on the bed, pulling her legs up and laying her head down on the second pillow.

Not wanting to be too forthcoming...actually wanting to be very forthcoming but instead heeding Dustin's warning, Sloane curled up with her back to Liam, feeling his warmth, and fell into a solid sleep.

~~*~~

Eyes slamming open, Liam inspected his environment. Regret simmered through every nerve. As Sloane might say, he was so fucked. Feeling the warmth at his back, he slid from the bed to the floor, crouching like a tiger to inspect his prey. Long, chestnut hair met his eyes first. Then he dragged his eyes down her voluptuous body. Closing them, he slowly dropped his head back. He opened his eyes again and stared at the ceiling. He had dug his grave deeper. Now she knew he'd stalked her. The fact that she was in his bed meant leaving her would be that much harder.

Rules. Always some damn rule to follow.

Liam stood, quiet as a ghost. He breezed out of the room, refusing to look back. Dustin was waiting for him in the living room, a friendly smile on his face. Liam strode over and held out his hand. Dustin took it, the smile never leaving his face. Liam shook his head.

"Thanks, Dustin. I appreciate it."

"No problem, man. Truthfully, I've been the recipient myself so…" he shrugged.

"Cool. I have to pick up my passport. I've booked her a flight out of here. I'll need to get her to the airport this afternoon."

Dustin raised an eyebrow. "She thinks she's going with you."

"She's not. I'll not bring her into it."

"You realize she'll come anyway?" Dustin asked.

"She can try. She doesn't have a passport."

Dustin nodded. "I do, however, have a passport."

With a wry smile, Liam took a step toward the door. "And your help is welcome, my friend. See you in a couple of hours." He thumbed toward the room Sloane slept in. "You fine to keep her until then?"

"Sure. She's a rascal that one. But she's got a heart of gold."

Liam's face dropped. He nodded and quickly left the apartment. Out on the street he breathed in the fresh air, cleansing his feelings, bottling them up to be tossed later. Focus was all he could allow now. If nothing else, to protect her from herself.

A few blocks away from the uncomfortable situation left at Dustin's house, Liam walked into a lingerie store. He headed directly to the back, ignoring the half-clad sales assistant who smiled seductively at him. Sometime in the last year he had lost his humor. He shook his head as he pushed through the swinging door to the back office.

Long legs covered in fish nets, a personal favorite of Liam's, greeted him first. Her feet were covered to the knee in shiny vinyl boots. Her ass, currently pointed right at him was in a short powder blue mini-skirt. As Steffie stood up from her desk, he could see her bare mid-drift and shiny black top. Or was that a bra? She turned to meet his eyes.

"Like what you see, Liam?" Steffie asked, voice soft and sultry. As her large brown eyes looked him over, she flicked her long blond hair out of her face.

"Of course," Liam answered, "a man would be a fool not to notice you."

Smiling, Steffie walked over and stopped mere inches from him. She ran a hand down his chest. Liam knew he was in trouble when his temperature didn't rise but if anything, dropped. Steffie frowned. She leaned in close, smelling his neck carefully before backing away. Her eyes became slits. She walked back over to her desk and leaned on it, appraising him.

"You've bonded."

Liam nodded. "Not on purpose."

"It never is, *Guardian*," she sneered, sitting back on her desk, legs open wide. "How will you be paying me then? Your normal payment will not suffice."

Great. She was annoyed.

"I was hoping cash might do it."

"You know I care little for such things. *You* were much more interesting."

"I know, I'm not sure what else I can offer."

"Well, I do. Send one of your friends in your stead. Tonight. One that is NOT bonded. They like coin, let them earn it through pleasure."

Liam wondered if she realized that her concept of pleasure wasn't necessarily the same as others.

He watched her and thought over it. Steffie liked them in their bestial form. There had to be someone who was interested.

"Deal," he said.

"Good," she purred. Taking his arm, she led him out of her office and into the store. Halfway to the door she stopped at the previously ignored sales assistance.

"Cherry," Steffie said, "we'll be expecting a guest or," she glanced at Liam, "*two* this evening to entertain us."

Cherry smiled, her large blue eyes glowing slightly. Her tongue slipped out of her mouth and seemed to just keep coming. Long with blue undertones, she flicked it at Liam before pulling it in and smiling innocently.

Liam chose not to react. He nodded at them both and turned away. Steffie grabbed him and yanked him down to her. She pressed her lips to his, biting as she pulled away. Liam stepped back and ran his hand across his bottom lip, pulling it away to find a streak of blood. He frowned at Steffie as she handed him the passport.

"Enjoy, my love," she said and sauntered back to her office.

Liam turned to leave and stopped cold. Sloane stood just inside the door watching him. *How had he not heard her entry?*

"How long have you been there?"

"Long enough."

Chapter 36

"Tea? How is tea going to prepare us?" Verity's lip trembled in apprehension as she placed her hand in his outstretched one. He cupped her hand and raised it up gently, pulling her from the chair. He paused and studied her hand, tracing her fingers with his. His touch sent a strange, unwanted thrill down her arm. He studied her hand as though the rest of her wasn't there.

"What?" Verity asked. Duran dropped her hand and motioned to the door.

"Join me in the dining room," he said and waited for her to proceed in front of him. Puzzled, Verity shook her head and left the room.

~~*~~

He set a tea cup in front of her before sitting across with his own. Verity became very interested in her cup. She brought it up and took a careful whiff of the contents. The brown liquid was deceiving. It smelled strongly like black tea.

"This is regular tea?" she asked, carefully avoiding his eyes.

"What did you expect?" he asked. She knew he was smiling without seeing his face.

"I don't know. A weird color? Maybe the scent of flowers? Or maybe even pretty swirls."

He laughed, rich and full. The smell of vanilla and wild flowers, always present around him, elevated, within her senses.

"Why do you smell like vanilla and wild flowers? Is that a cologne?" she asked. Duran stopped moving, cup midway to his lips. Verity wanted to smack herself. Or disappear into the root work below. Instead she took a long gulp of tea.

"Interesting," he finally said and took a sip. He didn't answer the question which was annoying and yet Verity was glad to avoid further embarrassment.

"So, tell me about you," Verity said pretending nonchalance while inspecting the dregs of her teacup.

"Another time, Verity. The child is ready." He stood and Verity followed, a lump forming in the back of her throat with each step toward the Queen.

The Queen was silent though the beads of sweat on her forehead told the real story. Verity wet a cloth and gently dabbed the beads away. The Queen's bright green eyes shone through slits, but her mouth turned up slightly at the gesture. Verity gave the Queen's hand a squeeze before placing her hands on the oversized belly. Closing her eyes, Verity *felt* for the activity. No matter how many times she had done it, the sense of it was always a surprise and sometimes still overwhelmed her. She could feel the life flowing through her hands and it gave her confidence. This would be ok.

She opened her eyes and found that King had snuck in. He was at his wife's side, holding her hand closely to his chest and blotting her forehead with the cloth Verity had left out. They looked at each other with such love, such caring. It was heartwarming on the one hand and so definitely odd on the other. Two completely different species with a bond that would test the trials of time. Duran's scent overwhelmed her suddenly and she realized he had moved up next to her. When she met his amethyst gaze, he gave her a *get on with it* look and she blocked him out. Taking up a pair of plastic gloves, she focused on bringing a new life to the world.

After grabbing a couple of towels, Verity lifted the Queen's knees and placed the towels beneath the Queen and between her legs. Then, Verity took olive oil and massaged the area to help elasticize the skin to allow for a watermelon-sized exit. The Queen shook with a contraction. Verity pulled off her gloves and placed her hands on the Queen's belly. She could feel the muscles straining and the movement, slow but sure, of the package within.

~~*~~

Four hours later the child had finally dropped into place, ready for the part that Verity had been dreading. Both the Queen and King had been silent, King being the anchor for the Queen's pain and attention. Duran too had been silent. He simply watched. Verity assumed he was an emergency backup.

When the next contraction came, Verity was ready. Using her own energy, she increased the small tear, staunching the blood and numbing the area to some extent so the child could push free. The black hair crowned then, and Verity waited for the next contraction. Thirty seconds later the child's head pushed through and a strange growl erupted from the fangless mouth. Human ears and nose, but a distinctly Goblin facial structure. With the next push the child was out. Verity wrapped him quickly in a blanket and put him in King's outstretched arms. She held the scissors out to him and he shook his head as he gazed upon his new son, tears welling in his yellowed eyes. Verity took care of the umbilical cord efficiently and turned back to the Queen. As expected there was blood but based on what Verity had read, it was an acceptable amount. Heart swelling with pride, Verity glanced at Duran. He was watching King, his face smug, eyes shining.

Eying the Queen's still large stomach, Verity wondered how large the placenta was going to be. The child was not as big as Verity had expected but being her first birthing, she didn't really have much to compare to. She waited for the Queen's next contractions to end this long wait.

The contraction finally came and along with it, another head of dark hair. Verity's jaw dropped. Her shock at missing this huge detail was evident in her wide eyes. She looked up at Duran who was smiling at her, eyes sparkling. A quick look at the Queen and King told her they had known. She shook her head before delivering what she would soon find out was the first ever female human-goblin mix. The King gave his son to Duran and took his daughter from Verity. Covering up a sob with a soft cough, he held her howling head gently to his own while Verity took care of the umbilical cord. When she finished, King showed the girl to her mother as Verity waited once more for the placenta to arrive.

Thirty minutes later there came blood. At first it was just a trickle, but it soon turned into more. Verity changed out the soaked towels quickly and rested her bare hands on the Queen's much smaller belly. She felt around until she found it. The placenta had only partially detached and was torn and bleeding. Focusing on the tear, Verity willed it to heal. Panicking slightly, she looked up at Duran. His face serious, he pointed to his chest. Understanding set in and Verity closed her eyes. She allowed herself to feel. She felt anger at not realizing there were two babies. She felt love for her profession. She felt her affinity for the couple that had trusted her to do the job right. A twinge in her chest told her she felt something akin to respect for the dark-haired man who so casually held the baby boy. She told the Queen's cells what they needed to do. Guided them. With emotion. And they listened.

Time flew but Verity couldn't have said how much. The tear was simple to handle since she was most familiar with its make-up. As Verity tucked fresh towels and blankets around the Queen, she noticed that Duran was gone. As she left the room, the healing Queen held her daughter and the King held their son as they whispered together, tired yet elated.

Noah was waiting for her just outside the door, concern etched on his face. Verity patted him on the arm with a smile.

"We did it," she whispered as they made their way down the hall.

"Complications I gather?" he asked.

"Yes, but it all worked out ok."

"Excellent. Well done, Verity. Really."

"Thanks, Noah. I am pretty proud of myself."

He chuckled. "So you should be."

"Yes, but now I need a shower and something to eat. I'm starved."

Noah grinned. "You shower up. I'll go see what I can dig up in the middle of the night."

"How can you tell what time a day it is?"

"I just know."

Verity shook her head at him and turned into his antechamber as he continued on to the kitchen. The shower was near the top of one of the best she'd ever had. When she came out wrapped in a towel, a plate of fruit and cheese was sitting on the bed. She inhaled it before getting dressed. She needed to check on the Queen before even considering a slumber. Noah was nowhere to be found when she left the room.

The Queen had two plates on a tray before her. One piled high with breakfast foods: eggs, bacon, potatoes, and toast. The other with a variety of things that Verity didn't recognize; lumps of what looked like green mashed potatoes, small brown sticks resembling green beans. The Queen was smiling.

"Congratulations, Verity. You did a great job. I feel better than I have in months." They laughed together. King held both children in his large, long arms. They slept under his watchful gaze.

"Congratulations to you both," Verity said and bulldozed to the next topic before she chickened out, "I'm assuming you didn't think it necessary to tell me you expected twins?"

The Queen laughed. "Sorry, King and Duran thought it would be entertaining. I played along. I must admit it *was* entertaining. You'll certainly know what to look for in the future."

"That I will," Verity chuckled. "It was a wonderful experience and I am really glad I was here for it. But now, I need a nap."

~~*~~

Verity left them with a bounce in her step and headed back to her room. She was halfway there when soft footsteps joined hers. Glancing behind she found Duran tailing her three feet behind. She paused so he could catch up.

"It was your idea wasn't it?" she asked.

"That depends on what you're asking," he replied. "Come. Walk with me."

"Why?" Verity asked and stopped, turning to him.

"To appease my curiosity," he smiled. Verity didn't buy it.

"How about appeasing my curiosity? I think you know enough about me. I think you need to tell me why you're still here. And why you keep following me around."

Noah came around the bend and into view. "Everything okay, Verity?"

"Yes, Noah, I'm okay. Just trying to get some answers. I'll be in soon."

Noah studied her for a moment before glancing at Duran, bowed his head slightly and left them alone again. Duran gestured down the hall.

"Please?" he requested. Verity was tired but started walking again anyway.

Five minutes down the path, Duran gently took Verity's arm and stopped her forward progress. He moved in front of her and brought his head down. Verity felt her eyes widen, her heart quicken and her insides churn with indecision, to duck or welcome the warmth of the approaching lips. But instead of a kiss, she met Duran's intense gaze and felt a single finger press on her lips while she watched his other hand press a finger against his own lips. Only when she nodded did he stand tall again. She was about to speak when his eyes widened in admonishment. She pursed her lips as he moved to stand in front of her, his back tall and muscular beneath his white tee shirt. Somehow his hand found hers and he held it gently behind him.

"She is mine," he said simply. Someone laughed, a deep sensual sound.

"I had thought it odd that the Goblin's Lair was suddenly teaming with humans. Oh, well. Another time then. I bring word from the Queen, an announcement that all must hear." Verity desperately wanted to peer around Duran's slender build but his grip on her hand kept her still.

"I had assumed so, seeing as how you are her messenger," Duran replied. "The King is indisposed at the moment, but his son will likely see you in the hall. I would be happy to let them know of your arrival, *Tague*."

"Thank you kindly, *highness*. I can make myself known, however. Enjoy your human."

Though she couldn't get a good look, Verity watched the shadow of Tague disappear around the curved wall. Their words had filled the air with tension and magic, only manners keeping their taught muscles in check. It was strange. Duran waited a moment before releasing her hand.

"Please continue with your plans on being a healer, Verity." He spoke as though nothing weird had just happened.

"You're not wondering what he's here for?" She waved a thumb toward the hall where the messenger had vanished.

"No. I have been the recipient of many words from the Queen. They are more often than not, to put it in your modern terms, bull shit."

Verity stifled a laugh. "Wow. Tell me how you really feel."

Duran moved to face Verity, his eyes narrowed. He lifted her chin with the tip of his index finger.

"You are quite the interesting creature, Verity," he whispered.

Verity swallowed hard as she met Duran's heavy gaze. His eyes were now a deep plum with flecks of gold like the sun bursting from behind a cloud. His hand left her chin, releasing her from whatever temporary hold he'd had.

"Yes, interesting," he said and continued walking down the hall. "Tell me of your parents."

"My parents?" Verity frowned. "You may not be curious about that messenger, but I sure am. You forget, a lot of this is still new to me."

Duran turned back to her, his eyes a bright violet once more. He rolled them at her. "Fine. Let us see what the Queen has to say today."

Verity smiled brightly.

Chapter 37

Liam walked past Sloane to the exit. He gestured for her to follow him out of the lingerie shop. Dustin was sitting on a nearby bench. Liam gave him a condescending look. Dustin shrugged. "She does what she wants."

Knowing that all too well, Liam turned to her.

"It's not what you think."

Sloane said nothing, but the steam developing in her blood was apparent. Liam sighed and turned away from her. He licked his lip and, as expected, found it to be almost completely healed. He turned back to Dustin.

"All packed?"

"Yep," he waved a hand at the bags at his feet. "'Bout time to kick some suppressive ass."

Liam couldn't help but smile. He walked to the street and hailed a cab. Once piled in, they headed to the airport. He noticed that Sloane had showered and changed into all black. She looked stunning and the warmth he didn't experience earlier with Steffie was now heating him to the core.

"Dustin, Steffie needs payment for my documents. I wasn't able to deliver her normal fee but was hoping you could ask one or," he cleared his throat, "or preferably two of your eligible boys to deliver?"

Dustin chuckled. "I think I know just the two." He pulled out his cell phone and started tapping the keys.

Sloane didn't meet Liam's eye or speak once during the drive. At the airport, Sloane wandered behind him, obviously lost in her thoughts. He could feel her presence as heavy as a dragon troll. Dustin trailed behind. He didn't approve of what Liam was going to do and yet he didn't pull authority or try to change his mind, which Liam appreciated. He'd found a new friend. Or at least someone with a common appreciation of Sloane. Liam's heart twitched slightly at the thought of someone else appreciating her.

They reached her gate before he could deliberate further on Dustin's interest or intention.

"Sloane, this is your stop."

Sloane came out of her reverie. She glanced at Liam, then at the gate to Tampa, then at Dustin. No emotion crossed her face. She watched Dustin lift a shoulder and purse his lips before inspecting the floor and then brought her gaze back to Liam. Her eyes met his with a determination that he loved. He held out her ticket. Sloane took it and looked it over before meeting his eyes again. She looked at him for a long moment before saying something in such a low voice almost *he* couldn't hear them. The words would haunt him.

"I trusted you."

She watched, waiting for it to sink it. Liam knew that nothing showed on his face but the pain inside made him feel like crumbling to the ground. When he didn't budge, she turned to Dustin.

"I know it wasn't you," she said to him, a small smile on her face. She opened her arms and *hugged him*. Him. Where had he been all this time? Liam knew his internal complaints were lost in vain.

Sloane turned and walked over to the gate. Liam watched her vanish into the jetway.

Standing for just a moment longer than needed, Liam waited. She didn't come back. And she hadn't said goodbye.

For the first time possibly ever, Liam felt regret. And the strangest pain pumped through his chest.

Chapter 38

Myra cackled as she swung the knife around her head like a lasso. Dr. J frowned. She wasn't heeding his orders well and he couldn't remember doing anything differently with her than he had with the others. Her bulbous eyes blinked over and over, and she cackled again. Finally, she put the knife down and sat heavily. Large tears started pouring from her eyes. She wiped them away and then gave Dr. J a hard stare. He backed up a few feet.

Hal moved in between them. Dr. J smiled. Hal had come through beautifully. He followed every order exactly. Never questioned a thing and never stopped when pain was involved. He would have been a perfect specimen if he wasn't a monster, Dr. J mused.

Moving suddenly and quickly Myra grabbed the knife and jammed it straight into her heart. Hal cocked his head. They watched her bleed out, slumping to the floor in death.

So, the mind treatment hadn't taken. That made sense. Dr. J shrugged and, with a pat on Hal's furry back, left to check on the rest of his patients.

Chapter 39

Fuming, Sloane found her seat on the plane and stored her bag in the upper compartment. Liam had sent her home and there was nothing she could do about it. The thought burned fire through her shoulders and neck. After everything they had been through, he decided to send her back.

Sitting in the aisle seat of row ten, Sloane's attention was drawn to the stewardess who was trying to close the plane door. She couldn't quite get it and it kept slowly pushing open. Sloane watched a hand shove in and hand the stewardess a slip of paper. She looked it over before nodding and allowing the person through.

At first, he was just a random good-looking guy. Olive skin, the kind that is natural no matter how much or little sun you get, sparkling green eyes and dark chocolate hair with copper highlights and the slightest of curls. His Hue was a soft silvery glow; a Guardian. Sloane stared at the seat in front of her and peripherally watched him come down the aisle until he passed, taking a seat further back.

Sighing and settling back into her seat, she wondered why in the hell Liam had sent someone with her. Seriously? She thought she was perfectly capable of sitting in a plane for two hours without getting into trouble. Maybe this guy was supposed to watch over her? She glanced over the little old lady next to her and out the window. They were just starting to move away from the gate. Fighting a deep burn of anger, Sloane grabbed a magazine and started through its pages though she didn't really see them. Everything was going numb.

Once on the ground, Sloane joined the sheep, jumped into the aisle to grab her bag from the overhead and get off the plane as fast as she was able. While flying she had come up with part of a plan but was missing a few key components. Like how would she get to Ireland without a passport? Why had she not gotten one before? Sloane blinked when she realized that she never thought she would survive long enough to go anywhere. But now, now that she knew how to block the feelings, her heart pinged at the thought, she wanted to see things. Experience things.

Exiting the plane, Sloane moved to the seating area to collect herself. She wasn't sure who to contact. Grief was slithering its way into her nerves and she fought to claim rationality. If she went to the Guardian's den, she would have to tell them what was happening. If she tried to go home, she would be in danger. Again, how would she get to Ireland? Sitting in one of the hard plastic chairs, Sloane buried her face in her hands and tried to decide a plan of action.

"Fancy meeting you here."

A soft, bell tinged voice came from in front of her. Sloane looked up and saw a beautiful, smiling face. Lunging, she wrapped herself around Nia, almost throwing them both to the ground. Nia hugged back. The tears ripped from Sloane and Nia let her cry for what seemed hours. Finally pulling it together, Sloane pulled away, brushed her red-rimmed eyes and they sat down together, Nia holding Sloane's hands tightly in her own.

"How did you find me?" Sloane managed to ask.

"I have my ways," Nia said with a smile.

Sloane smiled sheepishly at her friend. "You have no idea how good it is to see you right now."

Nia's smile broadened before a mischievous glint crept into her eye. "We have a lot to talk about, don't we?" Sloane nodded. "Then let's get out of here and you can tell me what the hell is going on."

~~*~~

Sinking into Nia's plush white leather couch, Sloane cradled the hot tea, taking sips and letting the potent liquid calm her nerves. Being a mountain nymph, Nia literally fluttered around her kitchen with her white gossamer wings before settling into the recliner next to the couch with a plate of scones and jam.

Biting into a scone, Sloane swooned before looking at her friend's face, marred in thought. She had told Nia everything. The relief in confiding was great and yet now she sat unsure of what to do with herself. Nia sat in quiet contemplation for some time before speaking. She cleared her throat, attracting Sloane's eyes.

"Sloane, I know how angry you are at him. I understand it, I would be furious too. But there is something else that I know all too well."

Sloane came to attention when she saw pain roll over her friend's face.

"There is nothing as sacred, as wondrous," Nia whispered, "as a soul-mate. Nothing. It is worth the heartache, the fear, the pain - to experience it even for a short time. Even for just a dance."

A rush of emotion flushed Sloane's face as she watched Nia gaze at the room but see something else. Nia abruptly turned to Sloane, her eyes filled with bittersweet.

"I can't let you give up so easily."

"Nia. After letting some biatch suck his face, he sent me packing. He made me leave without so much as an explanation. He doesn't want me." Her last words were choked. Nia frowned at her.

"Don't be stupid." Nia's words cut like a knife. Sloane pulled her head back in surprise.

"Pull back, Sloane. Stop looking at what he's done to you and look at what he's doing, well, *thinks* he's doing, for you."

Frowning, Sloane looked quizzically at Nia who smiled sadly and shook her head.

"You are so stubborn. He sent you away from danger. He's trying to protect you and that's what he felt was right. Don't you see?"

Sloane's shoulders slumped as the war between sanity, anger and betrayal swirled around her heart. She felt her ears flush as anger started to win. Nia rolled her eyes and leaned back in her chair. The scones sat forgotten on the coffee table.

Placing her tea on the table, Sloane rubbed her face and started pacing the elegantly decorated room. She finally stopped arms akimbo.

"Do you think Bob was right? I mean, is there truth to what he said?"

Nia's eyes narrowed slightly. "I don't know. I hope so."

Sloane cocked her head at the strange answer. Nia just shook her head.

"I received a message from the Shades once," Nia said. "It hasn't come to pass yet but I'm still hoping."

"That was a long time ago?"

"Very," she answered sadly.

"Nia, how old are you?"

A broad smile covered Nia's face. "Old enough."

Sloane chuckled, welcoming the playful banter. She clapped her hands together. "Well, I need a game plan. I think I know what I need to do."

Nia looked at her thoughtfully, a slim grin creeping along her perfect skin.

"Do tell."

Chapter 40

Liam sat in an aisle seat on the right side of the plane, head propped up on his hand, occasionally rubbing his forehead as he stared at the floor. He hoped she would eventually understand. The need to protect her overrode whatever the Shades might say. When he survived this fight, he would try to convince her.

Would he though? What kind of a life would it be? Could he settle? He hadn't looked at another woman since he'd met Sloane, let alone touched one. Of course, he didn't count Steffie. She was just being a bitch.

There was only one person he burned for and it was eating him alive. His brow furrowed, and he rubbed the bridge of his nose for the umpteenth time. Dustin, in the aisle seat to his left shifted in his seat presumably to get his large bulk more comfortable. Liam fleetingly thought about talking to him about her but couldn't get out the words.

The plane dropped slightly, and Liam squeezed his arm rests, glancing ahead nervously. Dustin chuckled softly earning him Liam's glare. Something landed on Liam's right hand. He jumped and turned to the young girl sitting in the middle seat next to him. He guessed she was about ten years old and her solemn face would have been funny if he wasn't terrified.

"First time flying?" she asked as she removed her small hand. Liam shook his head and she raised an eyebrow. "I hear it does get easier," she said before turning back to the book in her lap.

Liam rested his head back on the seat and started shoving his emotion into internal storage. Dr. J came to mind and he felt the growl deep in his chest. The girl glanced at him and he patted his belly. He watched her smile and nod before noticing her mother. She was very attractive, but nothing stirred in him. She smiled at him and he nodded before continuing to stare at the floor. His normal routine had been dumped upside down. Dustin leaned over and whispered.

"Stop your sulking," Dustin said, receiving a glare in reply. "Sloane is so far gone for you, you'll have another chance."

"What makes you think I'm worried about her?"

"Do I have a sign that says idiot on my forehead?" Dustin reached up and felt his forehead. Liam stifled a smile, intent on brooding.

"Jeez, you're definitely one of those stubborn fellows, aren't ya?"

Liam raised an eyebrow, his hands curled into fists. Dustin shook his head.

"Here's what I don't get. Why? Why lead her on, then push her away? Why not follow your heart?"

Anger shot through his system and Liam fought to control the heat.

"Because I was ordered to stay away from her." His voice was low and feral. Dustin leaned back and thought for a moment before turning back to Liam.

"You're not rogue," he whispered. Liam just looked at him. It didn't matter now. They were about to join the troops and Dustin would need to know what he was getting in to. He watched Dustin as the revelation sunk in. The muscles in Dustin's arms tightened for a moment before he stood and headed toward the back of the plane. Liam let his head hit the back rest and sighed. At the rate that he made friends, he would probably never have to worry about buying Christmas presents.

The plane hit turbulence and Liam found himself attached to the arm rests again. He was lucky the girl didn't use them. It would have been difficult to explain her broken hand. Dipping his head, he waited for sleep, appreciating the one thing that would stop his mind from churning at least for a little while.

Just before landing he woke. Dustin still hadn't returned. Wondering if he had lost a partner he glanced to the rear of the plane. He spotted Dustin's head several rows back. Rolling his eyes, he turned back in his seat as the announcement of their impending landing came over the speakers. Liam sighed in relief.

Liam made his way from the plane, leaving Dustin to choose his course. He was halfway through the airport on his way to the exit when Dustin appeared beside him.

"Can you hang on a second? I just need to make a call and then you can turn me in."

Liam scowled. "I'm not turning you in, Dustin. No one actually gives a shit that you're rogue. How can they not know this?" He whispered the last to himself. Dustin raised an eyebrow as he pulled out his cell phone. Liam stood a few feet away, out of body traffic but close enough to eavesdrop.

"It's Dustin. What's the update? A beautiful blond, huh? Well, keep it in your pants and stay on them."

Liam moved in and raised his eyebrows in question. Dustin gave him an irritating smile.

"What?" Liam demanded. Dustin's smile broadened as he pocketed his phone.

"I sent someone to follow her."

Jealousy raced down Liam's spine. He was a breath away from decking Dustin when he realized he was glad. He should have thought of that himself. He nodded at Dustin.

"Smart," he said, "where is she?"

"Apparently a beautiful blond met her when she got off the plane. He followed them to a car in the parking garage lot and slapped a tracer on it as they left. Don't ask me where he gets these things. He thinks he's 007. Anyway, he rented a car and caught up with them in some high-end neighborhood in south Clearwater. Why are you smiling?"

Liam laughed. "She's safe. The blond would be Nia. She can protect them both and then some. Probably even from me."

"What the hell is she? Is my spy safe?"

"She's a fae of some sort. She's a good girl. She won't harm him unless he does something stupid. If she was going to, she would have already. That girl's got some power, trust me."

Dustin scowled but seemed to acquiesce as he turned with Liam to leave the airport. Liam slapped him on the back cheerfully. A weight had lifted from his worried mind. He would go back to doing what he did best; finding and killing the bad things.

"Let's go see a Guardian about a war," he said cheerfully.

Chapter 41

"Oh, come on!" Nia hollered. Sloane jumped at the outburst. Nia was looking up into the darkness of the building roof tops as they took the relatively short walk to grab some dinner. Sloane glanced around for cover before she felt Nia's reassuring hand on her arm.

"Come out and join us or, in the words of my best friend, 'fuck off.'"

Sloane smiled and stared into the darkness, no idea who Nia was talking to. A shadow moved on the building to her left and she spotted the vague outline of a Guardian's horned head. Her heart skipped a beat until she realized it wasn't who she might have hoped. Sensing motion on the fire escape stairs to her right, Sloane shrunk toward Nia.

Bob appeared on the staircase just as the Guardian landed in the nearby shadows. The soft tinkle of Nia's laugh echoed around them.

"A rogue *and* a brownie," Nia said gleefully. She pointed at Bob in his squirrel form. "Very good, young one. Very good." Bob chirped and bowed. Nia turned to the Guardian. "You on the other hand need more skill in tracking the fae."

The Guardian backed up slightly despite the fact that he was five times the size of Nia. Sloane watched with great interest as he bowed quietly. Nia waved a dismissive hand in the air. *What's with the bowing?* Sloane wondered.

"Oh, please. No need for formalities. Just tell me your purpose and we'll see what happens next."

Sloane watched her friend's eyes sparkle.

The Guardian raised a thick, leathery arm toward Sloane.

"I'm to watch over Sloane Jacobs." His voice was rough and hollow.

"Name, rank and serial number, big boy." Nia sounded bored. She actually looked at her perfectly manicured pink nails.

"My name is Evan Smith and I was sent by Dustin Abernathy."

"Smith? Really?" Nia asked full of mirth. The gargoyle nodded. "And who is this Dustin person?" She glanced at Sloane.

"A friend," Sloane said with a smile.

"Well, good then, Evan Smith. Very good."

Sloane's heart swelled as she thought of Dustin. He was such a sweetie. Nia started walking again. "Go get changed, Evan Smith," Nia said, "and meet us at Nonny's for dinner. Bob, keep doing what you do."

Nonny's take-out area, in the front of the building, was bustling, but the rear sit-down dining was relatively open. Nia chose a table and sat with her back to the wall, with a view to both the front and rear entrances. The seemingly small move was not lost on Sloane. She had been to enough restaurants with Liam. She had just never noticed it with Nia before. Liam was always on the alert. Well, except those rare moments.

As though reading her mind, Nia grasped her hands. "Don't give up."

"I'll try, Nia."

"No. Promise me. You will not give up."

"Okay, okay. I won't give up. Yet."

Before Nia could retort, Evan Smith came in the back door. Sloane knew it was him immediately. Not only by his soft silvery glow but because he was the same Guardian who had almost missed her earlier flight. She had forgotten about him. Smiling, she waved a hand at the chair next to her. Evan grinned sheepishly and sat down. Nia ignored him as she released her friend's hands.

"I am guessing we are going to have to have to let him in on our plans. Otherwise, we'll have to kill him."

Sloane's brows shot up and Evan pulled back from the table quickly. Nia laughed almost hysterically. Sloane sighed and shook her head. It was weird enough to watch how people acted so delicately around Nia, it was weirder to see a full grown, capable man cower from her.

"Sorry," Nia sputtered, "I couldn't help it."

"After dinner, you owe me some explanations, Nia," Sloane said.

"One day I will," Nia said still laughing. The waitress came by and took their drink orders. Evan relaxed at the table. Sloane turned to him.

"I saw you on the plane."

"I figured you did," he smiled. He had a really warm smile. "One of the only things a Guardian can't hide from is an Aspie." He glanced at Nia, his expression wry.

"Yeah, we pretty much see exactly what's there. Except in some cases." She turned to glare at Nia who shrugged while she looked at the menu.

"How do you know Dustin? And how on earth did he get you on this wild goose chase?" Sloane asked him. They paused while the waitress took their order.

"Dustin met with a few of us..."

"Rogues?" Nia interrupted. Evan's eyes narrowed. Sloane frowned at Nia. Liam was Rogue too and even though she was mad at him, it didn't seem like it was *that* big a deal. But then again, it seemed that she didn't really know Nia like she thought she did. Nia smiled at her sympathetically.

"Don't give up on him," she said. Sloane raised her brows, eyes wide and shook her head.

Evan finally answered, his voice like steel. "Dustin met with some of us, *Guardians,* and let us know he had someone he cared for that needed to be shadowed. I was the only one without family or previous engagements, so I offered. Besides, I've never been to Florida. It seemed like a good opportunity."

"Well, Evan, I certainly appreciate you looking after me but," she waved a hand toward Nia who had sat back in her chair watching them both, "as you can see, I have a guardian."

Evan shrugged. "I see that, but it won't stop me from keeping an eye on you. I promised I would."

Sloane pursed her lips and nodded. Can't really knock a Guardian on mission. Stubborn creatures.

"She will need you, Guardian."

Nia spoke as though she was telling them about some upcoming weather, a light rain maybe, but to Sloane it was more like a hurricane.

"Why?" she asked dragging her *y* out like a teenager.

Nia smiled sadly. "I cannot go to the next destination with you, Sloane. That is for you alone."

Before Sloane could verbally bitch slap her friend, a plate of steaming baked ziti was placed in front of her. Starving, she dug into her meal, blowing on each bite before inhaling it. She was about to ask for an explanation, but Nia placed a soft hand on her arm.

"Let's tell Evan here about Florida since he won't be seeing much of it on this trip."

Sloane nodded. They fell into a pleasant conversation, one that anyone might have if maybe they weren't planning a trip through the Faeways.

Without a Fae.

Chapter 42

Sloane stared at the gigantic tree where Nia had vanished. Nia had told her that below the tree was a goblins lair, which was kind of scary. Nia said they were quite friendly to humans and Sloane wouldn't have any trouble. Sloane was not sure how much of that she could believe. Nia and Evan were escorting her to the Lair but only Evan would be coming with her through the Faeway. Nia apparently wasn't *that* kind of fae. Despite the heavy heat, a shiver coursed down Sloane's back at the thought.

Evan leaned against the tree, eyes closed, waiting. Sloane smiled inside with gratitude at Dustin's gift to her. She couldn't imagine going on this journey alone. She didn't think she would have gone through with it. Evan was a breath of fresh air. He was extremely well mannered, never cursed, and had eyes only for her safety. Then again, maybe that was weird too. Sighing and shaking her head, Sloane leaned against the tree next to him.

"You ever been through the Faeway?" she asked. Evan opened his eyes and squinted at her.

"This will be the first," he said. Before Sloane could answer, Nia reappeared next to them with a wide smile.

"All set! Let's go," she said. Sloane went to grab

her backpack, but Evan snatched it up first and slung it over his shoulder. Nia took Sloane's hand and pulled her through the invisible doorway into the cooler cavern of the tree. More chills slid down Sloane's arms. Evan was just a step behind her.

"It's a long trek down to the main entrance so let's move it," Nia ordered as she dropped Sloane's hand and headed down a long stairwell.

~~*~~

The cavern was enormous. Sloane had worried that being below ground would make her feel crushed and maybe even claustrophobic, but there was no chance. It was incredibly spacious, and it felt fresh, like she was meandering through a field and not lord knows how deep underground. Sloane made an appreciative sound as she followed Nia toward the front of the cavern. The throne was amazing but not as amazing as the goblin sitting it in. He was the scariest thing Sloane had ever seen and yet he put off such a happy hue of yellow that she couldn't possibly be afraid. Nia bowed to him before introducing Sloane.

"Matthew, thank you for welcoming us and with such short notice. Please let me introduce my dear friend and Aspicio, Sloane Jacobs."

It occurred to Sloane that she had no idea of the etiquette here, only that it wasn't the same as hers. She curtsied uncertainly, and the goblin laughed.

"Sloane the Aspicio, please be welcome to our home," he said with a perfect English accent, "I am about to share an announcement, please stay."

"Thank you," Sloane said as masses of Goblins started to file into the room.

Chapter 43

Verity scanned the room and noted that, as Duran had anticipated, the King and Queen were holed off in a room somewhere. Maternity leave for Goblins. The hall was filling with Goblins of all shapes and sizes. The King's son, Matthew stood and stepped away from the throne. Beside him Verity assumed, was Tague. He was trim and blond and had the ears of the Fae. Duran led her to the right, through the amassing bodies, but not too close to the messenger. Verity settled beside him and turned toward the entrance just in time to watch Noah saunter in. He stopped, scanned the crowd and found her easily. She gave him a quick wave and he made his way over.

"Any idea what this is all about?" he asked.

"No idea but it's interesting, don't you think?"

Noah gave a shrug in response as he continued to sweep the room with his eyes. Duran had walked a few paces away to chat with a Goblin who looked like he should have a walking stick to hold his ancient body up but somehow, he kept standing and managed to exchange words.

Verity turned back to Noah and got his attention with a poke in the arm. He gave her a smirk that not long ago would have melted her heart but now it only won a grin back. She spoke as softly as possible to still be heard over the din rising in the room.

"How come you now seem to be okay with me hanging around Duran but you get nervous as all hell when King's around?"

"I don't get nervous," Noah said with an insulted frown.

"Oh, please. I'm not blind."

"Trust me, it is *not* nervousness."

"Then what?"

Noah straightened and brought his eyes to the front. Verity felt a hand on her elbow and turned to see that Duran had rejoined them. She gave him a smile as Matthew addressed the crowd, hushing as soon as the first word left his mouth.

"Greetings, family and friends. Our ally, the Fae Queen has sent a messenger today. We are gathered to hear his words." Matthew flourished a hand toward Tague, who stepped forward and bowed.

"Goblins, Fae, Humans," he said and glanced at Verity with a grin at the last, "and *Guardian*." He paused, and Verity felt Noah stiffen slightly. She also noticed uncomfortably that Duran's hand had never left her elbow.

"The Guardianship has sent a plea of help to our realm. Our great Queen has acceded this favor. I am brought forth to ask your help to spread the word to all Fae in your realm. We are needed forthwith at the Castle of Tarnwool in the old land."

Chapter 44

When the news came, Andy was sitting in class. The morning announcements were just starting when the day's lunch menu was cut off. The sound of fabric rustling, and faint whispering came over the loud speaker. Then someone must have turned it off as it went silent.

Glancing at his English teacher, Mr. Glass, Andy saw his head tilt and brows raise slightly as he too listened to the silence.

A sharp squeal came from the speakers and then a soft voice.

"Teachers and Students, this is Joseph Barrows."

"The Director," someone whispered behind him.

"It is with great sorrow that I make an announcement today," he cleared his throat. "Mr. Shirtell, who many of you have had as your History teacher, has unexpectedly crossed the great divide. Let's give him a moment of thought, please."

Andy stretched his arms out and grasped the edges of his desk tightly as he watched Mr. Glass gape at the loud speaker. Andy was just in Mr. Shirtell's class yesterday. He had seemed his normal disgruntled self. He glanced at the rest of his classmates, twelve of them. None of them looked really upset but they all looked surprised. Andy frowned. Down the road, when he crossed the divide, he certainly hoped it would create a little more of an impact. He imagined Charlese screaming and throwing her body on the ground, tears flooding the room. Then he saw her skin through the tear-soaked clothes and...

"Thank you all. We'll be canceling the remainder of classes today and will meet in the great hall to give our condolences after dinner."

The room stayed frozen for a few seconds before chairs scraped the floors and one by one they filed out of the room, leaving behind a disturbed English teacher.

~~*~~

Andy took in the fading sun as he sat by the lake and watched the pixies play with the dragon flies. The pixies generally ignored him. On occasion they attempted a prank; he had learned quickly that they like to pull your hair or clothes in jest. Sometimes they threw clumps of grass or dirt at you. But it would seem that they could read his mood and stayed afar today.

Keppin sank down beside him quietly. He knew it was Keppin without looking, the telltale scent of the mint Keppin liked to chew wafted around him.

"There's talk that Shirtell was hunting when it happened. Nothing's confirmed though," Keppin said as he beamed a pebble into the water. They watched it skip three times before vanishing beneath the surface.

Andy knew that Keppin suspected foul play and he wasn't opposed to the idea himself, but neither of them were trained enough to be more than a hindrance. He turned to Keppin just in time to watch a pebble smack Keppin in the forehead.

"What the hell!" Keppin yelled as he palmed his head. Andy tried not to laugh but a snort made it through. He pointed to the water. Keppin stood and looked at the water kelpie lounging in the lake, shaking with mirth.

When she kept laughing, Keppin reached down and grabbed another pebble. He took aim and threw. The kelpie vanished beneath the surface.

"Friggin animals around here," Keppin muttered and sat back down. He stretched back, leaning on his elbows.

Andy saw what was coming. As soon as the pebble left the kelpie's hand he rolled his arm out, hand in front of Keppin's face.

"Dude," Keppin started, but the soft sound of the pebble hitting Andy's palm shut him up.

"They don't just 'be quiet and go away'," Andy said dropping the pebble to the ground, "trust me, I've already been through this. Just leave the pebbles on the ground."

Keppin muttered something to himself before lying fully back on the ground and rubbing his face.

"I know," Andy said, "I don't think it was an accident either, but it leaves me with another thought."

"What's that?"

"Did they just want Mr. Shirtell or are they going after Displacers?"

Chapter 45

"I thought the Fae would have like ESP or something, didn't think they would need to *spread the word*," Verity commented to Noah. He snorted.

"They definitely have extrasensory skills," he said, "but their magic doesn't go quite so far as long distant mind melds. They use cell phones and some of them are just as bad as the rest of us about checking messages."

"I *am* standing right here," Duran inserted. Noah ignored him, and Verity chuckled.

"So, what *is* up with the Guardianship, Noah?" Verity asked.

He shook his head. "Looks like I need to find out."

"Allow me," Duran said as he closed his eyes and placed an index finger to his temple. Verity watched intently as he frowned deeply. Opening his eyes slowly, he met her gaze and smiled.

"Just kidding," he said, his purple eyes sparkling, before sauntering over to Tague.

Verity grinned after him while Noah leaned in next to her.

"Why do you always attract trouble?" he asked. Verity frowned.

"Why do you think he's trouble?"

"He's Fae."

Verity vented a frustrated sigh and shook her head. "Seriously, Noah, what do you have against them? They have shown me nothing but kindness."

"Give it time."

"Gawd! Who are you?"

Noah cocked his head and frowned. His eyes caught something behind her and before she could turn he touched her arm.

"I'll catch up with you later on," he said and walked away, vanishing into the crowd. Duran appeared beside her.

"Apparently the Guardianship needs help to take down a *human*," he scoffed.

"Uh, hi, human standing right here," Verity waved at him. He smiled and caught her hand.

"Of that, I am well aware."

Verity felt the heat from his hand move through her arm like liquid gold and when his lips pressed firmly onto the inside of her wrist, her insides danced a jig. *What the heck?* He promptly dropped her hand. Verity squeezed her hand into a fist. Her nerves seemed to be in contrast to her personal feeling of defense.

"They wouldn't call in the Fae just for help with a human, but Tague does not have or will not share any further details," he murmured as he looked toward the entrance. Verity was just coming out of her momentary trance of thought, one that weighed heavily on the Fae standing before her, when she realized where Noah had likely gone.

"Noah will find out," she said softly.

"Yes, of course," Duran said sharply, "now I

believe we were in the middle of a walk…"

"I need to go speak to King. Or Matthew," Verity decided out loud.

"Why?" Duran asked his hand on her elbow again. Verity pulled away and headed toward the throne.

~~*~~

Verity watched Matthew as he delicately handled all manner of questions thrown his way about the odd announcement. He held his ground and asked for the Goblins to head back to whatever it was they were doing and to keep the announcement in mind when and if they ran across a Fae in their travel. Her turn finally came.

"Miss Applebee, what a pleasure," he said taking both her hands in his own huge furry ones. Verity dipped at the knees and smiled.

"Thank you, Matthew. Although the announcement was for the Fae, I fear it also announces the end of my stay with you."

"Are you sure? We had hoped you would stay longer," Matthew said, concern in his dark eyes. Verity smiled.

"You and your family have been incredible, and I am grateful for your hospitality. I would be happy to come back soon and check on everyone, but I believe my people may need a healer soon."

Matthew nodded kindly. "I do hope you come back very soon," he said sadly.

Verity squeezed his hands. "I will and thank you."

Verity took her leave and headed to the exit toward her room. Before she reached the hallway,

Noah entered.

"We need to leave now," he told her before coming to a stop. Verity gave him a half smile.

"I know. I've already told Matthew."

"Leave?"

Verity saddened at Duran's voice. Oddly, she didn't want to leave him behind. Before she could turn to him, she watched as Noah fixed on something over her shoulder, his eyes wide and frozen as though in a trance. Verity glanced at Duran who was turning back from that which transfixed Noah, his lips pressed firmly together.

Verity turned around and saw Sloane.

"Sloane!" she yelled and started forward, arms out. Sloane met her, and they hugged tight.

"I completely forgot you would be here," Sloane said with a wide grin for her friend, "It sure is nice to see a familiar face."

"Tell me about it," Verity laughed. "What brings you here?"

"Believe it or not, I need to get to Ireland for the war."

Verity's eyebrows shot up.

"And I don't have a passport to fly but apparently there's a Faeway here I can use to cross over."

"Oh perfect! I hadn't figured out how I would get there and if it's ok with you, I will tag along."

"Of course! The more the merrier," Sloane assured.

A familiar hand gripped Verity's elbow.

"Sloane, this is Duran. Duran, meet my friend Sloane."

Duran took Sloane's hand and dipped low before

kissing it briefly. "I am at your service," he said.

Sloane raised an eyebrow and looked at Verity who shook her head and lifted a shoulder. Sloane's gaze went over her shoulder.

"What's up with Noah?" Sloane asked.

Verity looked back and saw that he hadn't moved from where she'd left him, the same stunned look glazed over his face. "I have no idea." She turned back to Sloane and caught a glimpse of Matthew speaking with a tall blond. Sloane followed her eyes.

"That's my friend Nia. She's helping…"

"Nialla?" Noah's voice was clear and crisp. Both girls turned to see the glaze gone from his face. They turned to watch Nia whose hand, animated in conversation with Matthew, froze when she heard Noah's voice. The hand haltingly made its way to settle on her heart. She turned slightly to look over the goblin's shoulder at Noah.

"Is it you?" she asked delicately.

"I am dreaming," Noah whispered as he watched Nia move away from Matthew and come slowly toward him. Shifting her shoulders slightly, Nia's wings came forth and pushed out in shining splendor around her.

"I hope it is *my* dream," Nia said, her eyes shining with tears, her tone unwavering. Her mouth twitching slightly as she stopped in front of him.

Sloane backed away some. The air was thick with a vibrant energy. Verity joined Sloane for a better view while the towering Duran watched everyone curiously.

"Noah's Hue is changing," Sloane whispered to Verity.

"What?" Verity asked, confusion marring her creamy skin.

"Noah's gray Hue just turned into a metallic blue. What the…"

Wings unfurled from Noah's back, but they were not the veined gray wings that Verity expected. They were long and delicate with a stunning blue sheen. They were very similar to Nia's except that they had intricate webbing between the nodes. Noah's tanned skin took on a faint blueish hue.

Verity watched as silver tears slowly leaked from Nia's eyes. With a flash of webbed fingers, Noah took Nia's hands, and leaned in briefly to kiss her knuckles.

"The Shades…they were truthful," Nia said, her voice strong despite the tears. She lifted a hand from his and trailed it gently along his cheek.

"Another time, another life, you shall meet," Noah said.

"Another time, another life, you shall love," Nia finished before throwing her arms around him. A vivid yellow glow exploded into the room. Even Verity turned away, blinking her eyes painfully.

"Well, that explains a few things," Sloane commented as she rubbed her eyes.

Verity felt the faintest pang in her heart as she watched Noah lift Nia into his arms and walk out the nearest doorway.

"You can say that again," she whispered.

Chapter 46

During the cab ride to one of the gargoyle dens in Ireland, which masqueraded as a pub, Liam couldn't shake the image of Sloane's face, carved with disappointment. For the umpteenth time he drummed his fingers on his knee. He wondered how much longer he would be able to resist the bond and still maintain any sanity. He was stuck in a very uncomfortable position and he didn't know how to fix it. There was an invasion tomorrow for crying out loud. They needed to shut down Dr. J's crazy experimentation and he needed his wits.

"Dude," Dustin's low voice pulled him from his dwindling spiral. He turned and met Dustin's eyes.

"You've got to complete the bond. For both your sakes. Even if I wouldn't mind a crack at that action myself."

Liam growled low in his throat.

"Oh please. You have no sense of humor." Dustin turned to look out the window as they pulled up to the bar. The windows of the dirty two-story brick building were dark, and the arched entrance had a metal gate on the outside. Wooden lettering across the top of the door read 'Gargoyle's Tavern'. A faded sign was inserted between the door and the gate. It read "No Vacancies."

Liam handed the cab driver a bill and exited the cab. Dustin got out behind him.

"Clever," he commented as they got to the door. Liam smirked at him before entering.

The silence of the street was broken by the cacophony of blended voices. A long bar ran along the right wall, the wood hand etched with protection symbols. Above the bar hung a wide wooden soffit where a dispassionate gargoyle was carved, wings out, in front of a striped crest decorated with faded paint in alternating royal blue and light gray.

On the far wall was a sitting area with heavy couches and chairs on solid wood frames with well-worn red cushions.

In front of the bar were five billiard tables, set out in a "U" shape. Next to the sitting area was an office. Liam knew that beyond that were the restrooms, another room for darts and the stairs to the Tavern's rooms. The place was packed with Guardians. Some Liam knew and others he didn't.

The bar smelled vaguely of smoke and beer. Liam's lip curled as memories of past visits, some good, some great, crossed his mind. There was a time when you could bring dates to the Den. Liam thought of Sloane and his scowl returned. Dustin punched his arm. Liam was about to put him in his place when the loud speaker came on.

"Coordination commencing in ten minutes."

Dustin let out a long breath, Liam assumed it was Dustin's relief since no one had jumped him and tied him up for being rogue.

"I told you no one cared," Liam said. Dustin gave him a bright smile as he put an arm around Liam's shoulders.

"Then let's drink!"

Nine minutes later everyone gathered in front of the bar facing the office. Roughly forty Guardians were arm to arm, breathing down each other's necks.

Liam stood amongst them, Dustin to his right, when the office door opened.

Smiling, Liam's shoulders pushed back a bit, his head lifted higher.

"Hello, boys," she said with a smile, her eyes sparkling.

Varying responses from awed greetings to the Queen to the less intimidated hellos echoed through the room.

Mrs. Helen Barrows, Queen of the Guardians and Den-Mother of all Gargoyles laughed and looked upon the Guardians proudly for a few minutes. She made eye contact with each and every one of them before allowing her features to grow more serious.

"Thank you all for being here. As many of you know, we have a situation where a human has discovered the hidden world and deigned to experiment in what we believe to be an attempt to wipe us all out. By understanding the genetic makeup of various creatures, the human has been able to create chemically altered creatures from his own species. The man and his heinous inventions needs to be removed. For those of you who have assisted Liam to this point, I thank you. It was important for him to maintain rogue status so that he could access areas that might not normally welcome him."

She gave Liam a nod and he dipped his head in acknowledgment.

"There are roughly twenty more Guardians on their way and about the same number of the Fae are coming to help cover up the noise of our fight. We have four healers and a rumor that one more is on the way. Gentleman - do not underestimate the strength of these creatures. The humans have chemical technology that makes a person dull and unfeeling. This means they are apt to keep coming despite their injuries. Pay attention. Be swift and show no mercy. We assemble at the castle of Tarnwool tomorrow at 3:00PM. Any questions?"

"What types of creatures are we up against?"

"That is an excellent question, Aemon. The truth is, we are not certain, but that information should be here shortly. There have been massive quantities of meat, chemicals, water and other supplies delivered to the doctor's compound for weeks now. Nothing comes out and we know it's just a matter of time before we regret not taking action. We're being proactive but we are at a loss of information. Anyone else?"

Silence filled the room.

The Queen smiled. "Liam, come see me please. The rest of you, enjoy your evening."

Chapter 47

"Well, I am a little disappointed," Verity said, her hands made a flourish in front of her. "He was my Guardian here, and my friend." Verity fidgeted on the bed she had slept in for the last several weeks.

Sloane sat Indian-style next to her. She gave half a smile. "If there is one thing I can tell you, it's that the world makes less sense to me now than it ever did before and I didn't understand it then."

Verity laughed. "I completely agree but what's funny, is that I love it. I can't see it any other way now. And the opportunities that have arrived at my door because of it are..." she shook her head, "amazing to say the least."

Sloane nodded in agreement. "I'm with you there. I think it's a little more than I bargained for, if truth be told,"

"So true," Verity replied. A comfortable silence set in while they were lost in their thoughts when someone rapped on the door.

"Coming!" Verity popped up from the bed and opened the door. Duran stalked in.

"You were planning on joining the humans through the Faeway without an escort?" he demanded.

Sloane pulled back in surprise and Verity

nodded her head frowning. Duran continued. "Are you insane?"

"I have directions," Sloane squeaked out.

"Directions? What good are directions when the very threads of the lands can be altered with a mere thought?" Duran's face was slightly pink.

"A thought?" Sloane asked.

"Altered?" asked Verity.

"Yes!" he growled. "I should certainly know. Damn it, Verity. Were you not going to tell me?"

"Of course, I would have," Verity quipped, "I've barely had a moment to breathe since I made the decision. It seemed the easiest solution since she," she motioned toward Sloane, "is already going to where I need to be."

Duran's face smoothed as though anger had never crossed his path.

"Well, then. I shall guide you. We leave in two hours," he stated and with his chin held high, he turned and walked out the door.

Chapter 48

Oddly, the school decided to host a hunt in memory of Mr. Shirtell. They weren't meant to actually catch anything, it was more to learn the use of the senses to aid one in tracking. Andy was skeptical about doing an activity that spread them throughout the forest, but everyone was required to hunt in pairs so at least there was some strange logic to it. He stretched, reaching high into the half-light of the early morning. Energy buzzed through his veins as he felt the earth come alive around him. It had sort of creeped on him, this sensation of feeling his surroundings. He thought it must have something to do with hormones but when he had mentioned it to Keppin, the response was a mere raising of the eyebrows. Then he thought it must have something to do with being a Displacer, but before he had the courage to ask Mr. Grumpy Ass about it, he'd ended up in the morgue.

Low murmurs surrounded him as students poured out of the dorms and prepared for the hunt. Welcoming the chill in the air, Andy continued to stretch, testing out the new leathers he'd made in class. The belts wrapped around his waist and then up and over his shoulders like suspenders. He'd fashioned holders on his back for his axes, his weapon of choice. Versatile as a tool and a deadly weapon, he'd found that wielding the axes had a symmetry that worked for him. The bowie knife he'd received as a gift was tucked into a sheathe at his waist.

Having everything strapped into place would take some getting used to. They were all required to shield, thicken their skin, so that the newbies wouldn't accidentally take each other down. Still considered a newbie, Andy was thankful for the rule.

An inconsistent slurping sound made its way toward Andy. He continued stretching until the sound stopped nearby.

"Early as always," he said. A loud slurp and the crumbling of thick paper was his answer. He turned and smiled at Keppin. "Morning sunshine."

"Whatever," Keppin said as he dropped his empty coffee cup to the ground. "Why can't we hunt at sun down like normal people?"

"I hate to break it to you, Kep, but most people hunt early in the morning. Plus, we don't exactly fit into the "normal" category."

"I thought we were supposed to fit in," Keppin answered before laying in the grass and closing his eyes. A pixie appeared and scooped up the crumbled cup, depositing it onto Keppin's chest as she flew over him. She was gone before he could lob it at her.

"There is just no slack here."

Andy chuckled as the horn was blown. He kicked Keppin gently. "Come on, let's go track our prey."

Keppin's eyes popped open. "Now that is a better way to look at it. Which prey are we after? Pixies or Kelpies?"

Rolling his eyes, Andy shook his and headed toward the forest with the rest of the group.

As he closed in on the trees he saw Ben and Rashan in deep conversation. Ben saw him and waved but Andy was into the trees before Rashan could turn his way.

The forest behind Chateau le Gardien was around five square miles which was more than enough for the thirty plus guardians in training also known as high school students. As soon as they entered the forest, the chatter vanished and the training kicked in. Hours upon hours of practicing travel without making a sound, sighting the tiniest details; flattened leaves, broken branches, all to follow prey.

The groups separated and soon Keppin and Andy found themselves seemingly alone as they decided what to track.

"How about a wood pecker?" Keppin asked.

"Would be fun to hunt but doesn't really bring in the points."

"How about...squirrels?"

"Uhhh"

"I've got it. Boar. We should definitely scare up a boar."

"Now that will be fun and bring in the points," Andy said. He stopped and perused the area. Keppin, a few feet away, stopped to do the same thing. Keppin walked toward the right and gently touched his fingers to a low hanging branch. Some of the leaves had been nibbled. Slightly further away he kneeled and put a finger on a broken branch. He breathed in deeply, looking for the scent and when he got it, his lips stretched from ear to ear. He glanced at Andy who smiled and inclined his head slightly.

And they were off. At speeds meant to be seen as shadows, as a passing breeze, they raced toward their target. When they were almost on it, they stopped in the shade of a large Plane Tree and watched the boar nuzzling roots in the ground. Andy took out his phone and turned on the camera. He stepped away from the tree and quietly made his way toward the boar.

Charlese, the witch girl from the dance, stepped out from behind a tree to stand before him.

Andy gasped. She was dressed in a simple beige gown with a dark green sash which did everything to make her chestnut hair and eyes stand out. He closed his mouth.

"What are you doing here?" he whispered.

Charlese threw her arms over his shoulders and leaned into him. She smiled and gazed up at him.

"I missed you," she whispered. Andy wasted no time in dropping his head to meet those succulent lips once more. She leaned into him, one hand on his neck, the other moved down his chest and around his waist to rest on his back. She opened her mouth to him and flicked her tongue across his upper lip. Andy moaned, pulling her tight against his chest. He felt, more than heard her giggle.

On the outskirts of his mind Andy vaguely heard whispers.

"Oh, stop gloating."

"Okay! Geez, you won the bet!"

His mind started to form questions but he pushed

them away, ignoring everything but the girl in his arms. Her hands found their way to either side of his face, the soft touch relaxing him further. Charlese pulled away, smiling. Her eyes sparkled, and Andy realized there was mischief afoot. Before he could ask, she spoke.

"Until we meet again, handsome Guardian."

Before his very eyes she faded away like a ghost until there was nothing. He stared at the spot for a moment, waiting for something to happen.

A ferocious growl startled Andy and his skin started to swirl with the change on instinct. He turned to see that a small pack of wolves had also found the boar and were challenging him. Andy pulled his shirt off and changed. He growled back, faking a lunge toward the pack leader. The boar turned tail and bolted away from the pack but the moment it saw Andy, it turned and headed away from them both.

Keppin's clap and laugh pulled Andy back to himself again. He stayed in his gargoyle form and watched the wolves back away and then run into the forest before turning to look at a smiling Keppin who stepped out from the Plane Tree.

"Dude! That was awesome."

"Did you see her?" Andy asked, his voice a menacing growl to anyone else.

"See who? Have you seen yourself lately?"

The broad brows over Andy's black eyes came together. He stared at Keppin who slowly raised a hand and pointed over Andy's shoulder. Andy looked over his shoulder and found himself looking at a wing. He took a long blink and looked again. It was still there. He slowly turned back to Keppin who was grinning most annoyingly and then looked over the other shoulder where his eyes met the beauty of another wing.

Holding in an emotional outpour, Andy reached out and ran a hand over a wing. He felt the soft veined leather under his hands and the rigidness of the virtually unbreakable frame. But even more amazing was the feel of his hand, soft and gentle, running over his wing. He swallowed the lump in his throat and looked down so Keppin wouldn't see him blink away the sweet sting of tears.

Chapter 49

As soon as Sloane walked into the Faeway, she could feel it. The strangest buzz on her skin, life crawling over it in sporadic waves. The feeling was both sensual and unnerving at the same time. She wanted to dance and yet she wanted to hide. She glanced at Evan. He didn't seem to be affected. Verity was standing a few feet away with Duran. She was looking him over while he smirked at her.

"You look exactly the same," Verity commented.

"Was I supposed to look different?" Duran asked, the smirk never leaving his face.

"Well, I thought you would change somehow. You know, since we're in your world now."

Duran chuckled. "I have no need to use glamour in the caves. I'm afraid, Verity, that what you see is what *you* get."

Sloane felt his insinuation from where she was standing but Verity either didn't get it or didn't show it. She seemed withdrawn since his earlier explosion.

"Cool," Verity said before glancing around them. "Where are we?"

Duran had brought them through a doorway in the caves. One moment they were in the Goblin cave and the next in an enchanted hallway. The walls were old stone covered in rich green vines, flowers in various shades dotted the vines sporadically. As far as you could see, there was a door every twenty feet or so. Each door was unique. Sloane could make out one that was distinctly royal purple. The closest was extremely weathered, the door seeming to have been there since forever with a strange metal hinge and no knob.

Evan moved to touch the old door and Duran was there pushing Evan's hand down and away from the door.

"There are some places that you do not want to see, Guardian," Duran said before taking the lead and heading down the hallway. Verity raised her eyes at Sloane before turning and catching up with Duran's long strides. Sloane grabbed Evan's forearm and pulled him away from the door. They followed Duran in silence. He had passed more than a dozen doors before Sloane couldn't take it anymore.

"Seriously? These are all different realms of Fae?" she asked.

Duran slowed so Sloane could catch up. He continued to walk, but more slowly with Verity on one side and Sloane on the other, leaving Evan to trail behind.

"These doors are not each a different realm *per se*, but a different place. You might have twenty or forty doors that lead to the same realm but never in the same location. Some were set up long ago by a royal who wanted access without being seen. Some were set up to enter cities directly instead of having to traverse the land for hours. There are as many reasons to build a door as there are doors I'm afraid."

He chuckled then and slowed to a stop in front of a simple flat green door.

Verity frowned at him and then the door.

"Is this Ireland already?" she asked.

Duran shook his head. "I'm afraid this is just the beginning. This door leads to Tas'agee. If we cut through here it will take hours out of our trip."

"Is there a map of this place?" Evan asked. "I don't see how we would have been able to figure this out alone."

"No," Duran said with a lift of his shoulder, "you couldn't possibility learn these ways in your short lifetime."

Evan looked offended but said nothing.

Duran pushed the door open and started through as he spoke. "We will go through Tas'agee, catch the door to Tanyrd and then to your Swiss alps where there is a door to Domhnaill, our land, which will lead us nicely into Dublin, your land."

Sloane replayed his directions in her mind. "We have to go through four places to get to Dublin? How long will that take?"

"About four days," Duran answered.

"Four days?" Sloane sputtered. "But that would get us there after the fight!"

"It is only a fraction of one of your days. The Faeways run on a time of their own. In fact, four days is really only an estimate. Assuming all goes as it should, it will take about four days. If the ways are feeling mischievous, we may be here longer than anticipated but either way, we should get there in plenty of time for your battle."

"If the ways feel misch…oh wow. This is amazing," Sloane had followed everyone through the green door and gotten her first look at Tas'agee.

Rather than green, it was a lush lavender valley surrounded by a thick forest with pockets of black and white flowers swaying in a warm breeze. The leaves on the trees were a blend of colors more like the flowers Sloane was used to.

Duran was almost to the center of the valley before he stopped and beckoned them forward.

"Hurry. We don't want to get caught in the open."

"It feels so safe here. What might catch us in the open?" Verity asked. Sloane raised a brow and waited for the answer.

"Dragons," Duran answered. "Depending on where you are, some are to be avoided. This is one of those places."

"Dragons?" Sloane questioned expecting no answer. She *loved* dragons. But maybe not the ones hanging out in Tas'agee. When they reached the other end of the valley and entered the forest, the sun was immediately blocked out. Before anyone could panic, their way became lit by a plethora of glowing lichen on the trees.

"Incredible," Evan commented. His first words since being admonished earlier.

Up ahead, Duran gave an annoyed sigh and stopped.

"Hello, brother," he said.

Chapter 50

"Liam! Good to see you," the Queen said giving him a big bear hug. They were behind closed doors in the Den's office. Liam hugged back, she was like a mother to him.

"Please take a seat," she said when they broke apart. She gestured to the chair in front of a large desk covered in diagrams and other papers. He did so, sitting upright and at attention.

"All right, I've brought you here for two reasons, Liam. One, you know your part in tomorrow's raid, correct?"

"Mmm aye," Liam said, relaxing into his native Irish accent. There were no facades with the Den-Mother.

"Good. The next thing is a bit delicate. I've just learned that the boys were taking bets about whether or not you would be able to break a mate bond. I didn't ask for more details because I want to hear them from you. What is going on?"

"It was an accident. I didn't mean to bond with her, it just happened. When we were in the field."

"Doing what in the field?"

"It was a field test to see how she would handle things and observe as an Aspie. Circumstances made the test slightly, uh, intimate."

"An Aspie?" she asked rhetorically before heaving a sigh. "Liam, there is *always* something there, some invisible connection, before the bond will take. The bond doesn't make mistakes. It knows. And we all know of the one time that circumstances changed enough that the bond released the couple. People change, but not generally that much. Liam, you do realize that a bond is not a happenstance? That it recognizes strengths and harmony?"

When Liam shook his head, she smiled. "You really didn't pay attention in class, did you?"

"Apparently not in that class," Liam said as he fidgeted in his seat. She leaned back in her seat and folded her hands in her lap.

"So, tell me then, why do you think you need to break the bond?"

"Well, first? I was ordered hands off the Aspie. That obviously didn't work out and we ended up bonding. *It happened against orders.*"

She laughed out loud. "I'm sorry, continue."

Liam frowned before continuing, "I think one of the worst things I could do would be to bring someone into this style of life. I *love* it but how I can expect someone to bear with the schedule? The possibility that I may not return? Or worse, what if something happens to her because of what *I* do?"

"Liam, have you looked at the fact that had she… what's her name?"

"Sloane."

"Had it occurred to you that Sloane may not have survived without finding us? That she could have ended up in an institution to rot or thrown herself in front of a bus, convinced she was crazy?

Your concerns would have more merit if she was a regular human. But there is no way an Aspie could survive past thirty on her own. You know I speak truth, Liam."

Liam sat quietly, concluding what a dolt he'd been. The idea of taking Sloane and making her his was not only enticing, it thrilled him.

The Queen's soft tone interrupted his thoughts. "Bond or no bond, you're in love with her, aren't you?"

Liam's tongue felt numb, so he just nodded.

"Liam, I admire your integrity. Really, I do. But you're being a goofus."

Liam pulled back in surprise before nodding. "I was told something similar once."

She laughed. "That would be a smart girl. Liam, you have been with the Guardianship for over thirty years. As much as I hate to lose you, it would be okay."

She smiled at him warmly. "I know what you're capable of, but your happiness is important to me. You *can* retire. You *can* have a family. And it sounds like your soul mate has found you. Don't be a fool and lose one of the most beautiful things there is about being alive. *Love*, Liam. Love is one of the most fabulous feelings in the world, especially with a bond mate. I love you enough to let you go, my son."

Liam sat stunned in silence.

"I know you will do whatever you think is best. And I support whatever that may be. I leave you to it. I have a battle to plan."

Liam stood up and bowed to her. She waved him off with a smile and he left the room, closing the door softly behind him.

Leaning against the wall, he closed his eyes and sent out feelers to find her.

He was surprised to find that she was fairly close even if the feel of the pull wasn't as strong as usual. Then he realized he shouldn't really be surprised. That she was finding her way despite him depositing her onto the airplane only showed him how similar they were.

He frowned and scanned the room, wondered if she might be looking for him. After what he did, would she bother? Was she mad? Sad? She had learned to shut down emotion, so he couldn't tell, and it made him nervous.

Liam opened his eyes and met the eyes of the bartender across the room.

"Can I git ya sumtin ta drink, Liam?" the bartender called. Liam smiled at him and shook his head.

"Nah, Seamus. Gotta find the bonnie lass who makes me heart sing," Liam said.

"Ah, well. Don't lemme stop ya, boy. Tis luck for ye, them lasses." Seamus motioned Liam away and Liam headed to the door.

Chapter 51

A tall pale Fae man stood before them in the lichen lit forest. His translucent skin glowed softly but it was his smile that lit up the air around them. He patted Duran on the shoulder as his eyes looked over each of them. When they reached Verity, they filled with emotion. He reached a hand out to her.

"Verity Applebee," he stated.

Verity smiled, tears welling up in her eyes as he took her hand in his.

"Little one?" she asked. The Fae nodded and kneeled, placing a gentle kiss to the backside of her hand.

"Wow. You're all grown up," Verity said softly.

"I fear it is so, my Verity," he said as he stood straight once again and pulled his hand away. Duran bristled slightly. The pale Fae glanced at him only briefly before giving Verity his full attention again.

"I have only a few minutes to spare. Mother is keeping me terribly busy, but I knew that my brother was guiding you through the Faeways and I was certain I could find you in time and tell you myself how grateful I was for your help. You gave me hope where there was none."

Verity blushed as Duran moved closer to her,

putting a hand on her lower back. The pale Fae raised a brow and looked them over.

"It would seem my brother has given new meaning to repaying a debt," he commented without malice.

Verity blushed further, her cheeks heating from both the insinuation and the warm hand on her back. Her mind swirled in confusion. While her body flared with interest for the dark Fae standing so close, her heart was not in accord.

"Verity," the pale Fae said, "if you find that you ever need my assistance, I give you the name Rothald. Call it and I will come for you."

"I think that she will not be needing your assistance, brother," Duran sneered. Rothald raised a brow at him but smiled at Verity.

"I fear Mother is calling, but please tell me you will call if you need me," he said.

"I certainly will," Verity answered and reached out, giving his arm a squeeze. He winked at her and then turned and walked straight into a tree, vanishing.

"Let's move," Duran commanded and walked ahead of them all.

Shaken, Verity raised her voice at his back, "What is your problem?"

She jogged to catch up to him. Sloane and Evan locked eyes in confusion for a moment and then followed but left some distance for Verity and Duran to discuss their issues in private.

"What is your problem?" she asked, heat filling her cheeks with exasperation.

"I have no problem," Duran said his face

impassive.

"Like hell," Verity muttered.

Duran ignored her and increased his pace, leaving her to fall behind. Sloane and Evan continued to keep their distance. Verity snorted to herself and shook her head. She wondered if she would ever understand men. It didn't seem to matter what race or type of creature; the male and female versions just didn't seem of the same cloth.

The forest ended abruptly when Verity walked between two trees and found herself on freshly cut grass about twenty feet from a small cottage. Duran stood nobly next to its wooden door, his hand resting on a brass lever handle. Verity walked over and stood silently next to him while she waited for Sloane and Evan to catch up.

She felt Duran's hand grasp her upper arm firmly. She looked up, met his deep plum eyes and felt her heart tense with dread.

"Forgive me," he whispered. He flipped the latch and pulled her through the door.

~~*~~

Sloane saw the cottage just as Verity disappeared through the door, the latch catching closed behind them.

"Evan, run!" Sloane yelled as she took off toward the door. She knew Evan was just behind her when he grabbed her hand. Flipping the latch, they launched through the opening together.

Sloane felt the ground hit her knees and reverberate into her shoulders and teeth. Evan reacted much faster, launching over her prone frame and landing on his feet a few feet in front of her. He quickly knelt in front of her.

"You okay?" he asked. Sloane gave it a few seconds before answering. Her knees throbbed but nothing else was badly damaged.

"I think I skinned the hell out of my knees but otherwise I'm okay." She stood up and felt blood drip down from one knee, tickling her shin. Despite the throb she took in her surroundings. Evan was already scanning.

"I don't think they came this way," he commented. Though a half-smile twisted Evan's mouth, his hands curled into fists at his side.

"With a thought," Sloane said quietly. Evan raised a brow.

"Duran had said that the lands could be changed with a thought." Evan nodded understanding.

"Makes sense," he stated.

The desert before them was sunny, almost painfully so. There were mountains in the distance on their left and the rest was never-ending dirt and sand, yellow as far as you could see with one oddity. A door. It stood as a bright red beacon in the distance.

"Why do I get the idea we need to get to that door?" Sloane asked.

"I had the same thought," Evan commented as he started toward it, "let's hope we're right."

Sloane started after him. "Do you think Verity is okay?"

Evan turned to her, eyes slightly narrowed. "I think Duran will take care of her."

"I do too," Sloane commented, "unlike us."

Evan turned to her and rolled his eyes, nodding in agreement. It looked funny on a man with such dark, cutting good looks.

"I heard Nia tell you not to give up. What did she mean?" he asked.

Sloane shook her head at first but then she realized that getting a man's viewpoint might be helpful. She told him some of the story, mostly the part about getting ditched at the airport.

"Liam didn't even apologize. Just handed me a ticket. He could've gotten me a passport too. He could've worked with me," she told him.

"Liam?" Evan's head swung to her, surprise washing over his innocent face. "Liam McDougall?"

Sloane's jaw clenched. Of course he knew Liam.

"Yes. And how do you know Liam?"

"I don't, but I've heard of him," Evan said. The awe in his voice only further annoyed Sloane. Surrounded by good looking, single guardians and she was hooked on one who had serious internal issues. *Fucked up.*

"What's he like?" Evan asked.

Sloane waved a hand through the air like she was swatting at a buzzing mosquito. "I definitely do not want to talk about that, but I will tell you something."

Evan fixed his gaze on her.

"He *is* a total bad ass just like you've heard," her voice dropped, "and he's the ass that broke my heart."

Evan's mouth went into the shape of an 'o' before he turned to scan the area around them.

Something caught his attention over her head and he stopped, narrowing his eyes. Sloane turned to look. In the distance the mountains loomed tall while two airborne dark shadows headed in their direction. Sloane tried to make out the shapes unsuccessfully. She spun around to Evan just as he took her wrist and gave her a steeled look.

"Sloane, we need to run. I'm going to change and you're going jump on my back, okay?"

Sloane's eyes were wide as she nodded. Evan didn't even take off his clothes. His skin became churning gray leather as his muscles burst the seams and bulged. His bowed head elongated, and sharp teeth erupted from his mouth with a loud growl. Wings sprouted from his back, sinewy with barbed talons.

"Now!" he commanded. Sloane jumped up between his wings and threw her arms around his warm neck. Glancing behind as Evan shoved off into the air, her nerves buzzed when she realized what she was looking at. She held on tighter and wished for Godspeed. Evan's wings worked steadily, bringing them closer to the door, but the shadows were faster.

Sloane chanced another look.

"Evan!" she screamed. He twirled midair and faced the two dragons. Sloane tried not to tremble. Fire spat from Evan's mouth. Sloane almost let go, her grip loosening as she debated death by dragon fire or gargoyle fire or by falling from *really* high up. The dragons slowed down, hesitant.

"Let go," Evan growled. Sloane released her hands and fell. Evan grabbed her arm and started to free fall with her. It was only for a few moments, but it was enough to lodge Sloane's stomach in her throat.

Nausea came over her as Evan engaged his wings to soar straight at the door below them. He pulled her into his arms just as he hit the ground running. He didn't stop but wrapped his wings around her and barreled straight through the door. Sloane pressed her face into his thick-skinned chest to avoid the splinters and chunks of wood exploding around her.

Chapter 52

"What are you doing?" Verity yelled at Duran, she trembled, and her eyes were wide. The Fae that had so recently made her feel safe now made her skin go cold with fear.

"Welcome to my lands, Verity Applebee," Duran said with stately bow.

Verity's eyes narrowed as she looked around. The land was beautiful and lush with green grass, purple trees and the black and white flowers that she had seen before. The sky had an orange tint that made the large white cottage before her glow.

"What did you do?" Verity whispered. Turning back to the doorway out, she paused eyes wide when she realized the only door around them was to the cottage.

"Your friends are fine. I sent them through a door that will be more expedient for their needs. I'm sure they will figure it out."

"You're sure?"

"Yes, your friends seem fairly intelligent." A wry grin crept onto his face. Normally it would have been handsome, but Verity was not amused. She face-palmed with a loud sigh.

"Take me back to them," she snarled.

"But why? I wish to show you my home, treat you

to pleasures you cannot have possibly ever known."

Verity's eyes bulged. "You kidnapped me?"

"I assure you, I am quite certain you are not a child."

Verity's crossed her arms as she moved closer to Duran.

"You didn't invite me or ask my permission," she said, voice tinged with venom. "I have friends that need my help. Not just Sloane and Evan but many others going to battle tomorrow. I need to get to them!"

Duran frowned.

"I cannot predict the outcome of your battle, Verity," he said. "My wish is that you experience what I can do for you now, just in case it does not end well for you."

"You're worried that I'm going to die and you won't get to screw me first? Seriously? Fae men apparently think more like a man then even human men."

"That is *not* true," Duran commented with a shake of his head. "Fae men value honor and pleasure before all else."

Verity stood quiet, speechless and appraised him before taking his hand and speaking softly.

"Please, bring me back to my friends, Duran."

He rubbed circles on her palm for a moment, then he caught a stray lock of hair and tucked it behind her ear. He blinked and shrugged.

"As you wish, Verity. I shall see you again."

Verity gave him a wide smile. "Thank you so..."

The ground beneath her feet vanished. She fell into darkness and could hear only her scream as she plummeted.

Chapter 53

Dr. J stood in front of them all. They sat like school children in the gym seats, waiting patiently for instruction. Dr. J forced himself not to laugh. He didn't want to scare them. His creations were masterpieces and it annoyed him that no one worth sharing with would ever know. He should be receiving the Nobel Prize, not having to hide his science in the middle of nowhere.

But he was saving the world, so these things couldn't be helped. At least he could die knowing he had stepped up and taken the necessary action.

A promise of cake and ice cream would go a long way with these creatures. Under the rewarding influence of hypnosis, his favorite method of mind control, he had told them all that they lived happily on anything with sugar in it, but that monster blood was their favorite.

He knew the enemy would come soon. And he would be ready. They would be lunch.

He ended up laughing anyway.

Chapter 54

Liam found himself standing in a wide grassy dell. A Faeway door burst open nearby and the last thing he expected to see was Sloane wrapped up in another gargoyle's arms.

They hurtled from the gateway as if thrown. The gargoyle landed heavily on his feet before falling to the ground, holding her protectively with his wings. Liam watched her bury her head in the man's chest. A growl escaped him as he changed instinctively, his clothes shredding to the ground. The door abruptly tripled in size and was breached once again as two Domhnaill dragons came through, only to pick up another door on the other side of the clearing and vanish as quickly as they had come.

The dark night was dead quiet for only a moment before a brave cricket started his song once more. A low growl escaped Liam's chest as he watched the couple curled on the ground. The Guardian was not known to Liam and his internal alarms were screaming for action that he could not take until he knew what in the hell was going on. He growled again. Sloane's hands appeared on the prone Guardian's shoulder and she pulled herself forward to peer over them.

"Liam," she said. He huffed out a breath in

affirmation. "Evan, move," she whispered. The man didn't budge. "Evan, move. For crying out loud, it's Liam."

The man uncurled and lifted himself from Sloane's body. Still on the ground, he turned and appraised Liam. Liam stood tall, chest out, and allowed the grumble of a snarl to escape. The other man stood up, dusting his knees but his eyes never leaving Liam's. He retracted his wings and Liam watched his skin roil and turn deeply tan. The man's green eyes sparkled as he ran a hand quickly through his dark brown hair. Doubt started to ease through Liam as he realized he might be too late and a compliment short. Probably several. The man smiled, upper half man, lower half gargoyle and bowed casually. Sloane peeled herself from the ground, cursing softly. She squeezed the man's upper arm.

"Thank you, I'll be okay now," she said. The man, Evan she had called him, turned and touched Sloane's chin, lifting her head. Liam held himself in check rather than bite the man's head off. Evan, brows raised, just looked at her, waiting. Sloane gave him a small smile and nodded. The man pulled away and stepped back before giving Liam a deep, respectful bow. Sloane watched Evan retreat to the other side of the clearing until he stood at attention in the shadows beneath a tall tree and then she turned to Liam.

"Well, if it isn't my bonded," she said. Her beautiful eyes were marred with pain.

Liam took a step back.

Sloane moved to him. The anger poured from her, wrapping around him and squeezing. He found his skin numbing, his breath becoming short and strained.

"Now you know how *I* feel," she whispered to him. Pulling a compass from her pocket, she watched it for a moment before heading away. Toward *him*.

Striding over to Evan, Sloane took his hand and without a backward glance, entered the forest with Evan by her side.

Liam didn't move for some time. He was used to ignoring situations like this. Pretending they had never happened and moving on to the next job. It was always so easy. It was never like having a knife flaying the very skin from your muscle. Or like being burned by a thousand firescots, the Fae equivalent of a red ant. He considered his options. *Give up* wasn't really part of his genetic makeup. He vaguely recalled the story of the first Guardian. The blood and tears that the First had given to become the race they were today...but more importantly, to get the girl.

Liam pulled himself together. His option was clear. He would figure out the *how* on the way to the Den. Throwing out his wings, he leapt to the sky.

Chapter 55

Evan, human upper body minus a shirt with his lower body still in gargoyle form, and Sloane made it out of the clearing and about fifteen minutes down the dark and empty road before the cold hit her.

"Fuck!"

"What is it? Are you all right?" Evan asked in alarm.

"I'm fine, it's just fucking cold."

Evan chuckled. "I forget about such things sometimes."

"Sure, easy for you leather-skinned freaks to say," she mumbled knowing full well she had thought one such freak would lift her up and away.

"Ok, Miss Mind Reader, you too are a bit freakish."

Sloane punched Evan in the arm and laughed. "True!"

Glancing down the street, Sloane wondered how much longer they had to go when Evan's arm swung out and stopped her.

"What the...?"

"Shh!"

Straining, Sloane heard it. A shrill scream getting closer by the second.

"Get to the trees!" Evan shouted and she ran.

Tucking herself into a deep shadow, she sat and watched Evan push out his wings as he scanned the skies. Moments later he pushed off the ground, a wing aided power jump and caught the screaming something right out of sky. He landed gracefully and held the thing close.

"I gotcha," he said, "I gotcha, Verity. You're safe now."

Sloane scrambled up and ran over as Evan reached out and plucked Verity's backpack from the sky before it hit the ground. Tears were running down Verity's face, but she laughed when she saw Sloane.

"Oh, thank god," she said, her voice dry and raspy. She tucked her head into Evan's neck and sighed. Sloane reached over to squeeze her hand and as she did, she saw an interesting look on Evan's face as he gazed at the ashen Verity.

Since Evan made no motion to put her down, Sloane turned and took the lead, a ghost of a smile flitted across her face.

Chapter 56

When they arrived at the den, Sloane couldn't get in the door fast enough. Warmth. The one thing that she'd had more than enough of in Florida and only now could appreciate. As soon as the door closed behind her she turned to grin at Evan and Verity, who Evan had finally put down. Evan, smiling brightly at them both, offered to take their coats. Sloane put a hand on his shoulder.

"I think I need a minute," she said.

"Me too," Verity said, her voice a bit shaky.

His smile broadened just before his face jerked out of view as someone rushed past and ran smack into him. Cursing, Sloane jumped out the way, pulling Verity with her, only to find Evan and someone she didn't know rolling on the floor laughing. Evan caught her eye and still chuckling he pulled himself from the ground. His friend jumped up and looked over Verity and then Sloan before throwing out a hand to Verity who was closest.

"I'm Rusk and you are?"

"Verity," she said with a small smile.

"Hello, Verity. Lovely to meet you and you are?" he asked as he held his hand to Sloane.

"Sloane," she said and took his hand. He pulled it away quickly looking a little guilty. Sloane tilted her head and frowned. Evan patted him on the arm.

"It's cool," Evan said. Rusk turned back to Sloane.

"Some of these dolts can run faster than the wind, others can create thunder *or fire*," Rusk stopped to roll his eyes at Evan, "and some can even run through walls, but me? I can feel bonds." He motioned with his hand into the room before continuing, "I imagine you'd be wanting to get back to your bonded. I'm happy to take Evan here off your hands for a bit."

Sloane turned around and appraised the room as Rusk was asking Evan why he was half changed and where on earth he left his clothes. She felt the odd tingle, the pull toward Liam. She wondered if the feeling would vanish when he was really close. She had never really paid attention before. She was still deciphering the strange emotional tugs and pulls she experienced so often. She knew he was nearby, but he was nowhere she could see. Since he was rogue, it did make sense that he wouldn't be hanging out at the den. But then, Evan was rogue too and he didn't seem the slightest bit concerned.

A hand gripped her shoulder startling Sloane from her inner monologue. She turned to meet Evan's concerned eyes. Before she could attempt a syllable, someone grabbed her elbow and turned her. The sight of a handsome dark face with a long scar from chin to temple greeted her. Sighing in relief Sloane threw herself at him. Kam caught her, and his deep chuckle shook her as she held on tight. Kam had been one of the first Guardians she had ever met, and he had never judged, just always had a smile for her.

Kam finally pried her away and looked into her

face. He brushed away a tear and shook his head.

"There will be none of that, ya hear?" he said.

Sloane nodded.

"Good, then let's get this bungling coat off you and play some pool!"

Sloane smiled weakly and let him help her out of the coat. She noticed Evan had pulled on a shirt and she waved him and Verity off with Rusk. Kam hung her coat and led her to the bar, ordering them each a beer. Once the beer was set before them he grasped her hand and towed her to a table where two guardians had just ended a game. They nodded at him as he quickly set up the table. Sloane wondered about Liam *again*. She could feel him close. Her blood boiled a little when she thought of him but at the same time, she wanted him. He had a corn cob stuck so far up his... she took a couple swigs of beer as the quiet anger threatened to get a bit louder.

"You've played before?" he asked.

"Uh, once, Kam. Honestly, I'm not really cut out for this," she answered.

"Well, let's see how you do with an expert teacher," he commented and took a shot. Sloane watched the balls fly across the table, two balls landing in pockets.

Chapter 57

"It looked to me like her friends must have dared her to do some magic," Andy said. Laying on his back in bed, he threw a ball against the wall and caught it over and over as they went over what had happened in the forest.

"A dare?" Ben asked, brow rising toward his hair line.

Keppin, who was perched on James' bed, shrugged.

Rashan sat backward on Andy's desk chair. "Why would they do that?" he asked.

Keppin frowned at him. "Seriously, dude? If I could magic my way over to chicks and knock them senseless with a kiss, I sure as hell would. Dare or not."

"So would I," Ben said nodding seriously.

Rashan raised a hand in mock-surrender.

Sitting up, Andy put the ball on his desk, next to his computer. "I would too. I just keep getting surprised by the number of things in this world that are really true."

"Join the party, man. From the moment we're approached by a Guardian," Ben's eyes widened as he cocked his head left and spoke, "life gets weird."

Rashan snorted.

A heavy knock on the door grabbed their attention. Before Andy had finished standing the door swung open.

The collective gasp was loud. Andy stood at attention before the others though they followed quickly.

"Director," Andy acknowledged.

The Director took two steps into the room and looked at each of them before resting his eyes on Andy.

"You boys need to work on your Stance," he said. The Stance was what they called it when a Guardian was not fazed by anything in their environment, or at least didn't look like it.

"Yes, Sir," they intoned.

"Andy."

"Sir?" Andy said, his back straight as a rod.

"Congratulations on your wings."

"Thank you, Sir."

"Please report to Joy. Directly."

"Yes, sir. I'll be on my way right now."

"Good." He nodded toward the others, "Boys," and then stepped back into the hallway, closing the door behind him.

"WTF?" Ben was the first to ask.

Andy's face contorted into confusion.

Keppin dropped back onto the bed. "He doesn't know. And for once, it wasn't me who's in trouble."

"How do you know he's in trouble?" Rashan asked.

"Why else would he be summoned? Hey! Who is

Joy?"

Andy was lacing his boots. "She's a Secretary in the main office."

"The main, Main office? *The* office?" Ben asked.

Andy shrugged. "I guess."

"Damn. I don't think he's in trouble, dude."

"Well, what else could it be?" Keppin glared.

Andy stood. "I don't know but whatever it is, I'm not keeping anyone waiting. I'll see you guys later. Kep, fix James' bed before you go."

He closed the door calmly behind him, but his nerves were on fire.

"Andy. Good of you to come so quickly," the Queen said with a quick smile.

She met him at Joy's desk. The office was bustling with activity and Joy had one phone held to each ear. Andy nodded, a little speechless. The Queen waved him to follow her into her office.

She shut the door and turned to him.

"Sorry that I don't have more time to indoctrinate you, Andy, but this is very important."

Andy nodded.

"We have a situation where the abilities of a Displacer would be very desirable. You know that Displacers are rare, correct?"

Andy nodded again.

"Good. You're the first new Displacer we've seen in probably sixty years, Andy. George was last."

At Andy's quizzical look she backtracked.

"George Shirtell."

"Ah."

"We have two others, older and in the field. Both of which are on critical missions and pulling them now would have consequences that I do not want to see come to pass. That leaves you, Mr. Chamberlain. I've already spoken with Brick. He feels strongly that you are up to the job. Considering your wings have found their way to your back, that will certainly make it easier."

She stopped and studied Andy for a moment. That weak smile appeared again briefly.

"Your father was a warrior, Andy. He would be so proud of you."

Andy's bottom lip quivered.

"Now. I have a building that we need to map out. I need to know what is on each level, how it's arranged, and anyone living there. It's not going to be pretty. Experiments on humans have been taking place there and the results are less then savory. Am I clear so far?"

"Yes, Ma'am."

"Good. You will have a Pixie with you. Shimmie?" The Queen paused and a familiar five-inch-tall winged figure soared in from the balcony. The Pixie landed on the desk and smiled at Andy.

He recalled her little window dance and frowned.

"Shimmie will be with you on the mission. She'll be casting a blanket spell over you. It helps you blend in to the area without being seen. It's not perfect. If someone has the least bit of Fae blood running through them it will waiver, and if they have a lot of the blood running through them, well, they'll see you just fine. It's not likely but you should know before going in not to be overconfident."

Wide-eyed, Andy nodded once more.

"Do you think you can handle this, Andy?"

"I can."

"Good. There is much to do. You'll pack a bag and leave. Now. I have a Fae," she glanced at Shimmie, "a full-size Fae waiting at the back door to take you through the Fae paths to Ireland. I'll see you when you finish at the building."

This time her smile was true. She squeezed his arm gently.

"Let's go, kid," someone said from behind him. He turned to see the Director.

"Sir," Andy said and followed him out of the office. He felt an odd scratching on his shoulder and turned to find the Pixie crouched there, her face solemn as she held onto his shirt for balance.

Chapter 58

Kam hit the cue ball and smiled as it slammed the purple solid into the side pocket. Sloane shook her head and smiled.

"You called it," she said with a raised voice to combat the stream of music and voices in the hall. It felt just like your standard pool hall which Sloane had been to once in all her life. It was much nicer when you couldn't read most of the people in it. Kam took a tricky shot and Sloane watched in amazement as the ball bounced off the side, clicked the blue solid and sent it hurtling into the corner pocket. Kam went to shoot once more and glanced at her before purposefully missing. Sloane laughed and stomped a foot in pretended glee.

"Oh goody, now I get a turn," she said sarcastically and hefted up the long stick. Kam made a motion for her to chalk the end. Sloane rolled her eyes and did as he had shown her. She pretty well sucked at the game, but it did take her mind off a few things.

Kam had explained that before a big fight, the Guardians would often hang out together, have some fun to keep up moral and camaraderie. It made sense to Sloane; living life gave more reason to protect it. The only thing she thought was wild was the fact that they were going up against a simple human.

How hard could that be? She tried not to think about the fact that the human was married to her mother.

For what felt like the hundredth time, Kam stood close and showed her how to hold the stick. She knew it wouldn't help but tried again. The stick sat aimed in the crook of her left hand and she pulled back and gently pushed forward. The stick tapped the white ball and slowly moved a few inches toward her target. Kam went to retrieve the Q ball so she could try again. She placed a hand on his arm and shook her head.

"Kam, I *really* suck at this. Maybe we should try darts?" she asked. Kam laughed.

"Tell you what. I'm going to line up the balls and you take a go at hitting each one. If you still feel that way, we'll try darts."

Sloane took a swig of her beer and gave Kam a shrug. "If you think it'll help," she commented. As she watched him line up the balls she found herself wondering if Liam was okay, which pissed her off again.

Once more, Kam was ready to show her how to hit the ball. Pulling her thoughts away from the confounding redhead, she got into position and hit the Q ball with intention and force. It slammed into one of the balls and Sloane yipped in excitement.

"I hit something!" she exclaimed. Kam laughed and clapped. He leaned down to her.

"See?" he said, "miracles *can* happen."

Laughing, Sloane continued down the line, some went well and some didn't, but it was a hell of a lot better than before.

"I guess there is hope, Kam."

<h1 style="text-align:center">Chapter 59</h1>

When the bartender added a bit of Irish Cream to her hot cocoa, Verity finally started to feel her insides thaw. Despite being cradled in Evan's warm arms, between the long fall and then the walk to the Den, Verity would have preferred a full five minutes of brain freeze.

What a strange twist the day had taken. When she thought of Duran she felt mostly pity with a taste of sorrow. He was too old, too bored, and too much Fae for her. The otherworld folk were fascinating, and she loved working with them but in the end, when it was time to put up your feet and take in the night, a good old human life was just fine.

Evan laughed heartily, and Rusk shook silently after some joke they shared. Evan had found some clothes and they were sitting at the bar as they caught up. They obviously hadn't seen each other for a while. Verity, who had taken a stool to the right of Evan, couldn't help but smile. Even though there was a battle tomorrow, of which she could barely fathom as even real, everyone seemed to be having such a good time.

She took another sip of her cocoa and sighed. Now that was good. Glancing up, she met Evan's gaze. She thought something smoldered there, but it vanished when he winked and replied to something Rusk said. Verity frowned and blinked. She stared at the dark-skinned man for a moment and when he met her eyes again, he just smiled. No spark or heat. Verity took a gulp of her cocoa when a shadow fell over her.

"Verity the Healer?"

Looking up Verity swallowed and nodded at the huge hulk of a man in front of her. He had to be at least six and a half feet tall with arms so thick it looked like the muscles wanted to be on the outside.

"I'm Halsey, a Master Healer. I'm running the healing team tomorrow and wanted to say hi before we're all shoved together in a panic tomorrow." He had a deep Texan accent.

Verity held out a hand and smiled. "Nice to meet you, Halsey. I assume that healing is your special gift?"

"You assume correctly," he said with a broad, friendly grin.

"I am guessing sometimes they think you're there to break them in half?"

Halsey laughed. "I admit, sometimes that does happen. It is somewhat ironic that I ended up this size with healing hands." He wiggled his fingers in the air.

Verity chuckled. "Try ending up human with healing hands. It's got the Goblin's interest."

Halsey cocked his head. "That could be good or bad depending on which way they look at it."

"Lucky for me, they're intrigued. I've found some friends there."

"Definitely lucky for you. Do you have a few

minutes? I have some things I want to show you before tomorrow." He glanced over at Evan and Rusk. Halsey raised his brows. Verity looked over and frowned. The men were quiet and watchful. Shaking her head, she smiled and slid off her stool.

"Of course, Halsey," she said, "guys, I'll be back soon."

With a wave, she followed Halsey across the Tavern. In the next room there was a closet between two bathrooms. He opened it up and Verity was greeted with rows of shelves, each neatly stocked with vials and bottles, band-aids, salves and other medical supplies.

"Oh, wow!" Verity said as she inspected some of the vials. Frowning she held one up. "Dandelion Root?" she asked.

"For humans it's for digestion but for the Fae it's like an antibiotic."

"Hm. I don't know anything about herbs really. I've only been around the medical industry and they don't put a lot of stock into herbs."

"Well, they know some things when it comes to healing, but with the Otherworlds', herbs are really the only way to go. Perhaps when we're through this particular week, you might like me to teach you a few things?"

"That would be great, Halsey. This is fascinating. I won't be able to help with this tomorrow but these hands," she held them out, "can do some damage."

They laughed, and he pointed out some of the key things that would be in the packs handed out for each of the healers.

"How many healers are here for this?"

"There's five of us. I will be surprised if we all catch some action though none of us are really sure what we're up against."

"I've been wondering about that," Verity commented as she felt someone standing behind her. She glanced back and found Evan's beautiful face peering over her shoulder. She smiled and turned back to Halsey.

"I keep hearing that it's a..." she held her hands up in quote signs, "*human* that we're going after but I would imagine that the Guardianship wouldn't go through this much trouble if that's all they were dealing with."

"And you would imagine right," said a female voice. Verity turned to watch a tall blond woman approach. Halsey and Evan bowed deeply so Verity quickly curtsied though she didn't know why.

"Gentlemen," the lady said, "Miss Verity," she continued with a nod to Verity before disappearing into the lady's room. Verity turned with a raised brow to Evan.

"Our Queen," he said, his teeth a brilliant white against his bronze skin as he smiled, "Come on, let's play some darts."

Verity gave an apologetic smile to Halsey, who chuckled and waved her off. Taking Evan's outstretched hand, she followed him back to the game room.

Chapter 60

She was laughing. Heat rushed into his neck as Liam watched. Kam leaned in to take a shot and she grabbed one of his arms, holding it down. Kam didn't back down as he went for the shot anyway. Sloane reached around and hit his arm, causing him to miss. They laughed together, and she skipped around to the other side of the table. She picked up the chalk and Liam moved. He found himself standing next to Kam as Sloane leaned in for her shot.

Liam leaned down to Kam's ear and whispered so she wouldn't overhear even through the loud din.

"Mine."

Kam turned to him, a smile appearing. Sloane looked up and met Liam's eyes. They rolled over to Kam. He gave her a wink, patted Liam on the shoulder and left the table. Sloane hadn't moved. She was leaning over the table, stick loosely aimed at the cue ball. Liam could almost see the thoughts stumbling over each other as her eyes roved the table top. He leaned down and placed both hands on the table, causing her to look at him.

"We need to talk," he commanded.

Sloane's face pulled back in surprise just before her brows shot up and her lips pressed together, hard. She searched his face. He laughed inside, knowing she had no idea what was happening.

"Go fuck yourself," she said.

Sloane put the cue stick on the table and folded her arms across her chest. She stood and glared at him defensively. Liam forced himself not to smile. She was so damned hot. Her hair was piled up and clipped out of her face, but a few strands were hanging loosely around her cheek. And she was his.

"No. We need to talk," he said. Never taking her eyes off him, Sloane slowly walked around the table. Liam turned to face her. She stepped up to him, only a hair's width away from his chest. His heart raced, he had to admit.

"Go. Fuck. Yourself." she said and turned away. She started across the floor toward the lady's room. He was struck by her stubbornness and admired it. He shook his head. It was too late for her. He walked up behind her, grabbed her by the waist, twisted her body and tossed her over his shoulder. She must have been stunned into silence as she didn't say anything or scream or *something*. As he entered the hallway to the dorm rooms, he turned to the now quiet crowd and waved. He heard the hoots and snickers as he headed up the stairs.

"Put me down," she finally spoke when they reached the top of the stairs. He let her down and they continued in silence until they reached the door to his room. He turned to her.

"Now, we're going to behave and go inside and have a nice wee chat," he said.

"That's fine, but there's just one thing," Sloane answered.

"What?" he asked. Sloane smiled sweetly at him before raising her arm and smacking him audibly across the cheek.

"I had that coming," he said and rubbed his burning cheek. Opening the door to his room, he waved his hand with a flourish and followed a frowning Sloane inside.

There was a Queen-sized bed on the left wall next to a small closet. Soft moonlight glowed into a window set above a simple desk and chair. A tall chest of drawers was opposite the bed leaving just enough space to walk around.

Liam closed the door, locked it and turned in time to watch Sloane step onto the chair and sit down on the desk, the chair an ineffective barrier in front of her. Her feet on the seat of the chair, she watched him. No smile, no frown. He couldn't tell by her face, but he could hear her heart quicken and he watched her unwittingly clench and unclench her right hand.

"I really did manage to upset you this time, didn't I?" he asked, his accent no longer hidden.

Sloane raised a brow and smiled without mirth. "Yeah," she said, "You kinda ditched me, Liam."

He walked over to the stand in front of the chair and put his hands on his hips. He drank her in before crossing his arms over his chest. Sloane put her hands on her thighs and sat straight. Her eyes never leaving him.

"I'm here," Liam said his voice low, "and this time, I really am yours. Completely." Sloane's eyes closed as she took in a deep breath and let it out through her nose. When she opened her eyes, they were wet, but her voice was full of anger.

"Are you fucking serious? *Now* you say this? After putting me through hell and back, *now* you're claiming me?"

He shook his head. "I'm not claiming you. I'm saying, I am yours. Whatever you decide to do is your choice. But. I am yours. Finally."

He watched the anger boil in her eyes, but he refused to give up. Her nearness made his knees weak, his heart dance.

"I'm a Guardian, Sloane," he said, his eyes never leaving hers, "I know how to protect. I know what to do in a battle and I know how to kill. But..."

Liam paused and glanced away, gathering his thoughts.

"I have no idea how to be a bond mate."

Sloane shook her head. "I can't have you running away every time we get close. As much as I know you're meant to be with me, you can't keep running, Liam. It will break me."

He watched a single tear run down her cheek. She brushed it away with a lift of her shoulder.

"That's just it. I get it now. The thing is, Sloane, since the moment I laid eyes on you, I knew you were the one. I fell hard and not only did I have no idea how to handle it," Liam starting pacing between Sloan and the door. "I didn't even understand what was happening and on top of even that, I was ordered *not* to go there with you. I've been doing this job for thirty odd years, Sloane. One thing I *do know* how to do is follow orders."

"Who would order that? Why would someone even *have* to give that order, Mr. *Rogue*?"

"Yeah, not really Rogue. I had to keep everything

under wraps, but that's another story. You may have figured out that I have a reputation with the ladies, but it is completely superficial, and Brick told me to keep my hands off you. He was protecting you but not realizing that he was also making our lives miserable."

Sloane couldn't help but smile. "That's actually kind of sweet."

Liam snorted. "Yeah, sweet. I've had blue balls for six months."

"You really haven't been with anyone since…"

Liam moaned and shook his head. "I don't see anyone but you, Sloane. Your scent, your eyes, your love of chocolate. The way you smile when you're in your own world and don't think anyone is watching…" Liam chuckled. "I'm fucked."

He sat on the bed and rubbed his face.

"Show me," Sloane whispered. Liam looked at her and realized his barriers were firmly in place. He stood before her and moved his arms outward, palms up and released his emotion. Allowing just a hint to seep out at first, he watched surprise ripple across her face as he allowed the flood gates to open and shared himself completely, things he had never let her see before.

She stood on the chair and placed her hands on his shoulders. A broad smile took over her face and minimized the streaks on her cheeks.

He hesitated. He knew what he wanted to do right then but wasn't sure of the effect it would create. Women were confusing.

"Liam?" she whispered. He nodded, words lost in his throat.

"If you get the opportunity to kiss me, will you leave again?"

He shook his head slowly, never leaving her eyes. A growl built up slowly in the back of his throat as an image of Sloane with Evan wrapped around her crossed his mind. When he spoke, it was a much lower timbre than he expected.

"You're mine."

He watched her wipe a stray tear from her face, her smile broadening.

"Yes. I am," she whispered as she traced his lips with her finger, "and you are mine."

Liam felt a satisfied warmth blossom in his chest and start to slowly spread into his extremities.

"Aye lass," he breathed out softly. His hands flew up and gripped her waist while his left foot kicked the chair out of his way.

Sloane hissed in surprise and dug her fingers into his shoulders relaxing them the moment her feet hit the ground.

Pulling her close, Liam devoured her lips. Sloane wrapped one arm around his shoulders and the other around his waist. She could feel the threads of the bond wind itself around her, pulling them together. Moaning, Liam sucked her bottom lip before moving his lips along her jaw to her ear.

"I missed you," he whispered.

His tongue danced around her lobe while she fumbled in a haze to find the bottom of his shirt. She finally found the hem and the hard muscle beneath. He sucked in a breath as her hands smoothed over his warm flesh. She pushed the shirt up and with one hand he had it off. Sloane's teeth grazed his chest and she followed with light kisses. Taking in a deep breath his scent filled her and fueled the flame already roaring within.

Liam's hand found the hem of her shirt and Sloane slowly lifted her hands into the air. He grinned lasciviously as he put his hands beneath her shirt. One hand slid behind and moved up her back pushing her flat stomach into his groin. His other hand lifted her shirt and he growled when he grazed her breast. Sloane's breath caught, and her eyes closed unbidden. His lips found her neck and nibbled away all her inhibitions. He stopped nibbling and Sloane fleetingly wondered if he actually had six hands, all gentle and making her feel things she didn't know was possible and definitely never wanted to stop.

Forcing her eyes open, Sloane found him drinking her in, the lust in his eyes palpable. She smiled. It was like a trigger. Liam ripped her shirt right off. He snapped her bra off and twisted them around, laying her on the bed and suckling her hungrily. Just before she lost herself in luxury, he moved to her lips again, gently kissing her while he unfastened her jeans.

He pulled away and ran a finger from her lips down her throat, between her breasts and down to her jeans. He slid down the bed and pulled off her boots, then started to peel back her jeans. He paused for a moment when he realized she wasn't wearing underwear, meeting her eyes. She just smiled mischievously and licked her lips.

Liam growled in response and pulled off her jeans. After dropping his jeans to the floor, he sat on his haunch, hidden from her view and admired her.

Sloane watched his chest, heavy with heated breaths and taught with years of training and the nature of his beast.

The silvery glow of Liam's Hue brightened. Sloane blinked a few times to be sure. Slim strands of silver reached toward her entwining themselves with another Hue, a bright yellow. Her eyes widened when Liam reached over and ran a finger over the pulsing Hues. She looked at him and found him smiling at her. She looked at the strands again and realized the yellow was her. Reaching out she touched them, felt the energy and warmth as they continued to intertwine and blend into each other.

Her body dripping with need, Sloane reached for Liam who leaned in, taking in a deep breath of her before meeting her eyes. Sloane ran a hand over his cheek bone as he slid himself into her. Digging into his shoulder, pleasure shot straight through her and the strands of the bond pulled taught. Liam breathed out in surprise.

They became entangled in color and light as the bond completed.

Chapter 61

Verity found herself fully clothed and tucked carefully into an unfamiliar bed. Soft sunlight glowed from the slits in the curtained window. Morning. A mild throb in her head told her she'd had a bit more to drink than she was used to. A lazy smile crossed her face when she thought about Evan's dart teaching antics.

All evening he had stayed close. It was like he had turned Sloane over and been given a new target to protect. Oddly, Verity didn't mind. It helped to take her mind off Duran's turncoat behavior and if what she'd seen so far was any evidence, Evan was sweeter than pecan pie.

Sitting up, Verity froze halfway through putting her feet on the floor. She blinked, rubbed her eyes and blinked some more.

Evan lay on the floor, shirt off, jeans slung low with one arm resting behind his head and the other with a thumb tucked into his front pocket. The slow breathing was easy to see on his tanned chiseled chest. Verity was beside herself with the sudden urge to lick his skin.

Eyes wide she pulled her feet back onto the bed and stared at the wall in front of her, thoughts racing. One side of her knew that if she threw herself on him he would respond in kind. But the other side was scared to death of rejection. And though her body was reacting now, what of the future? What would she be committing to? Verity didn't do things like that but oh, god he was right there and begging for her hands to touch him. Was he?

Distracted by commotion in the hallway, Verity strained to hear what was going on. The noise passed, and she realized it was just people heading out of their rooms, albeit loudly.

"Verity?"

She stiffened at his voice, soft and husky, before peering down at him. He was propped up on his elbows, green eyes gazing at her lazily. He smiled when she came into view.

"I heard your heart beat quicken," he commented. Verity looked away. She knew exactly why her heart had sped up.

"I heard people in the hallway, it startled me," she said.

"Hm. Yah, breakie time," he said as he pulled himself into a sitting position, purposely facing away from her. "I hope you don't mind that I brought you back to my room. I wasn't sure if you had a place or not and you weren't talking very coherently."

Verity laughed. "Yeah, I don't usually drink so it hits me pretty hard. It's ok that you brought me here. I actually slept great."

"Good," Evan said as he stood fluidly. Verity couldn't help but admire his back once more. He turned to her with a smile.

"I hope you slept ok," she said suddenly remembering that he had been on the floor all night.

"I'm almost used to sleeping anywhere at any time," he said grabbing a shirt from his dresser and pulling it on. Verity hid her disappointment. "They will be serving breakfast down near the bar. I'll leave you to do whatever girls do in the morning and see you downstairs?"

"Great, thank you, Evan."

She watched him leave before laying back on the bed with a sigh. She mockingly fanned herself and wondered if she had missed a good opportunity or avoided a bad situation. The door opened abruptly, and Verity's body jumped. Evan took a step in and his eyes raked over her.

"In case I don't get the opportunity again," he said, "I wanted you to know that you are absolutely beautiful when you wake up."

Verity blinked, and her mouth dropped open slightly. Evan gave her a warm smile before closing the door again. She waited to see if he would return and when he didn't after a few minutes she scrambled up and over to the mirror to see what he saw. Her thick black hair pointed every which way and the kohl black lining her eyes was smudged against her naturally white skin, leaving her to more closely resemble the ghost of a raccoon. Shaking her head, she frowned at whatever Evan thought of as beautiful and went to get cleaned up.

Chapter 62

When Sloane woke she didn't dare open her eyes right away. On her side, she clutched the soft sheets in her hand letting memories of the night before bring a sly smile to her face. The musky scent that was Liam started to awaken parts of her body that she thought surely needed more rest. Liam chuckled next to her and she felt his warm hand on her hip. His feelings for her, raw and unfettered, smoothed over her skin like a luxurious silk.

"It was real," she whispered.

"Completely," he said as he leaned in and peppered her neck with hot kisses.

An hour later Sloane found herself being hand washed in the shower by her bonded. An hour after that she was fed and then dressed from head to toe in black leather. Liam tightened the straps and handed her two knives to nestle on her thighs with leather straps, a 9mm gun that holstered on her right side, and a short sword that fit into the harness on her back.

"I don't even know how to use this stuff, Liam," she complained.

"That may be so, my lass, but you will figure it out if you need it. Your goal is to get to your mum and get out. Period. I certainly hope you never have to use any of it." He looked her over and slowly blew out of his mouth. "You look so good right now, I seriously want to rip that right off you."

"As much as I support that comment, we have a battle to get to, remember?"

"Fine."

Sloane giggled. She couldn't help it. She knew she was going into danger, but she couldn't help but believe that everything would turn out perfectly.

Liam picked up two swords and slipped them into the scabbard on his back. He had knives strapped to his calves and on his boots plus he had a gun on each hip which he called Glock 45's. Sloane whistled in appreciation.

"I am bonded with one sexy mother fucker," she said. Liam looked up and her heart skipped a beat. He grinned and slapped her on the bum. Squealing she went to get him back when there was a rap on the door. Laughing, Sloane opened the door and saw Brick filling up the opening. She smiled and waved him in only to find Kam saunter in behind. The room seemed to shrink. Brick wasted no time.

"The reason the Fae were called in is to screen the building from the humans. They will handle it so that no matter what goes on, people will see a quiet closed building and nothing else."

"Impressive," Sloane commented.

"They are good for some things, that's for sure," Brick said with his deep bass chuckle.

"I'll be with you, Sloane," Kam said. She glanced at Liam.

"I'll be on the first wave in, babe. I need someone

I trust to get your back."

"But who's going to get yours?" she whispered.

"I will," Brick said. Sloane gave him a weak smile. Reality was digging its ugly, sharp fingers into her skin and squeezing just a bit too tight.

Chapter 63

As the Guardians filled the tavern to splitting seam level, Sloane found herself surrounded by Liam's protective arms and she liked it very much. They were gathered for the final briefing before heading out to the castle. She spotted Verity across the room with Evan and waved. Verity smiled brightly and waved back. Sloane was relieved that she was ok now. She had looked pretty rough yesterday.

The Queen popped out of her office wearing white cargo pants and a light blue shirt. She oddly reminded Sloane of her friend Nia. Frowning to herself, she wondered whatever happen with Nia and Noah. They had just left, without a word. Pressing her lips together Sloane realized that if she had found Liam after that much time had passed, she would probably do the same thing. If her family weren't directly involved with this battle, she might even suggest it now. She glanced up at Liam and found him watching her. He lifted a brow which earned him a smile.

"Good afternoon everyone," the Queen said. A tall dark-skinned man stepped out of her office and settled to the Queen's left next to another Guardian. Sloane squealed, bringing several eyes to her before the Queen continued.

"Some of you know Andy here," she flourished a hand at the dark man, "and the fact that he is a Displacer. He was exactly what we needed to better understand what we were dealing with at Dr. Johnson's office. Last night we confirmed my fears. Our kind is not the only non-human that he has captured and experimented with. Fortunately for us, his tests and attempts at grafting *our* kind onto humans did not work. Unfortunately for other kinds, it did work. Many times."

The silence in the room was palpable. Sloane looked at Liam and saw the pain in his face. He had lost a good friend to Dr. J's work.

"There are six floors in the building," the Queen continued. "The top three of those floors are dorms for these creatures. There are twenty on each floor."

She paused to let it sink in. "The third floor is a cafeteria, a gym, and some other office size rooms. The second is the medical facilities and the first contain a few offices and a small loading dock. The doctor keeps a bedroom and personal office on the west side of the second floor. No one ever comes out of the building except Dr. J and his wife."

Sloane's heart jumped at the mention of her mother. The Queen's eyes found her, and she gave a sympathetic smile. "It's been two days since we've seen any outside activity."

The Queen shifted back and forth on her feet before looking over the room again. "I know most of you would prefer it if we captured these creatures and helped them to live a life in hiding or in one of the Fae worlds, but the doctor has ensured that they won't be able to. Based on what Andy has overheard, and experience from someone who once worked for him, they are drug hypnosed into believing they are human and that we are the creatures that need to be destroyed. There is the chance that once we take out the doctor, that will vanish but since it's a mind alteration rather than a spell, it's not likely. You will need to kill to end this vicious cycle and I am sorry about that."

Sloane didn't care. She had seen firsthand what this man had done, not just to her mother, but to innocent people and Guardians. He was going down and she was glad to be a part of it.

She looked Andy over. He did not resemble the boy she had met many months ago. He had filled in and gotten much taller. He caught her looking and gave her a toothy grin. She smiled back and found herself really glad to see him.

"All right everyone, you have your marching orders. There is a Faeway open in the back alley that goes straight to the Castle of Tarnwool. Let's go build a battle, shall we?"

Sloane frowned and looked at Liam. He laughed. "She means let's go kick some arse but she's being nice about it."

Chapter 64

The Castle of Tarnwool and its rich green grounds was breathtaking. Verity was blown away. On the outside it boasted beautiful timeworn, dark stone that was clearly in need of repair, but the inside? It had the character and build of the original style but with all the modern amenities. The Fae were nearby keeping a cloak over it to hide the masses of armor covered and weapon packing men and women coming through the Faeway. Once Verity was properly through the gateway she saw Liam and then Sloane hugging a Guardian she hadn't met yet. She walked over with Evan and Rusk while she scanned the grounds for Halsey and the medical equipment.

"Verity," Sloane said as she pulled away from the hulking man, "this is Dustin. He's the one I told you about that sent Evan to watch over me."

Verity turned in time to see Evan and Dustin clasp hands and do the man hug thing. Evan winked at her as he pulled away and she reached out to take Dustin's hand.

"My pleasure, ma'am," he said as he shook it gently. Evan backed up and placed a hand on her lower back. Before Verity could question it, Dustin spoke.

"Liam, I will be on your team."

Liam nodded. "Good to have you, my friend."

They started to shake hands and Verity turned her back to them to scan the crowd, searching for the medical crew. She spotted Halsey going through a door in the back of the great room they were in.

"Excuse me, I'm going to get my med kit. Back soon," Verity said. Evan followed her.

"I don't think I'll be hurt surrounded by Guardians, Evan."

"Just keeping you company."

"Well, in that case, how do you know Dustin?"

"He's my mentor. Long story short, I finished school but didn't show up for assignment at the Guardianship and then ended up in New Orleans where I met Dustin. He took me in, trained me further and helped me. He's like the dad I never had."

Verity stopped walking and looked up at Evan's vibrant green eyes. "I'm so sorry about your dad, Evan."

He shook his head eyes darkening, "Oh, I have a *father*. I'll tell you about it one day over a cup of coffee. Right now, my mind is on you and on this battle."

Verity cocked her head at him and let the barest of smiles show. She wanted him to know that she was pleased he was thinking of her, but not too much in case he was doing the guardian, protective thing. She couldn't really tell but she did notice that as she turned to continue across the room, she felt his hand briefly on her lower back again. It was warm and inviting and when he pulled away, she felt cold.

As she walked through the doorway she had

seen Halsey go through, she barreled directly into his back. Evan stopped a hair away from running into her and grabbed both her arms to pull her away from Halsey. Interesting.

Halsey turned and smiled when he saw her, but it was Evan he held a hand out to.

"Evan, good to meet you."

"You too, Halsey." Evan smiled. Verity frowned. She did not understand Guardian behavior. Or was it man behavior? She shook her head and decided to ignore them. The room was set up with ten beds like a hospital, along with equipment that Verity was not only familiar with but knew how to use. There were two large glass door cabinets where the herbs and medical needs were kept. She looked back to Halsey.

"I wanted to get my med kit and find out where we're meeting when they give the green light."

"Sure. The med kits are on the table in the corner and when we move out, we will be the next to last group brought over to the office building to wait with one of the Fae. If we're needed, we will have these nifty ear bud radios that will call us in. You can find yours in the kit."

"Cool," Verity said and walked over to get a kit. She grabbed one, the size of a kid's lunch box and headed back over to the boys who were chatting amicably. She took in Evan's black clothing, strapped with various weapons and frowned as she realized something. After they left Halsey and the room she stopped Evan and pulled him out of the way of bustling Guardians.

Quizzically he looked at her concerned face. "This may be a dumb question," she asked, "but if you need to…ah, *change* quickly, how on earth do you do it all decked out like that?"

Evan laughed and brought a hand to her cheek. The heat from his touch startled her as it moved down her nerves like a zip line. Evan stopped laughing and pulled his hand away looking at it for a moment before lowering it and explaining.

"If you look carefully at the weapon belts and straps, you'll see that they have extra length and wrap around. Each Guardian has custom belts so as they expand, the belts give. Some even get their belts magically adjusted so they don't have the weight of the extra leather."

"What about the clothes?" Verity asked.

"Well, some just let them tear off. Some only shift part of their body so they save their clothes, and others get the stripper style clothes."

"The what?"

"You know clothes made for strippers, that come apart easily?"

Verity felt the heat rise into her cheeks. Now she *really* wanted to know what *he* wore but instead she nodded before turning away to get back to the group. She could feel him close by. Something tickled her ear and then she heard his whisper.

"I just let it tear off."

The blush went deeper and started to burn her neck and shoulders.

A loud screech filled the air and Verity stopped in her tracks. Evan's arms went around her and pulled her behind him. She peered around his bulk to see what was going on. Half the Guardians had weapons pulled and the other half were frozen in some kind of fighting pose. Verity searched the room for the culprit. She saw Liam with Sloane tucked into his side and a large dagger held out. It was his face relaxing that brought a quiver of a smile to Verity's face. She watched Liam lower his dagger and release Sloane before she started searching again for the source of the odd noise.

It didn't take her but a few seconds to see Kam sweet talking a beautiful lady who was obviously irritated. She was easily six feet tall, as tall as Kam, with long blond hair that had vines or something similar entwined throughout it. Kam was clearly imploring her, and she was having no part of it. In the woman's anger, Verity watched as gills on her neck flapped periodically. That was the giveaway. She pushed away from Evan and headed straight to Kam.

"Verity!" Evan exclaimed.

"It's ok, I know her," Verity said as she came up next to Kam, Evan stayed right behind her.

"Ha!" the lady said when she saw Verity. "You take a soft human like her but don't allow me? The man killed my *family*, Kam."

Chapter 65

Sloane let Liam lead her over to Kam. Quite the crowd was gathering around the quarreling couple. Verity was speaking.

"Why can't she come, Kam? She would be one hell of a fighter."

Kam sighed and gave Verity devil eyes. "She is one of the last Siren's on earth, Verity. She should be protected, not brought into battle."

"I choose what I do," the siren said, "*not* you."

"Come on, Jaws, you know I'm just looking out for you."

Sloane felt the slightest of a warning squeeze on her arm from Liam and stifled her laugh. The fish lady, apparently called *Jaws,* had a sudden and distinct change come over her face. She took Kam's hand and held it gently in her own.

"I know you are Guardian, Kam. I know that you take care of the humans and your family and protect them ferociously. *I* am not one of your humans. I am a *predator*. I must be allowed this. I must have my vengeance."

Many of the Guardians that had gathered around moved on, continuing their business in the great castle but Sloane, Liam, Verity and Evan hung nearby. Sloane knew this fight and knew without a doubt that Kam would not win it. A woman, a siren rather, scorned and all that.

Kam finally let out a very loud growl and threw his hands up. "Fine. But you need to stick with one of the Guardians. I've already promised to look after Sloane."

Liam stepped up. "Kam, Sloane can take Dustin. I'm sure he won't mind and then you can look after Jaws here rather than worry about her."

Kam looked at Sloane. She smiled and went over to him, placing a hand on his arm. "It really is ok, Kam. I understand these pesky women things more than you know."

Jaws laughed as she removed Sloane's hand from Kam. "Almost, young girl, almost."

Sloane watched the water woman's webbed fingers run down Kam's neck before withdrawing and resting on the short blade belted at her side. With a nod, Sloane withdrew and backed into Liam who must have moved in close.

He pulled her away and whispered in her ear, "Don't trust a Siren, ever."

"Ha, I don't but, damn Liam. He's really fallen for her, hasn't he?"

"Oh clearly," Liam said and laughed. Verity joined them.

"Now there's something I wouldn't have seen coming," she said.

Sloane noticed Evan move discreetly to Verity's side and she smiled.

Chapter 66

It wasn't long before the horn sounded and Sloane knew it was time to move. The Fae had set up a Faeway to run from the castle directly to a grassy plane near the office building, where Dr. J and her mother were holed up. The Fae were already stationed around the building and projecting the magic that turned the building's activity into a loop so that what was really taking place would be covered up. Sloane wondered how many Fae it would take to cover so much area.

A strong grip tugged her arm and Sloane knew it was Liam. She turned to look in his face and felt the tingles cover her skin. She was so damn happy that he had finally come around. His lip quirked up as he took in her face but then went solid again. Business mode it is.

"I have to leave now, love. Dustin's right behind me and he'll help get you straight to your mum. You remember what to do?"

Sloane nodded. "Of course, I remember. Don't worry about me, I'll be fine."

"Good. I've got plans for you later."

Before Sloane could think of a witty reply, he pressed a hard kiss to her mouth and then turned and vanished into the crowd. The nerves around her lips throbbed and she pressed her hand to them gently.

"Don't worry, he'll be fine," Dustin said as he appeared beside her. "Did anyone ever tell you about the time he blew up a field of miter bugs? They're flesh eaters you know. His crew stupidly ate some bad berries and he was the only one conscious enough to handle the rampage."

Sloane frowned and shook her head at him. Dustin laughed. "I know there's some weird stuff out there."

"I guess so."

"I think we're going to see some of that today."

"Yeah, I think so too," Sloane whispered as they finally surged forward to the Faeway. Several other groups including Liam's had already gone through but once they were at the entrance, Sloane and Dustin had to wait for their turn. Looking over the crowds behind her, Sloane spotted a familiar face.

"Andy!" she hollered. He turned and waved, his lanky yet toned body made an effort to come through but the heavy Guardian bodies separating them were a bit too thick. He cupped his hands to his mouth.

"Good luck!" he hollered.

Sloane smiled and waved just as she was told it was time to go. Turning back, she stepped into the Faeway with Dustin at her side.

Chapter 67

Dr. J still had his secret weapon. Hal stood near, head cocked, listening hard.

But they were being slaughtered.

He had been so certain that his team would be able to destroy these hideous, unnatural beasts. At least he would always know that he had done his best. And since the humans running his government were so hell bent on leaving these creatures to roam around free, he would not allow the love of his life to get into their heathen hands.

"Do not let anyone come into this hallway until I return," he told Hal, who nodded in turn and let a low growl.

Dr. J gave him a weak smile and turned toward the stairs at the end of the hall.

~~*~~

"You understand that if I can't have you, no one can?" Dr. J said to his wife Clara, his breath heavy.

She smiled at him. "What are you going on about, Reagan?"

"I love you, Clara," he said softly and brushed a lock of hair from her cheek.

"I know that," she said and leaned in, placing a

gentle kiss on his lips.

He held her close and looked into her eyes.

"It is for the best," he said searching her eyes, her empty and lifeless eyes. He sucked in a sob. He had done this to her. He blinked. For her protection. To keep her safe. He straightened his shoulder as she gazed up at him.

"Of course, it's for the best," she said as his knife slid between her ribs and up through her heart. He watched her patiently as she took her flight to the heavens; the blood soaked his clothes before he finally lay her gently on their bed. He removed the knife and gently pulled the covers over her.

Chapter 68

In the Faeway, Sloane followed a line of Guardians, making her way through a doorway, down a short hall to a blue door that deposited her directly on the grassy field next to their target's building. Despite the strange emotional energy she felt coming from the building, Sloane marveled out loud that travel could be so simple.

"Yes, but only if you know where they lead. They can also be a world of trouble. I'd be happy to guide you some time."

Sloane glanced around for the voice and found an extremely handsome light-haired Fae standing about twenty feet away, his hands held palm up in front of him.

Sloane raised her eyebrows at him. "Shouldn't you be shielding the area or something?"

He raised his brow up and licked his lips. "I am quite capable of multi-tasking, little beauty."

Sloane pressed her lips together and turned back to trudge through the grass toward the building. She heard an odd noise behind her and glanced back to see Dustin unsuccessfully hiding his laughter.

"Whatever," Sloane said under her breathe and kept moving forward. Ahead, two guardians opened the front doors to the building and the low roar of voices and scraping weapons burst toward them and then vanished again as the doors closed. Sloane started to run but Dustin's hand on her shoulder slowed her. He came up next to her.

"We're not here to fight, Sloane. We're here to get Clara, if she's even here, and leave, right?"

Sloane nodded. "Right, of course."

"We're going to the back door."

"Yes, I know. Sorry Dustin. I think it's because I know Liam's in there somewhere that I automatically want to jump into the fray."

He nodded sympathetically.

"Not like I would have a fucking clue what I was doing," she added.

"And would likely get yourself killed."

"Thanks for the vote of confidence there, Dustin."

"There are some things that I don't sugar coat and during times like these, there is no good time for it."

"Point taken," she said as they turned the corner of the building. Fae were lined up about twenty feet apart circling the building and the surrounding field. They all held out their hands palm up but otherwise looked pretty bored.

Sloane commented as much as she moved toward Dustin's side and made her way to the single back door.

"This should take us to the stairs and directly up to the doctor's quarters," Dustin said softly. Sloane nodded and waited for Dustin to open the door, check the inside and then wave her in.

Some alarm was beeping in the distance and the faint smell of smoke filled the air. Sloane couldn't tell if it was an old smell or something new, but she hurried anyway.

The stairwell was exactly where it was supposed to be. Sloane rushed up the steps.

Chapter 69

The first wave of injured came through but it was a group of humans that had been inside. They had apparently been kept locked in a cell together and not been treated well for weeks. All were dehydrated, some were dangerously malnourished, and others were sick. One had a seeping open wound which looked suspiciously like a dog bite. There were twenty-seven of them and Verity worked diligently with the healing team to help them get well enough to travel through the Faeway and out of the area.

As she crossed the grass to the next patient she passed Halsey.

"How does it work with humans?" she whispered. "They're not supposed to know."

"We have someone who is versed in the mind. It's not the best solution, but it's better than the alternative."

Verity didn't fully understand and made a note to clarify it when she had more time.

She knelt by the man who had a bite taken out of his calf. It was clearly infected, and he was in the throes of fever.

Using her Med Kit, Verity pulled out disinfectant and gauze and placed them on the grass next to him before placing her gloved hands on the laceration. Eyes closed, she could immediately feel the oddness, the strange lust of the bacteria to take over, to mutate the healthy cells. Once she had her bearings, Verity urged the white blood cells into overdrive. Imagining an evil eating vacuum, Verity helped to pull the bacteria from the gash while the white blood cells attacked and consumed from the other side.

The man moaned in pain, but Verity ignored him. She felt him jerk but she held fast. She wasn't sure how much time had passed before she felt they had purged enough of the bacteria and that the man could now heal on his own.

She opened her eyes and was startled to see that three of the healers where holding the man down. They were smiling and nodding at her which Verity thought was a little odd, but she gave a small smile back and then dressed the lesion, now more like a large cut, knowing that he would be okay.

The healers let him go and moved on to other patients. Verity stood.

"Thank you," she heard a whisper.

She saw that the man was awake and smiled.

"You're welcome," she said and knew once more that *this* was her calling.

Chapter 70

In the hallway upstairs, some of the lights hung down haphazardly as though there had been an explosion or someone had come at them with a large weapon. Others buzzed and blinked incessantly.

Joy and fear coursed through Sloane's body as she rushed toward the room on her right, the one that Andy had said was her mother's. The drug hypnosis could have done permanent damage to her mother over such a long period of time and Sloane didn't know what to expect.

Dustin held a hand out, stopping her. Her body buzzed in anticipation, but she knew he wouldn't let her through the door until he had checked the room. He quickly swung open the door and blocked her entry until he had swept through. He waved her in.

Someone was on the huge wooden bed centered on the far wall. The person was facing the other way, a blanket pulled up past her neck. Sloane knew it was her mother by the soft blond waves covering the pillow.

Slowing, Sloane walked over and put a gentle hand on her mom's shoulder. She was so cold. She gave a little shake.

"Mom?"

Nothing.

She shook a little harder. "Mom?" she said a little louder. Her heart thumped with fear and any warmth she had felt earlier drained. She gently moved her head to see her face. Clara Johnson's face looked young and calm in her final rest.

Sloane had to blink several times to believe what she was seeing. Dustin moved her gently out of the way and pulled the blanket down. She saw that it had hidden the dark puddle on her mother's chest and covering the bed. She couldn't stop the heave that pulled at her stomach and the tears that poured down her face. She couldn't even breathe.

"Sloane."

His words were solid, commanding. She stood there, sick to her stomach, and stared through glassy eyes at her mother. Even though she had been checked out mentally for years now, Sloane always had hope. Now there was none. Dustin's arms curled around her then and she allowed him to hold her until she saw the empty easels and unused paints. She pushed him away. Her eyes found the dark puddle on the floor and the drips that fell from the bed. She needed air.

Rushing away from the horror and into the hallway, tears streamed down her face.

"Sloane!" Dustin yelled but she kept going.

She neared the end of the hall and slowed only slightly before flying around the bend to the next one.

Someone walked out of a doorway directly into her path. She tried to stop but her legs just didn't slow in time. She ran full body into Dr. Johnson. He slammed into the doorway behind him and wavered slightly before catching his balance. He held her close with one arm for just a moment to steady her and then pushed her into the room and stepped away, looking her over, appraising. He was covered in blood. Sloane's stomach curled.

"Hello, my dear. Such a surprise to run into you here of all places," he chuckled as he waved a hand in the air, "and my, it looks like a bomb hit you." He laughed. Sloane stood, eyes narrowed while she tried to catch her breath. Dr. J made an odd motion with his hand and a large scaled creature Sloane had never seen before stepped out from the corner and walked out the door.

"Where is she?" Sloane heard Dustin growl from the hallway and then she only heard the grunts of a fight.

"Cat got your tongue, young one? Well, you never did have much to say," Dr. J said as he walked closer and reached out as though to touch her face. Sloane pulled away.

"Don't touch me," she hissed. Anger tickled her ears but hadn't quite warmed her blood.

Dr. J shrugged. "I don't suppose you'll be interested to know that in the end, your mother didn't remember you at all."

Sloane's mouth gaped. "What?"

"She only needed me."

Dr. J moved his right arm and that's when Sloane noticed the long metal staff with a sharp point at the tip. She stepped back. The anger left her and sorrow overwhelmed her insides and flowed thick like honey through her veins.

"How can you do this?" she managed to whisper.

"Quite simple really," Dr. J shrugged, "You are unnatural. It is my duty to restore this world to its natural place. No one else seems to observe this catastrophe in our midst. I take it very seriously." He gave her a condescending smile.

"Your concept of a natural place is wrong," Sloane argued. "This world contains many creatures and they are meant to be here. You're a fool to think differently." She shook her head at him.

"I'm afraid, my dear, that you are the one who has been fooled." He lifted the staff casually and pointed it at her chest. Adrenaline replaced the sorrow and surged through her nerves. Sloane took a step back only to hit something solid. She glanced up to find an enormous creature covered in green fur standing directly behind her. It resembled a sweet, furry monster she had once played poker with but instead of being cute, it had a human face merged with some qualities of a bird. The scream tore from her throat as she struggled to run but was locked in its iron grip. She watched in terror as Dr. J plunged the staff into her chest.

Chapter 71

Slashing out with the dagger in his right hand, Liam removed the head of one of the abominations. His left hand flew behind stabbing another through the heart.

He looked for the nearest *thing* and discovered that they were far and few now. Excitement rushed over him as he realized it was almost over.

Brick was battling two, but he looked like he was playing more than fighting. Amused, he shook his head and looked for someone who needed help. He watched Helen take down four easily when something hit him deep in the chest.

The stabbing pain pulled through his lungs, dropping him to one knee. He dropped his blade and pressed his chest heavily expecting the thick warmth of blood.

The pain was close to unbearable but looking down, there was only his smooth leather skin. Clasping his chest, he glanced around as his other knee dropped to the ground. He heard rather than saw his dagger clatter to the floor. His heart pumped, and pain seared through him. He caught his fall to the ground, hand slamming to the floor. Eyes pinched shut, he tried to take in air calmly but with each breath, raw pain coursed through his body.

Someone growled as they pulled him up. Liam lifted his head, and opened his eyes to find Brick holding him up. Brick looked him over quickly and then turned.

"Evan!" he yelled, his words echoing throughout the room. "The girl!"

Liam vaguely heard heavy steps rushing from the room. His mind blurred, his thoughts wouldn't articulate. Brick carefully set Liam down to the ground. Liam pulled his legs inward, his wings flapped periodically on the floor, slick with various shades of blood.

Resting a hand on his shoulder, Brick spoke, his voice a soft guttural hum. "I'm sure she's fine." He patted Liam's arm as he knelt beside him.

Images started surging through Liam's mind. The time he bought Sloane ice cream. The time he lost control and smothered her with his passion only to turn and run away. Her face, the smell of her hair. The way she danced just for him. His heart was slowing, but the pain kept coming. His body suddenly chilled to the bone. Sloane.

His scream was a rafter shaking roar. The remaining fighters stopped to see what new creature had joined the battle. Liam forced his body up. Brick stepped away. Liam growled again and bolted, down one hall, up the stairs, and through another doorway.

When he reached the hall, he saw Dustin laid out on the floor, eyes closed next to a scaled creature that seemed to be bleeding out.

Evan was fighting the biggest creature Liam had seen yet and he wasn't winning. Behind their battle, Dr. J was cowering against the wall, covered in both dry and fresh blood.

A glance inside the room confirmed his worst fear. Sloane lay on the ground, pinned down by a long spear of the strange dark wood that was somehow able to penetrate the skin of his kind. A scarlet puddle was growing around her.

Grabbing the twin blades strapped to his legs, Liam ignored the pain coursing through him, ignored his bonded and walked over to Evan. Liam growled and Evan stepped back, his breath heaving from exertion. A terrorized scream from down the hall called Evan to move quickly once more.

The strange green creature had an odd humanlike face. It laughed and brought up its sword. Liam grabbed the massive arm and held it away. The creature stopped laughing and started to bring down its other arm. Liam's blade entered its stomach and sliced clear up to the chin. The creature gurgled, eyes wide, before collapsing to the ground, its arm never hitting its target.

Liam's eyes met those of Dr. J. They narrowed as he stared. The good doctor was cowering and sputtering out excuses. Liam felt only phantom pain as it seared through his chest. He considered how to deal with the doctor. He considered pulling off each limb, slowly, one by one before finally biting off his head.

The doctor must have taken Liam's hesitation for mercy. He ran. Liam waited a few moments. Savored the battle. The doctor only made it a few yards before Liam was on him.

Chapter 72

Agony. More pain than she had ever known in her entire life coursed through her chest. Sloane blinked away the darkness that had stunned her and reached a hand over to gently touch her chest. She pulled it away with a sharp inhale and felt the slick blood on her fingers.

Her chest pulsed in distress when she tried to move. Breathing suddenly became labored and Sloane fought to relax and pull in the tiny breathes she needed.

Turning her head slightly, she watched Liam slam Dr. J into the wall. The scream didn't quite cover the cracking and crunching of bones on impact. Turning away from the wall in haste, Liam let a still screaming Dr. J tumble into a distorted pile on the floor. Even covered in a mix of dark blood and other things Sloane didn't want to think about, Liam was the most beautiful creature she had ever seen.

She startled as he lunged forward, soaring over her and hitting something with a crash. She heard a growl, followed by a sticky crunch and then he was leaning over her.

Despite the pain, she smiled. He showed his sharp teeth in response and even then, she could read the concern etching his structured leather face.

"Can you hang on one more moment?" he asked with a deep, velvety growl.

Sloane nodded. He started to rise.

"You should look away," he said. She didn't.

He walked over to Dr. J and looked down at the bloody, broken body. The body started to tremble, and Sloane could just barely hear the softest laugh.

"Look away, Sloane," Liam said, louder this time. She didn't.

He knelt and took the doctor's head in his hands. He whispered something she couldn't hear and then gave an abrupt twist. The doctor's body stilled.

He came back to her side.

"He deserved worse than that. More," she said. Tears fogged her vision as the image of her mother clouded her mind. She blinked them back in favor of concentrating on the short breathes she needed so badly.

"Yes," Liam said as he wrapped a clawed hand around the staff protruding from her shoulder. "But I'm not one to drag things out."

He pulled the staff from her body. She screamed.

He tossed the staff away, bunched as much as he could of her tight shirt near her skewered chest and scooped her up. Through the throbbing pain, she felt him practically fly down the stairs.

Despite the pain, she started to calm in his arms, anticipating escape, only to find herself falling. Liam pitched, and her stomach clenched in fear and pain.

Falling forward, Liam caught himself with a grunt before twisting around. The motion made Sloane's head whirl. Her chest pounded in agony as he squeezed her close with one arm and reached away with the other.

Prying open her eyes, Sloane saw the beady eyes of a blue beast as Liam thrust his one-fisted sword downward and into its head. The creature paused, its eyes rolling in confusion before the furred thing toppled to the ground. After removing his sword from the body, Liam turned back and continued his course. Moments later Sloane knew they were outside by the soft drizzle kissing her face. The pain in her chest seemed to ease slightly. When she cracked her eyelids, she almost smiled at the sliver of a sun rise in the distance. Liam kept running, her body curled into him.

Something in the corner of her eye caught Sloane's attention. Blinking she reached out to touch Liam's leathery chest. She stopped when she realized that she was looking at the tip of a spear. Panicking, she inhaled roughly and then was coughing and crying, the pain in her chest secondary to her fear. It was *IN* him.

She looked up at his face. His lips were pulled back, fangs exposed as he ran.

They went downhill toward the Faeway but at the bottom he slowed. She felt him start to tilt. Was he tripping? She heaved in a sob. There's no way... She did her best to land on her feet as he went to his knees. Her foot slipped sideways, and she cried out but the sprain was nothing compared to the pain in her chest. When she turned back to Liam, the ache in her chest was nothing compared to the agony of her heart.

Liam was on his side and bursting from his chest was the staff.

"No!" Sloane cried out and scrambled to him. His breath came out in a gurgle as his eyes followed her. She watched the blood flow from around the staff. Shaking her head, tears dribbled down her cheeks.

"Help!" she screamed but the Fae surrounding the building only looked on in curiosity.

She looked into his black eyes and placed her free hand on his cheek.

"Do not leave me. Don't you dare. I can't have you leaving me, do you hear me?" Sloane realized she was screaming.

"Please, Liam. Please," she begged.

His hand found hers and gently pressed it closer to his cheek.

He breathed in, the sucking sound tearing a fissure in her soul. She leaned in to hear what he was trying to say.

"You are *mine*."

He shuddered then, his hand falling away, his black eyes staring but seeing nothing. Cradling his head, Sloane howled.

Chapter 73

Sloane lay next to Liam, holding his lifeless hand. Brick's voice came through like a soft waterfall. "It's alright now, girl. Everything's gonna be just fine."

Kam's smooth voice took over. "He's going to need you now, more than ever."

Sloane's head snapped up to look at Kam. The nerve in her neck bit and tingled so she laid her head back down and scanned the room. She found Kam's face through the fog in her mind and turned slowly to look at Liam. Her chest flared in pain, stopping her motion. Dustin and Evan were setting up some type of gurney, industrial size, next to him. Her eyes roved back to Kam. He was a bit more in focus.

He touched his heart and then pointed to hers. "Can't you feel him?"

Her hand went to her chest automatically. She felt the damp blood soaking her clothes but could tell her shoulder was healing. He had told her she might heal faster after the bonding. It still hurt like a bitch.

Closing her eyes, she started to breath in deeply, cursing at the pain and then forcing herself to relax once more, to let her mind expand. She mentally felt over the hurt and used body that she wore and searched for anything that could ease her heart. And she found it.

Eyes flying open, she met Kam's eyes. He smiled.

"The bond," she whispered, "it's still there." Kam nodded.

"How can that be?" she demanded weakly.

He shook his head. "I have no idea. Let's get you two out of here, ok? The Fae are getting restless. And our work here is done."

Sloane nodded.

"Touch him as much as you can, it will help," Kam said, "At least *I think so.* Now close your eyes and hold tight to him because what we're about to do is not going to be pleasant."

Sloane frowned but did as she was told. Except for the closed eyes part. She was not going to miss anything.

Brick took a spot behind Liam, and Kam held Liam's shoulders while Dustin and Evan stood back, hands full of gauze and tape. Brick took hold of the staff protruding from Liam's back. Sloane yelled as Brick threw a foot onto Liam's back and pulled. A sickly slurping sound ensued as the staff slid through Liam and exited with a pop.

Dustin and Evan rushed in, covering the wound on both sides and quickly taping it up. Blood started to seep into them immediately. The four of them lifted him away from Sloane and onto the gurney. Kam scooped her up and at the same time, shoved her hand around Liam's. She held tight as Kam tucked her onto the gurney next to Liam. Dustin and Evan picked them up and started toward the Faeway, Kam running alongside.

Heart racing, tears flowing, Sloane held Liam tight and let her own pain take her into darkness.

Chapter 74

Blinking away the sleep, Sloane could make out stone ceilings and walls. She felt the warmth of a soft blanket tucked around her aching body.

"Welcome back," a gentle voice said to her right. Sloane was relieved to find Verity propped in a nearby chair nursing a coffee.

"Thanks," Sloane said her voice scratchy. "Liam?" she asked.

"He's..." Verity frowned thoughtfully, "Fine?"

Sloane went to sit up and Verity rested a hand on her shoulder, pushing gently back down. She shook her head.

"Not so fast there, Sloane. Luckily the spike just kissed your lung and missed anything else major, but it still ripped through you pretty nicely. You're mostly healed up, but you need a bit more rest before you can go gallivanting around the castle."

Sloane relaxed back with a sigh. Her arm hit something cold and clammy. She pulled away in disgust and looked over to find Liam in his gargoyle form stretched out next to her.

His gray skin was pale. He didn't seem to be breathing or moving. At all. Sloane sat up anyway and hovered over him, touching him, feeling for a pulse and finding nothing. Tears sprouted, and a low moan came from deep within.

"Hey, hey, it's ok, Sloane. He doesn't look like much now, but he'll be ok."

Blinking back the tears, Sloane met Verity's eyes.

"He looks dead," she whispered.

"I know, he does. But you know how each of the Guardians have a special talent? Like Andy is a displacer and Brick is all tornadoey?"

Sloane nodded, and Verity smiled.

"Liam's talent?" Verity shrugged. "He comes back. So technically, he *is* dead."

Frozen, Sloane stared at Verity waiting for the terrible joke to be over.

"We moved him away from you at first but the healing process within him, coolest thing to watch externally by the way, anyway the process slows dramatically. Once we put him back next to you, it becomes steady. It's like you're the battery he needs to recharge."

Sloane couldn't help but allow a small smile. She turned back to him and peppered kisses onto his cold shoulder and neck.

"That's because he's mine," she whispered before settling down and dozing off.

Chapter 75

When Andy landed at the Bergerac airport in southeast France he found himself well rested but fidgety. The trip to Ireland had been empowering and yet here he was, on his way back to school. He wanted to go on more missions, but he knew that without proper training, he was less help and more in the way. He needed to study hard, train hard and get himself ready.

He smiled to himself as he stepped outside the door of the airport. He could literally fly now.

Mr. Songue was already at the curb waiting for him. Even though he knew HQ probably already knew, Andy had texted the guys his arrival info and asked them to let HQ know so he would be picked up. The rest of the Guardians, including the Queen, wouldn't be back yet. He had been brought to the airport and sent home just moments after giving Sloane a wave through the crowd at the castle, not having been allowed to join the fight. Andy had been reconnaissance and nothing more.

He smiled again when he opened the Morris Minor's car door. The experience had been frightening but it had also been awesomely fun.

He sank into the leather seats of the back seat and glanced at the driver. His back went straight.

"Where's Mr. Songue?" he asked as he observed the pale and strangely luminescent person sitting in the driver's seat. The person turned to look at him. Everything about him was light, his hair, his skin, even his eyes were a blue that was almost white. Andy got the chills.

"He's been detained; helping with an altercation in the lake. The Secretary asked me to pick you up."

Andy nodded and closed the door. He hadn't been around long enough to know the secretary. Was that Joy the snake lady or someone else? As the car pulled away from the airport, he wondered what kind of being this was. Not one he'd learned about yet, that was for sure.

As expected, the small town disappeared in favor of the quaint forests and green hills that was the beauty of south France. He loved it, but every now and again, the hard streets and noise of the city called to him. He decided he would request a city assignment for his apprenticeship when he finished school.

He frowned as he thought about Brick. Where did Brick live? Was that where Andy would visit for holiday breaks? Were there breaks?

The trees flashed by in his periphery. His room would be quiet when he arrived. He had arrived midafternoon and everyone would still be in class. When classes ended, he knew his friends would want to hear about everything. He thought about what he wanted to say. What the trip to Ireland had done to his outlook on the future.

He briefly thought about what it would be like to bring a girl into his life. He shook his head. As much as girls were interesting, that would be a smart thing to leave as something to look forward to. Liam had been lucky, finding an Aspie to steal his heart, someone that needed his kind. But what if Andy wasn't so lucky? What if he bonded with a human?

A bump rocked the car, pulling Andy's attention from his head to the road before him. He didn't recognize anything but then it wasn't like he'd been there long enough to know the terrain yet.

"Excuse me?" he asked the driver while he scanned the road ahead. "About how much longer until we reach the driveway?"

Once they were at the driveway, Andy would have a much better idea of what was to come. The strangest sensation rippled through his body. Something felt wrong.

"Any idea?" he asked the silent driver.

A glowing flash of light on the side of the road caught his gaze. It was there and then it was gone.

"Sir, slow down, please! I think this may be a trap," Andy said. *This was not right.* The car seemed to pick up speed. Andy grabbed his phone and hit a speed dial number.

"Sir? What is going on?" Andy pulled closer to the seat in front of him.

A glow flickered in the road ahead, this time a figure appeared in the glow before fading once more.

"Stop!" Andy yelled. The driver ignored him. Andy tried to open the car door, but it was locked. He ground his jaw slightly. He had really liked this car. Slinging his bag over his shoulder, he kicked the door.

"Hey," the driver finally said. The car slowed

slightly before picking up again.

"Screw you," Andy said and slammed his foot into the door again. It flew open, dragging along the dirt road on one hinge. He jumped. The ground was harder than Andy expected. The movies made a drop and roll from a car seem easy. It wasn't. It hurt.

The car screeched to a stop as Andy stood and searched the road for the glow. He walked slowly to where he thought it had manifested. Frowning, he concluded that he didn't have the first idea of what to look for. Would someone who was projecting affect the environment, show foot prints or trampled grass?

A loud engine pulled his attention from the road. He turned, and adrenaline flooded him. The car was only feet away and backing toward him at full speed. Moving might keep him from being hit full on but there was no time to avoid being hit. He phased.

The car passed through him and kept going before the strange man inside realized he had missed his target.

Andy watched the car while he debated running or flying or trying to take down the driver. Since he didn't know what he was dealing with, going after the driver did not seem to be the smartest move. If he ran, he had no idea where he was and could end up in Spain or Italy for all he knew.

He didn't know if the person in the glow was for or against him.

Andy bolted into the trees. It was probably better to hide and try to use the GPS to get to the school. The car stopped and idled for a few minutes before driving away.

Leaning against a tree, Andy breathed out a long sigh. He pulled the phone from his pocket and looked at the screen. The call had been disconnected. Andy checked his outgoing calls and saw that it had gone through. Whoever had answered Keppin's phone had listened for a minute and twenty-two seconds before hanging up. That was eight minutes ago.

Andy felt the slightest breeze before the wind was knocked from his lungs and he was pushed into the tree behind him by a force he couldn't see, and it was strong. He struggled before remembering he could phase when something dropped out of thin air onto the ground before him.

"Is that him?" a gravelly voice that sounded a lot like Keppin floated in the air around him. Andy looked around in bewilderment. On the ground, curled in a fetal position was the pale man from the car.

"Yes," Andy said.

"Awesome," the voice said as an unusually huge gargoyle misted and formed in front of him. The gargoyle removed its hand from Andy's chest and chuffed. The large, clawed hand whacked Andy on the upper arm.

"Keppin?" Andy asked. The gargoyle nodded.

"Don't you tell anyone, dude. I'm keeping this skill under wraps for as long as possible. The things I get to see and hear…"

"How did you find me?"

"Duh. I tracked your phone."

Andy blinked in disbelief before recalling the few times Keppin had hijacked his phone. He nodded before looking at the pale, limp body on the ground.

"I sure am glad to see you," he said and stood up straighter.

"Glad you're home. Come on, let's get back. I'll carry this idiot since you're such a pipsqueak."

"What?"

"You know I'm bigger than you and everybody else, it's cool."

"You are so..."

"Realistic? Truthful?"

Andy laughed as he pulled off his shirt and shoved it into his bag. He released his wings, stretching them out and then he jumped into the air to follow Keppin.

Chapter 76

Verity packed up the rest of her belongings and looked around the small room, preparing to leave for her visit to the Goblin's Lair. Watching Liam's healing process was the most amazing and strangest thing she had ever seen, and Verity doubted she would ever get the opportunity again.

She smiled at the thought of Sloane's face when he had finally opened his eyes. Verity may not be very experienced, but she knew what that look was. Wistfully she thought of Evan. He had stayed a few days to make sure she would be taken care of but then he had to leave, a patrol of some sort. The Guardians were ensuring no creature had escaped. Some of the Fae had even stayed to be rid of the "foul beasts." Evan hadn't committed to being a "non-rogue" but he seemed to love helping out. Dustin had stayed until Liam woke and then vanished, presumably back to New Orleans.

Picking up her small medicine bag, Verity couldn't help the smile it evoked. Evan had given it to her before he'd left. It was already full of labeled tinctures and glass bottles of herbs. A small booklet explained the uses of each. Her smile faltered ever so slightly when she wondered if she would ever see him again.

Taking her small suitcase in her free hand, she gave the room a last glance and left. The hallway to the stairs and then down to the grand entrance of the castle seemed longer than usual but there was no reason to draw out her visit. The last human, the one with the bite in his leg, had left two days ago, fully healed and his memory just slightly tweaked to remove the hideous monsters from his memory and leave him thinking he had been in an auto accident. He had referred to her as "Doctor".

After a visit with the Goblin King and his Queen, Verity would decide whether to attend school to become a doctor or study at the Guardian's school, taking only the science and health care classes and become a Master Healer. She had to decide which world she wanted to focus on.

She stopped to breathe in the old and natural smell of the castle. She knew a guardian waited out front for her. She would be on her own once she was dropped at the airport but until then, she would not be left alone.

The thought of more freedom put a spring in her step.

Footsteps thundered behind her and Verity turned, shocked to see Evan running down the stairs toward her, without a shirt on. He slowed as he reached the bottom step but still moved quickly until his graceful stop in front of her.

She gazed up at his bronze face and frowned to find it missing his classic smile. He was looking over her head.

"Oh, hey Evan," a guardian said from the front

door.

"Hi, Sam. I'll just be a minute, cool?" Evan asked.

"Sure, sure. No worries."

Evan brought his eyes back to her. He took her suitcase and doctor bag from her and placed them on the ground beside them.

"What *are* you doing?" she asked. He stared at her for the longest time before reaching up and slowly trailing his finger down her face from her temple to her chin. When he pulled away she felt a spark and a stream of warmth spread down her body.

She'd seen it once before. That same surprise when he looked at his hand and then dropped it to his side.

"I was wondering if it was just me or if you felt it too," he said. "I don't really understand it, but I felt like I should say something. You know, before you left. "I mean, what if...what if it was true? I've always hoped. I don't want to miss out on it, but I don't know how I'm supposed to know for sure..." he trailed off and looked away.

He closed his eyes and mumbled. "Sorry, I'm babbling."

His words brought a boldness to Verity that couldn't be ignored. She reached out and placed her hand in the middle of his chest. He looked down, searching her eyes. She smoothed her hand down his body and stopped at his naval.

"I feel it," she whispered.

Evan brought his hands to the sides of her face. She reached up and grasped his wrists.

"May I?" he asked, the longing and fear of rejection evident on his face. Verity grinned. His beautiful lips parted and the smile she had grown to look forward to spread across his face, vanquishing any doubt.

"Please do," she said.

He leaned in and whispered, "With great pleasure."

His lips were warm and soft. Verity responded immediately and molded into his embrace, bringing her arms up and around his neck to better fit into the perfection of his body. The heat in his chest was soothing and exciting. Verity had never felt more at home. She traced his lips with her tongue and he groaned, pulling her closer.

Sparks started to fill the corners of her closed eyes. His growl rumbled deep into her groin and her blouse suddenly felt constrictive.

Vibrant colors swirled through her mind, deepening her pleasure. It was so beautiful and she wanted more.

Her lips went cool when he pulled away and his voice, his beautiful voice of an angel pulled her back to the present.

"I had hoped," he whispered and kissed her again. When he pulled back again she could see the sparks in the air. He smiled brightly at her.

"If I wasn't sure before, I certainly am now. Verity, may I accompany you to your next destination?"

"Of course," she said, her heart swelling with joy. She took his hand and squeezed. When there was no response, she met his eyes. He had stopped moving. He had frozen in place as though she'd hit a pause button.

"Verity, my dear. I do apologize for disturbing

such a fascinating exhibition of love, but I do need to borrow you for a while."

The joy fled from her heart and was replaced by fear.

"Duran." She said before turning slowly to meet his eyes. He bowed.

"At your service."

"Leave him alone."

"There is no question as to that occurring. I have no need for him. It is you I want."

He reached out and gripped her upper arm.

"Get your hands off me," Verity growled.

"Just as soon as we arrive."

And then the world shut off and all Verity could see in any direction was blackness. It lasted maybe thirty seconds.

"Ah, here we are," Duran said and as though a light switch was flipped, Verity could see. She was standing in front of a large bed where a young lady was tucked in, pale and lifeless.

Verity turned to Duran. His lips were firm as he stared at the girl. He knelt and took a sallow hand into his own.

"Fix her," he commanded.

Chapter 77

Nia lounged in the pool, the heated water lapping gently around her naked body. Surrounded by stones and lime, she imbibed the strength and let it fill the remaining gaps in her being. She watched a blue streak on the other side of the pool come nearer, slowing as it glided along her legs, up her torso arriving at her side.

Noah shook the excess water from his hair and smiled at her. The same smile that had taken her heart so many years ago and gripped it so painfully that her very breath seemed like it would not come again until he smiled once more.

"I am still awed that you are here," he said. His voice always so calm and soothing with just the slightest gruff edge just for her.

She laughed gleefully. "I too cannot believe it." She looked at the paradise around her, the warmed pool, the natural stone and elements of her home mixed with the elements of his home. "I cannot believe you built this for us," she whispered and covered his mouth with her own.

He pulled her close and nuzzled her neck.

"I had hoped it was only a matter of time. I couldn't stand the wait, so I created what I thought would be our perfect home. Away from the prying family, away from the cold. But with the things that we need to be complete. And now that you're here, I am complete."

"You know, every weekend I would venture into the forests and try to rejuvenate," she said. Noah slid behind her and gently rubbed her shoulders.

"I tried so hard, searched for the elements I needed, but they were so far and few between, that once I finally found them, I would suck the essence from them. It would take too long for them to return so I never stayed in one place."

"I searched for you," Noah said as he moved to massage her scalp, "probably in those very forests."

"I kept moving. I had to. To find new essence to survive. I feared that though I loved Florida, I would have to leave again, and then I had finally found a friend."

"Sloane," he said.

She nodded, and he dropped his hands to pull her to his chest and gently kiss her shoulder. She sighed.

"Yes, that was something that I never really had, and she has no idea how much it meant to me. One day, when we finally take a breath of each other, I need to tell her."

He laughed. "Don't wait until then, love. I fear I shall never want to take a breath without you near, for fear that I will lose you again."

She spun around and met his eyes.

"Don't even think it. The Shades spoke, and it was true. We are complete."

"That we are," he said with a wry smile and pulled her closer.

Chapter 78

Waking up to the smell of bacon was a pleasure that Sloane had not experienced in longer than she cared to remember. Dragging her naked self out of the king size bed in their temporary home, she picked up Liam's shirt from the floor and tugged it over her head. The shirt rested mid-thigh, and Sloane did a happy dance before walking out of the room toward the kitchen.

His back was to her as he stood at the stove. Sloane stifled a giggle when she noticed the ties of a black apron hanging over his bare bottom. Smiling gleefully, she did something she had wanted to do for a long time. Sloane slid her arms around his waist, resting her head against the nape of his neck and sighed. Liam's head leaned back and gently rested on her own.

"Morning, beautiful," he said before pulling up his head and resuming cooking.

"Good morning," Sloane whispered. She had determined that she was physically incapable of releasing the smile plastered to her face. It was kind of embarrassing. He was so confident and amazing... and skilled.

Then she saw the elixir of the gods. The coffee pot pulled her like a ship to a Siren.

"I made your coffee when I heard you get up. It's the black cup next to the machine."

Sloane froze halfway there.

"You *heard* me get up?"

Liam turned off the burner and walked over to her. His fingers trailed lazily down her jawline.

"Yep. I heard," he said and flashed his crooked smile. Sloane thought about her happy dance and wondered what that sounded like.

"Well. I don't know how I feel about that."

"Well," Liam said as he leaned in and kissed just below her ear. "I feel," he kissed her neck, "fine." He brought his head back up and kissed her forehead. Sloane basked in his warmth for a moment before he pulled her attention to two plates on the counter. Crepes filled with cream and strawberries covered most of the plates with crispy strips of bacon arranged to one side.

Sloane picked up a fork. "You actually made this?"

"Sure, love," Liam shrugged. "I can make a few things here and there."

She took a bite of the crepe and swooned.

"Chocolate. You put chocolate in it. *Divine.* You're truly heaven sent, you know that?"

Liam appraised her so intently, Sloane felt the inner flame start licking the seams of her skin. He took the fork from her hand and tossed it into the sink.

"They're good cold too," he growled as he scooped her up and swung her around to sit on the counter top.

Chapter 79

Helen Barrows, the Queen, was alone in her bedroom suite. She sat slumped in a heavily cushioned love-seat, staring at the map that took up part of the wall in front of her. The lights of her Guardians, spread across the nations, usually filled her heart with a joy unmatched. As each were one of her own blood; she bared the pain of their pain, the joy of their joy and the death of their death.

After so many years, she could feel it and funnel it away, but it was always there. Always present, a constant hum of life. Every loss and every birth the most noticeable and yet, sometimes undefinable. Sometimes it was such a strong life force that she could feel the string of the bond snap into place and easy to locate, yet other times, it was a slowly formed ghost line that held them to her, barely visible.

Maybe it was magic, or the natural Faelines. Helen couldn't be sure and though she tried, she knew she couldn't save everyone.

She felt the earth's tug beneath her and searched the lines once more for the one she needed most right then.

Since the birth of the first Guardian, there had never been a time that the Queen didn't find her Princess in time. And yet. Helen worried that the unshakable bonds of the Guardians would crack away and diminish without a Queen.

Her door opened, and the Director walked in. She gave him a tired smile. He knelt in front of her and took her hand.

"Helen," he started, he rarely called her by her formal name.

"Don't, Joseph," she said and gave his warm hand a squeeze. "You know I can't stop trying."

"Helen," he repeated. "You must sleep."

She felt an unbidden tear roll down her cheek. "I cannot. I must find her."

He gave a great sigh while staring at her knees. He stood and leaned over her. "Then let me help."

He met her lips with his, warm and full of emotion and care. Despite his humanity or perhaps it was just the strength of raw love, the Queen was able to use his energy to fuel her power. He let it pour into her, the colors streaking around them in a slow dance.

A thin band of blue energy shot down through the floor, tearing through the earth below, down and away. A moment later an answering stroke of energy touched them and vanished.

Helen pulled back in surprise, Joseph grunted and squinted at the flickers of energy around them.

"She's alive," she whispered, "but something is hiding her from me."

Would you like to receive a free short story about the Origins of The Guardians?

Just go here to tell me where to send it!
http://tinyurl.com/LbarryFreeBk

I hope you enjoyed this book as much as I lovedwriting it. If you did, please leave a review, it helps so much!

Also, I really do love hearing from my readers, feel free to reach out!

Email: LB@authorlisabarry.com

authorlisabarry.com

facebook.com/authorlisabarry

About Me

From the age of five, I grew up in Florida which I quickly found was not a good enough reason to avoid wearing black. A daily color choice, I constantly pine for weather cool enough to wear boots but I generally just stay locked indoors. :)

I live with my incredibly supportive (and hot) husband and amazingly awesome kidlets. I count it a blessing that they still love me despite the deafening sound of my music muse throughout the house.

Whether I am reading, writing or doing other bookish things, I count on my many gargoyle companions who listen carefully when I read to them aloud. As you might have guessed, I collect gargoyles and books. I also LOVE to travel (always planning my next trip to Ireland!) and enjoy time with friends and family.

More books by Lisa can be found here:

authorlisabarry.com/books

**The Gargoyles Den series is a
complete trilogy.**

The Guardians
Rogue
Found

Protect your Mental Health Rights

Unscientific Mental Health Diagnoses

One of the fundamental flaws of psychiatry is its unscientific diagnostic system. Unlike proper medical diagnosis, psychiatry categorize symptoms only, not disease. The American Psychiatric Association's Diagnostic and Statistical Manual is notorious for its low scientific validity. In it, even "spending much more money than intended" is listed as a symptom of a mental illness— for which psychotropic medication is often prescribed.

Harmful Psychotropic Drugs

Drugging with psychotropic medication is a preferred treatment of psychiatry. These drugs are synthetic chemicals that pass the blood-brain barrier and can cause serious side effects. Here are but a few of the warnings for one of the most commonly prescribed anti-depressant drug:

- Hypertension
- Increased weight
- Varicose veins
- Amnesia
- Hallucination
- Suicidal tendency

And even though the drug is classified as an "anti-depressant", one of its FDA listed side effects is—depression.

There ARE other Solutions

Many Non-Profit organizations and individuals are concerned about the excesses and harmful practices of psychiatry. The Citizens Commission on Human Rights (CCHR) of Florida is a non-profit organization that investigates and exposes psychiatric violations of human rights. CCHR Florida also educates Americans about their mental health rights, including the right to informed consent.

CCHR Florida works side-by-side with like-minded groups and individuals who share a common purpose to stop abuses in the field of mental health. Together, they have formed a strong movement that is especially active to help protect the rights of children. We invite you to join our efforts to bring compassion and decency to the field of mental health.

The Right to Say "NO"

A fundamental human right is the right to be fully informed of the possible consequences of a medication or treatment. Part of this right is the right to say no to a drug that you don't want to take or that you don't want your child to take. Call or email CCHR Florida if you want to know more or need help. 800-782-2878; info@cchrflorida.org